THE SHELTERING STONES SERIES
4

CALL TO ARMS

A NOVEL OF HISTORICAL FICTION

JOANN KLUSMEYER

innovo
PUBLISHING

Published by Innovo Publishing, LLC
www.innovopublishing.com
1-888-546-2111

Providing Full-Service Publishing Services for Christian Authors, Artists &
Ministries: Books, eBooks, Audiobooks, Music, Screenplays, Film & Curricula

THE SHELTERING STONES HISTORICAL FICTION SERIES

BOOK 4

CALL TO ARMS:
A Novel of Historical Fiction

ISBN: 978-1-61314-734-4

Cover Design & Interior Layout: Innovo Publishing, LLC

Printed in the United States of America
U.S. Printing History
First Edition: 2021

Has God called you to create a Christian book, ebook, audiobook, music album,
screenplay, film, or curricula? If so, visit the ChristianPublishingPortal.com to
learn how to accomplish your calling with excellence. Learn to do everything
yourself, or hire trusted Christian Experts from our Marketplace to help.

CONTENTS

Chapter 1.. *7*

Chapter 2.. *27*

Chapter 3.. *47*

Chapter 4.. *67*

Chapter 5.. *87*

Chapter 6... *107*

Chapter 7... *127*

Chapter 8... *147*

Chapter 9... *167*

Chapter 10... *187*

Epilogue 208

Excerpt from Book 1 in the Footsteps in the Canyon Series...225

Additional Book Series by Joann Klusmeyer..........................230

CHAPTER 1

HUGE CHANGES IN THE AIR

Old Miz Carlile was dead.

It was practically impossible for anyone to believe that she was no longer to be found on her rocker in the shack located at the corner of State Highway and the road to Argyle.

It was inconceivable that she no longer sat there…where every curve of the rocker was shaped to fit her lumpy body while dispensing coffee (or something similar) and the latest gossip. She no longer sat with her pleasant wrinkled-face smile while the customer (neighbor) helped himself to coffee and maybe a cookie before checking his own particular mail hook.

Not much was known about Miz Carlile except that she was possibly older than the prairie itself and was certainly here before the great Land Run in 1889. Her establishment was originally located where small stream of water crossed a buffalo migration route, or so it was said. But things, as well as stories, had to start somewhere.

The corner where her small building was perched actually belonged to Matthew Wilson who won it in the Land Run, but she didn't care who it belonged to. It was her spot first, and certainly Mr. Wilson didn't care if she was there. Actually, she made it handy for Mr. Wilson and all others of the community to collect the mail…if someone had happened to have gone to Argyle and brought it back.

But this was the day of great changes.

Today, someone had opened the door and realized Miz Carlile's closed eyes did not mean she was asleep, as sometimes was the case, but it indicated that she had gone onto her reward. Quietly and with no fanfare, she had gone on, in the same way in which she had chosen to live her life. Uncomplaining…serving when she could and asking nothing of anyone. The coffee on the potbelly stove was still warm, so she hadn't been gone very long. The knowledge of her passing, however, was spread through the community with the speed and ferocity of a prairie wildfire.

Old Miz Carlile was dead. Unbelievable, actually! There had seemed to be thoughts that she might possibly live forever.

Gwendollyn McLaughlin, age 13, darted a glance at her sister, Krystallyn, barely a year older, in wide eyed surprise. Now that they had graduated from Miss Josie's Prairie Academy, the high point of the day for the sisters had been to go to the "Corners" to check the family mail hook and see if any excitement was to be had. This needed to be done before their mother found her own sort of activity for them. Summers were long enough, what with the weeding, picking, shelling, drying or canning, and other boring work.

What, for heaven's sake, would now happen to the mail? These two particular girls who had just graduated, with honors, from Miss Josie's school and the assignments there that were a fair sight harder than harvesting sweet corn in August, and having been primed in this way, their minds were as sharp as a pair of tacks.

As a matter of fact, either of them was qualified, test-wise, to take over the education of elementary children and would be snapped up in a moment by the Board of Education in the infant Oklahoma Territory. The girls were not ready for that, and neither were their parents. That was the worst problem with educating girls. They could then support themselves and that could be a scary position for parents of young ladies hoping to keep them nearby.

These two girls' minds were so attuned to each other, that, without a word, they turned to the door and saw approaching old Miz Gray Owl, the tiny, wrinkled Kiowa lady, who filled the role as the only doctor in the community. She had other talents. The girls had hardly opened their mouths to her that she answered their question. Yes…she knew that Miz Carlile had passed on.

With a nod, she sent them for help in the form of Matthew Wilson, the owner of the land under Miz Carlile's shack.

A crowd gathered around in no time at all, each trying to find something to do to feel needed. Matthew Wilson took charge, as was his duty, and produced a wide board for use as a stretcher. With speed and due reverence, they moved the remains of the founder of Carlile's Corners to his own house.

Kristie's shy request was seemingly ignored when she asked, "Who's gonna clean up here and watch the mail hooks?" As no answer was forthcoming, her sister provided one, directing it to the one who seemed to be in charge. "Don't worry about anything, Mr. Wilson. We'll clean up and watch the mail till someone comes."

Mr. Wilson had not been concerned about the mail hooks at the moment but was relieved for the problem to disappear before he had noticed it. "Thanks, girls," he responded.

His two words were permission enough for the moment, and the girls eased through the door, checked the fire in the potbelly stove, and inventoried the cookies and the money jar. They noted the mail hooks had mail, and the shelf beneath it contained a catalog or two, and a small, wrapped package. See there? Someone needed to stay and keep watch over things. Perfect job for them. Now they had only to inform their parents of this fact, which they did with skill and finesse.

With bright eyes and smiles, they rearranged the interior of the shack to please themselves, looked at the tiny living quarters at the rear and exchanged excited smiles. Bed. Bureau with drawers. Cracked mirror on the wall. Cabinet with the makings of sugar cookies. Tiny cast iron cook stove with a miniature oven.

"Do you think we could…?

"Of course! We just have to figure out how."

"Overnight…and everything?"

"Absolutely! Starting tonight! We have to go for clean sheets and our pillows. Ma wouldn't want us to…uh…."

"Let's make a list."

Of course. That was what Miss Josie taught them at the Prairie Academy. Before any project, get your thought organized. Do first things first, and then make long range plans. That would include a list.

"Gwinnie…!"

"What…?"

"This could be a job, with money. Miz Carlile got along all right, and so could we. We'd need to figure a way to make more… of course…."

"Besides, Papa isn't too agreeable to us going away for a while, so maybe he'd…?"

"And we could make it bigger…."

"We could maybe find something else to sell…."

"Maybe candy or something. Folks gotta stop here anyway. We'll think'a something.

The subject was picked up later by James and Maidie McLaughlin, the parents. Maidie was concerned. "A new buildin'? What'd that cost? And it'd be settin' on the Wilson's land…how'd that work out?"

Then James. "Done started to think on it. I'll have to check to see if Matt'll sell that corner. We'd been thinkin' on when the girls would be havin' to split up and leave here…well, this here might be the answer."

"What's the question?"

"How to keep them girls around till they get old enough for their brains to kick in. They got book learnin' but they could use a little horse sense. You know we got that money we got put back to help their husbands get started when they get married? Well, we could use that and…."

"But they ain't even got no steady fellers…!"

"Don't need none. This'a way, that money'd grow. Land prices can only go up, and a good corner like that'll always sell. Two, three, four years from now it'd give the newlyweds a good start. 'Sides that, they're right in sayin' someone's gotta look after the mail hooks. It could be them girls and then we'd know where at they were, most times."

"Sounds good. Let's sleep on it. My brain's plum wore out." When the sun came up the next morning, the plan seemed to be not only a good stopgap measure, but possibly a long-term investment. A fellow had to stay flexible when raising up his girls out on the prairie.

That was essentially how Misses Kristie and Gwinnie McLaughlin became business owners. Matthew Wilson could, indeed, be persuaded to sell…not only the corner, but the whole half mile strip bordering his tract alongside of Argyle Road. A 100-foot-wide strip made lots of room for a new "Corners" building and a good six or eight more businesses. It'd be good for the Wilson's and certainly an answer for the community.

The new building was at least four times as large as Miz Carlile's shack, with a counter, stools, and a better variety of cookies, also sandwiches (packed in a lunch sack, no extra charge, you furnish the sack) and an array of small cup hooks if a "regular" customer wanted to leave his own special cup handy to be ready when he wanted to use it. Very popular, that was!

The back part of the building contained a much bigger kitchen, counter workspace and a stove with a very large oven. The tiny bedroom held two beds, wardrobe closets and a bureau with drawers. Out back was a spacious, two-hole privy. (How did Miz Carlile get along without one? Everybody's gotta go sometime!)

All the younger set of the community were eager to see what was going on, and it immediately became THE meeting place. There were even three of the tiny ice cream tables with two chairs each. The delicate wire construction looked fragile but was known to hold a two hundred and seventy-five pound man with only minor squeaks of protest. It was wonderful for couples not wanting to be part of the crowded, noisy counter group.

The Mason jar with the hole in the top for the nickels turned into a metal box with a proper money slot (compliments of the blacksmith shop) and outfitted with a small padlock. Wall shelf lamps were provided for the extra lighting ("You girls gonna pay for your own kerosene, you know, don't you?") and a small kerosene heater for brewing the coffee in the summer to keep from unduly heating the room by firing up the potbelly.

Mama McLaughlin made up and hung cheery yellow flowered curtains at the small windows that were placed high for better ventilation of the hot air that accumulated at the ceiling. Then, she seated herself on one of the ice cream chairs and enjoyed a cup of tea…which she had brewed herself.

Kristie caught her sister's eye and mouthed, "You tell her…?"

Gwinnie nodded. This had been discussed. She seated herself comfortably at the table with her mother. "We're glad to have you stop in for tea or anything. Anytime. Likely this'll be a nice place to have a visit with your friends. Kristie and I, we thought about it and we'll be glad to have you anytime, for free, but if you have a friend here with you, they'll have to pay. Not free, like as if they were at your house at home. Reason is, Papa says we must pay for the cookin' kerosene, even if we get it from him. Our cookies are gonna be extra special, once we get better at cookin', and there could be so many lady friends here that we couldn't make a profit. We decided we weren't gonna work for nothin' and we gotta pay for what we put into the cookies. We plan to sell a lot'a cookies." She tempered her rules with a dimpled smile.

Mama was a bit surprised, but as she sipped her tea, she saw the truth in it. Fact was, she was proud of the girls for being so businesslike…and all…even if it seemed a mite impolite to charge money for what should be thought of as friendliness. With a smile, she remembered that if they were going to work for nothing, they might as well be doing it at home!

The girls had learned from Miss Josie about profit and loss, about keeping a record and developing a budget. Nevertheless, they packed up their record book and asked her to help them set up their business.

The former teacher, Miss Josie, smiled. Pleased, but knowing very well they could do it themselves, and that they now only wanted to show her that they could do it. After a fun hour as their teacher shared their excitement, she sent them home with an order.

Could they make her two dozen of those cinnamon cookies with chopped up raisins? She decided it wouldn't hurt to toss them a bit of business and cooking never was a pleasurable thing with her.

You bet! They sure could make the cookies, soon as they sent over to Argyle for raisins! They were too expensive to keep around all the time because the girls liked to eat them right out of the box! Maybe they should think of locking them up with the sugar that had to be locked up to keep it away from the ants? Or get some self-control!

Miss Josie stood at her window and watched them leave, walking side by side up the road. Their wavy light brown hair topping their blue dresses, and their heads turned about as they chatted with each other. The memory of their excited, but serious, faces as they had talked with her intrigued her. What would it be like to have a sister for a friend? She would never know, of course, but…one could wonder.

The girls had done very well in her classes and passed their teaching Certification with a good score, just as had their classmates, Patricia O'Day and Bridget O'Grady. The Irish girls were very busy now, learning to sew, being instructed by Bridget's mother. It would be interesting to see what they did with that skill.

The test scores of these four girls was not so high as those of her first class containing her own cousin, Carmelita Wilson, Carlotta Owens and the sisters, Rosalie and Francine Canfield. That was all right, though. They had fully qualified, and not everyone was a teacher at heart. Fortunately. The Territory also needed cookies.

In fact, actually, Miss Josie had been looking forward to the girls being successful, and for her to have such a good place to watch their progress over a cup of coffee at their little tables was just a bit extra.

Speaking of progress, Mrs. O'Day was just relating to Mrs. O'Grady, "Zillia, let me tell you, there's got to be some changes at my house. That Patricia, she's got scraps'a her sewin' everywhere. Seems worse now since the girls got back from visitin' Francine at Shady Ridge and saw how many women liked their sewin'. Don't get me wrong, I'm glad and all for what you taught 'em. It's just that the mess is everywhere and she's fussy about anyone a'gettin' close to it."

Response. "Say no more. I got the same thing at home. That Bridie, she's plum taken over the house. Thinks she's so important, now, that we all gotta steer clear'a whatever them girls got goin'. Don't get me wrong. I glad and all, too, but I fear it's getting' worse."

"I know what you mean. What'll we do?"

"I don't know. I threatened to make 'er move to the barn, only it'd not work for the dust and dirt."

"You know somethin'? We still got our old covered wagon that we come out here in. Seems it ain't shaped right for farm work, and there it sets. Still got the cover. Wouldn't you think that'd work for the summer…maybe?"

Smile of agreement. "Why not? Mostly that mess is the stuff they bought ahead and is still on the bolt. That'd make a place to store their supplies anyway. I thought'a somethin'. If they would'a had that when they went to Shady Grove to see Francine, they could'a took a lot more and stayed longer. A few hours in the middle of the day for lookin' ain't much time for women that's got duties at home. Thing of it is, we got our wagon, too. If the men folks was to build in the sides with lumber they could make it warm enough for most of the year. Wouldn't you think?"

They sipped their tea there in the Cookie Jar (formerly Carlile Corners), and it was almost as good as they would have made at home. Just couldn't get used to that stuff called coffee the youngens thought they liked. Nice thing about the Cookie Jar was that the price of a cup of tea entitled one to stay as long as one liked, but the bad thing was, it didn't get housework done.

Zilla O'Grady began to squirm guiltily on the flimsy-seeming chair made of curled wire. Seemed too fragile for her sizeable girth, but it had held up so far. Table was tiny, too, but it made for more private conversation.

Sarah O'Day noticed the restlessness of her closest friend. "Yeah, I gotta get with it. Things to do. We gonna speak to the men about this?" Meaning, "We need to team up on the men if we expect to get something done."

Nod from Zilla. "I'll see what he says." Meaning, "I'll say it so he can't get out of it and I'll let him know to be prepared for me to keep at him till we get something done."

It was the fellows, however, who decided that neither of them had room to board both wagons at their houses, so they talked with McLaughlin who now owned the land under the Cookie Jar. Favorable response.

"Tell you what, fellows. I like your idea, and it'd be good for the girls to be close, case one needed the other. I'll say this to ya, move them wagons on over on the next marked out lot to the north. If you fellows'll put up a shed and privy, and punch a well on the lot, you can leave them wagons there, rent free, until all my other business lots are full. Then I'll have to either rent it or sell it. We ain't knowin' if your girls'll stay with it, any more'n my girls. Good for 'em if they do, though."

Nodding on their agreement, the respective fathers began work on the covered wagons. One of them had only to be reinforced and covered with another coat of liquid tar. Cold wouldn't bother the girls' cloth, pins and thread. A better closing was created for the ends. Couldn't afford to let their product get wet. Tightening up and repainting the wheels and axels helped the looks because there it was, right on the corner of State Highway and what was beginning to be called Canfield Road. Needed to look good.

The other wagon was boxed in on the sides, with a full-length side bench created over the wheels where the wagon sideboards were spread to give more inside room. A full length "clothes pole" was extended down one side. It stretched over the benches, making a place for hanging items in work. The other side had a double row of hat hooks extending the full eight-foot length. Hats might soon become their best product, and many of the creations were quite crushable because of bows and feathers. Four hooks for hanging lamps would ensure that the girls could see what they were doing. Four stools of various heights were added.

Both of the wheeled enclosures were towed to the space just north of the Cookie Jar, facing Canfield Road. As per the landlord's requirement, a generous two-hole privy was constructed, and a punched well was dug.

The well drillers were new to the community and were certainly welcomed by the women. Currently at work were the four small donkeys who were led in circles. The "weight" at the end of a chain was lifted and dropped, again and again, with each revolution of the donkeys.

As the weight was lifted and allowed to chunk down, slamming itself against the ground again and again, it dug itself below the surface a small amount at a time. This was more efficient than "dug" wells, as the pointed weight made a uniform sized hole, easy to fit with a steel casing. The moved soil was packed against the edges of the hole, making a strong wall against the casing. This aided in steadying of the casing which was the major cost of the well.

When completed, the well was outfitted with a cylinder bucket ten inches in diameter and a foot and a half-long. A very efficient design. The punched well went a long way in lessening the work of the women, who had often been obliged to carry water as far as a quarter of a mile, and even farther. Now the well could be in their own back yard! Such luxury!

Mr. O'Day and Mr. O'Grady stood back and admired their work with the feeling that they had done something that might keep their daughters from going elsewhere. At least for a year or two. Both fathers were aware that any one of their girls would be snapped up in a moment by the Board of Education. If the girls were only willing.

The "move in" was the excitement of the week. Cookie Jar customers gaped with wide eyes and passers-by stopped for a look as bolts and rolls and folded piles of cotton and satin were carried from the family wagon to the covered transport of several years ago. Boxes of thread and pins, scissors, patterns and tape measurement were piled into the wagon.

With joyous giggles, the Irish girls sorted their supplies, determined the best way of storing, and decided what their next plan would be. Miss Josie's Aunt Sharon in New York had sent new fashion magazines. There were hats and hats, and more hats. This must be the year of the "hat," and they intended to be ready. There were hat styles to be wondered at, hats to be giggled at and hats to study for possible changes that would make them more acceptable to the women of the territory. Also, hats to be assessed, price-wise, as the passed-on cost of materials was always a concern.

Other interesting concerns had arisen. First, there was limited money for most families to invest in hats that were made for dress-up, as well as those to protect from the sun or other weather. Second, most ladies did not really want a hat that seven other women had. They wanted one different and were reluctant to buy if there would be a dozen more made just like theirs. Third, heads were a variety of sizes and not all styles could be adjusted. Just things to be considered, but the two girls felt themselves well able to do it.

There was, however, a wonderful plus. Anything, absolutely anything, could be put on a hat as long as it could be made to stay securely in place. Another thing, the newer hats were not necessarily meant to cover hair that was sweaty, dirty and wind-blown. Hats were not bonnets and were not meant to be. Newer styles were meant to be perched up there somewhere to make a fashion statement of some sort.

Uppermost in their minds was the search for styles that were different, inexpensive and quickly made. Both girls, before their eyes closed at night, gave the matter a bit of thought and minds remained open to help from Above. More than once, it turned out, that one or the other would wake up in the dark of night with a full-fledged new idea. Grabbing up a piece of their ever-present sketching paper and lighting a candle…or even sketching a design in the moonlight coming through their window. They could now sleep, having committed the new idea to the security of the paper that would be there in the morning.

A game. That's what it was and winning or losing the game was determined by the weight of their money jar. There would be a time in the future when coins would mean shoes for the children and new straw hats, etc. At this time, however, they could play their games, giggling together as they had since they were toddlers.

Across the Atlantic Ocean coins were viewed in a different light. Emil and Lucille Forrester hoarded their pennies carefully, counting them often, and checking on the availability of affordable passage on a sailing ship to the new country.

They had to go. For them, it was like a tree that was planted in a container…it eventually needed space for new roots and greater height. They were like that tree.

Consequently, in the old country, Lucile cleaned houses and ran errands for anyone who had money, and Emil's cart, outfitted with a padded seat and a sun and wind cover, plied the streets of London. The pony and the man were available to transport anyone who had coins.

They did not expect a large, luxury ship. That was far beyond their means. Many small ships made trips back and forth, back and forth until they were torn to pieces by wind and water. They were patched, refitted, and trimmed with new sails, then advertising again for passengers to the new colonies.

The Forresters studied these advertisements. When a ship with a new name became available, it was almost certain that it had been patched up after years of plunging through the waves and being tossed about like a cork in the Atlantic storms. When this was to be considered, one must take care to inspect the patching and refitting, and especially the main mast. It would be hoped that it would be made of new timber, a scarce item becoming scarcer in England, and it must not be a mast that had been patched, spliced and wired together.

Angel Gabriel became available. Its former name was *Albatross*, and the new mast was tall and thick, well able to manage the expanse of canvas it would take to get through a storm. The price for passage, luckily, was almost affordable, meaning that it would be very crowded, but the Forresters could live with that.

So their names were added to the list, and the sailing date would be in the spring, four months away. Good timing. That gave them the opportunity to get together the last-minute supplies with the certain knowledge that they would actually need them.

At it happened, though, it might not have been such good timing. Lucille discovered that their future plans for a family would be moved up a bit. She was truly and wonderfully pregnant.

They looked at the calendar, adding four months to the usual three months of the voyage and came up with a few weeks to spare. They could make it. They would go ahead, because passage was becoming harder to get and their migration might then be put off for several years. They assured each other that the baby was more easily carried within the body of the mother rather than in arms, requiring food and diaper service, as well as costing an additional charge for passage. It would work.

They were both young and strong, and when they docked, they would just stay on the coast and work to save money to go west, just as they had planned. Two years, maybe, and things would be better. It would work.

As it turned out, the *Angel* was indeed too heavily laden for its "wings." Although the sheets of canvas were stacked high and the ropes were thick and new, cargo weight was now a problem. But what matter if she rode low in the water from the number of the passengers and the necessity of live animals in the hold that would be used for food?

It was on the second of March in the year of 1888 that they weighed anchor and sailed down the Thames River on the outgoing tide. Weaving through the cross-currents of the channel islands, past Guernsey and Jersey, then the Skilly Islands, finally seeing, in the distance, "Land's End." That location was well known as the last piece of solid earth that they would see for many days and nautical miles.

The deprivation and crowding aboard the small ship was a story that could be told over and over during the late 1800's, and it could describe many of the other ships.

The heavily canvassed *Angel* flew low, wallowing in the troughs during a storm when the canvas must be hauled up or risk the ship being tipped over into the briny. The three months of the voyage turned into four and the food must be threaded out thinly to make it last, even when supplemented with over-the-side fishing. Whatever living thing the nets brought up, that was what was eaten. And gratefully.

There was a lot of complaining, but Emil and Lucille Forrester had never had an easy life, and they plodded along, day by day, concerned only with the length of time the trip was taking.

Conversely, the child within her seemed to want to appear earlier than expected. The one good thing for Lucille was that she was not alone. Hers would be the third child born aboard ship on that trip, and for the bored and restless older women, this was an event. Something to take their minds from the routine.

The little girl made her appearance a day and a half out from the shores of Virginia, and her proud mother named her America, the land they could almost see as they peered over the yardarm. A brave and proud name, and her parents would never know about how brave and proud their little scrap of a girl would have to be but they would not have been surprised that she would find a way to overcome. Had she not been made of their own flesh and blood?

There was money to be made in the new colonies. On the shores of Virginia there was more work than there were hands, and good money seemed to be available for work performed. The ships bringing passengers took back cotton, wool and tobacco. Loading and unloading. Work for all. Money for all. Much needed coins for those with a purpose. Like the Forresters.

Kitchen help was so scarce, Lucille was able to find a job where she could keep little America with her. Coins were hoarded and counted, and lists were made of things they felt they would need when they could finally go west across the big river.

Emil was dismayed to learn that he was only months too late to be part of the Land Run in a place called Oklahoma Territory. It seemed that, if a man had been fast enough, he could get free land. Too late for him, though. He did realize, however, that there would be work in that new land, so they would go there as soon as they were properly outfitted and ready.

Then Lucille was pregnant again. Well, they would wait until she was too far along to work on her job, and then they would move on. If they needed more money, he would find work at the big river. At least, they would be that far.

The following October, they reached a place called Saint Louis. It was located on the big river and was called the gateway to the west. Good omen.

They could not yet afford to go through that "gate," but Emil found work as a stevedore on the big river. Their little boy was born in January and, as an act of faith, he was named Oklahoma, the destination they held before themselves. He would be called Homer.

The work at the big river paid well and they put away every cent. Just the way they had always done. It was six years later that they were on the road heading for the Oklahoma Territory with a small amount of money and a great amount of faith. They had trusted that the Good Lord would not abandon them now, and He hadn't. For hadn't they obeyed every commandment that they knew?

The family of four settled onto a farm near a small town called Argyle in a settlement called Carlile Corners. They were lucky because the former owners of the land had to give it up for some reason, and their savings of coins were enough to pay for the land. At this time America was nine years old and Homer was almost seven.

And there was a SCHOOL for the children! *Thank you, Lord*…for the parents knew that the unexpected existence of the school made it worth all that it had cost.

It was two years later that Lucile was again pregnant. Things were not going well, and even the nearest to a doctor that the community had, Old Miz Gray Owl, refused to give Emil any hope.

"Is wrong," she insisted. With a hand held low, barely above her head, and a sad shake of her head, she advised Emil, "Too much not big and work too hard. Baby not…uh…."

But she had no more words to tell him that things would not go well, also that neither he nor Lucile could do anything about changing it if she did know. Even Old Gray Owl could not help, and when the time came, she gave Lucile the "no pain" drink and let nature take its course. Mother and too-young, too-small baby were buried on the back of the property. Emil plodded on...alone.

America had attended the school for two years and had learned a lot. She had been tested at age twelve and was qualified to teach school in the Territory. Even eleven-year-olds were accepted by the Board of Education if they could pass the test, and they were called "teachers in training." How these teachers were being "trained" while they taught others was a puzzle no one could solve. Homer had attended for three years and had completed the course when their lives were to be irrevocably changed.

That was the year of the terrible drought, there was no water on the land that was not carried in by the barrelful. The animals must be cared for. The house must be cared for, and Emil, ever provident of his family, put pencil to paper and decided, with a sigh, that a change must be made.

Over the supper table, scanty though it was, he told the children of his plan to go to Oklahoma City and look around. If there was a way to find a job, he would come back, sell out the farm and take them and their plunder to the city. What else was there to do? In stunned silence the boy and girl nodded that they understood. Papa always did what he said he would do. They were confident of his ability.

Papa took the best horse, a change of clothes and the six shooter...and he left in the night. At first, the boy and girl did their best to keep things going, trying to hide their concern from each other. When the waiting time became three weeks, they could be brave no longer.

Back at the supper table, the fried eggs and boiled potatoes were eaten, and America took the problem to a piece of paper and a pencil. The answer was somewhere. It had to be. Something had happened to Papa or he would have been back. One way or the other.

"I could get a job…?" Homer's voice was thin with worry and hesitant with fright.

"No. You're not even thirteen. It has to be me. You have to stay here."

"All alone? But I…."

"I know. The only other thing to do is to go to someone's house and beg to get to stay. I've been thinkin' we might do better in Oklahoma City, but if Papa couldn't get there, how could we? Besides, I don't think that old horse could make it. We still have a little money but its goin' fast."

The girl did not mention that she could get a job immediately as a teacher, but where would that leave Homer…as the teacher was "boarded around" among the parents of the students.

For want of something to fill the silence, they lifted cups of steaming unsweetened tea to their lips. Tea was free…it grew in the garden. Flour and sugar were expensive.

At breakfast (more eggs and fried potatoes), the subject was discussed more thoroughly.

America began, "I've been thinkin' all night. There could be one more thing. Maybe two things. This farm is worth something, and it can be sold. But then I don't know where we would live, and the money wouldn't last forever. Papa thought he might have to work on someone else's farm instead'a buying' this. He didn't have to, but there might be someone else that would work for a place to live and that'd be money to be takin' care'a us. Course, then we'd still have to find a place to go."

"How'd we find out about that?"

"I don't know. Here's what we'll do. First off, I want a chance to see if we can get help here where folks know Papa wasn't a person to go off and leave us, and where they know we've never asked for a thing we couldn't work for. I'm gonna ask you to stay here and do what you can to make the barn and sheds look better. Cut some grass or something. If you're busy, you won't worry so much. I promise I'll be back today but it could be after midnight. Or maybe first thing in the morning. Then we'll figure out what to do next."

Homer drew in a deep breath and let it out slowly. She sounded so brave. He felt his fingers crossing themselves "for luck" and nodded. He could do what she said. Fact was, he rather liked using the big scythe and he would cut grass for hay. Papa said he wasn't big enough to swing the scythe, but he was growing fast and Papa wasn't here to object. The huge meadow behind the house had tall grass that Papa would have been cutting if he had been here.

"How're you gonna get where you want to go?"

"I was going to tell you. I'll take the horse and ride up to the corner. I can leave him tied at the blacksmith and walk on. I'm thinkin' that'd be better. Can you saddle him up while I get ready?"

Watching her brother stand and leave the room, head high and walking determinedly, she was relieved. She didn't see the crossed fingers.

What to wear? Older dress. Bonnet. No, not a bonnet. Her bonnets looked too girlish. Scarf? No, a shawl. There was that short blue and white striped one her mother had liked to wear over her shoulders in the house in the winter. Kept off a chill, she said.

America settled the three-cornered shawl over her head and drew all the points back to the nape of her neck. Tie a knot. Straighten the ends. They hung down among her mane of honey-colored waves. Nodded. Looked about right.

A jiggle and a snort outside the window, and she saw the ancient animal being led to the front door. He would be slow, but it would keep her from being so tired when she got there, what with all the walking she had ahead of her. At least two miles, maybe a little more.

Sitting sideways on a regular western saddle was not comfortable, but it was possible, and the animal swayed and lurched as he ambled down the rutted and cloddy Cedar Bush Road. Reaching the corner, she asked for and got permission to tie the animal to a tree in the yard of the blacksmith shop.

Which direction? Toward Enterprise, three miles south? West to Shady Ridge three miles west? North toward Argyle? Why not.

Traveling to the farther most one of the business establishments on the road to Argyle, she walked up to the well driller. Equipment was spotted about, parked here and there on the lot. Mules munched quietly on the side grass, and fortunately the owner was around, a rare occurrence.

"A job? For you, you mean?"

"I love animals, 'specially horses and mules. I'm good with animals. I really need a job."

A sigh. "I could sure use someone, but I'd be doin' wrong to take you on. Wouldn't be safe, a girl that looks like you with the ragamuffins I hire to do the work. It's dirty and hard, but I couldn't have a girl around here even if she wasn't a pretty one, like you. Wish't I could, though."

America smiled her bravest, thanked him and walked away. Next business south was the grist mill. They had small mules... actually just little donkeys. She didn't know much about them, but they were like horses, weren't they? They were hitched in pairs and walked around and around, pulling the chain that turned the heavy grinding wheel over the grain. They needed time-consuming care. She could do that.

The grist mill had certainly been a welcome business to the community of Carlile Corners. Cornmeal. Wheat flour. Rye flour.

Mr. Bramwell stopped his work and listened. "A job, huh. Well, I could use help. Couldn't pay much but there'd be place to eat and sleep. Thing is, you're, well...I'm thinking you'd not be able to do the liftin' up high that I'd have to have along with care of the animals. I'm needin' a boy. Taller. They just naturally got more liftin' power. Regret havin' to say it, and I hope you'll get luckier."

America put on her smile and her nod and turned away before the tears welled up in her eyes. *Walk south, and get the tears out'a your eyes*, she chided herself. She shook her head in disgust. She was acting just like a girl'd be expected to... squallin'.

A few yards ahead of her was Canfield Grading and Dirtwork. Tall cottonwood tree there by the entrance. A big, flat-topped rock in their shade. Sitting down on it, she concentrated on gaining control of her discouragement. Drying her wet eyes. Just across the fence were Raymond's Canfield's Clydesdales, four-legged beauties with coats shining like a greased skillet, steaming and ready for hotcakes.

Snorts and contented crunches as they ate grass today because they might be pulling a dirt slip or grader tomorrow. Whole herd of them. Two more coming up the road, and they turning in at the entrance.

"Whoa, up there!" The horses stopped at the sound of the commanding voice, and Johnny Black leaped down from his perch. "Miss? Oh, it's…America? Is that you?"

She sniffed, firmed her chin and found the strength to speak. "It's me. Just restin' a minute."

Her response didn't sound quite right to Johnny. He came over and sat beside her. "You been walkin' far?"

"Not too bad, just headin' on south."

Girl, out walking on the road a long way from home. Dressed like she was, she was certainly not visiting. He turned to look into her face and she could no longer pretend. Eyes filled and tears came down her cheeks. Swiping her sleeve across her face did not help much.

"Girl, I see you got yourself a problem and I ain't too good on them. Never was. But I know who is, and you're gonna come on in and rest in the shade and get a drink. Could be you'll find an answer." Reached for her hand.

Totally discouraged, America allowed herself to be assisted, and she followed the operator of the grader the short distance to the building belonging to Raymond Canfield, former schoolmate.

"Found Miss Forrester at the gate, plum wore out. Told 'er she could come in and get a fresh drink and rest a bit." With that explanation, he left to care for the animals.

"America! How are you? Haven't seen you since school days, I don't think…."

Tears! *Oh, America,* she agonized with herself, *how'll you convince anyone you can work if you keep crying like a girl?* A swipe of the sleeve again, slightly smearing the road dust that had settled on her cheeks. Like a spring rain, words tumbled out of her mouth, ending with "I was just admiring your horses when Johnny made me come in. I'll be runnin' on, now."

CHAPTER 2

Wait. I can't help, but I know someone who might. Anyway, you've got to have some help somewhere. I wonder about what Mr. Bramwell said, 'If you were a boy.' I remember Homer being strong built. Why couldn't he work there?"

A sniff and a hiccup. *Now, why didn't I think of that?* "Well, I could go back and…."

Raymond butted it, "You really like my horses? You don't think they're too big and dangerous?"

"Oh, they're gorgeous! So shiny and so strong looking. I could just look at them all day! Takin' care of animals is my very favorite thing, and horses are my favorite animal. Papa always let me do it unless Homer insisted it was his turn. Thing is, I'm better at that than sweeping or ironing. My mama could'a told you that." Paused for breath. A rosy cast arose from her neck as she realized, with embarrassment, how she had gone on!

A serious moment for Raymond, and a pause. "Likely shouldn't say this to you, but I could really use someone. Right now, those beasts have to be taken care of by whoever has a minute, and sometimes it's my father. Feeding, moving about, checking on health problems in their coats, like cuts or burs. Or sometimes they get infected fly bites."

While he talked, he watched America's face. Eyes bright and shiny, intent and interested. Maybe…?

"Now, what I would like to find is someone to tend to those things. I don't have a place for that person, but I could take care of that. Fact is, I need to tell my father about your problem. He's really good at problems like yours. I got a good idea, I think, but he'd be the one to…Well, let me say this. Why don't you go back home and come again tomorrow with Homer? Least ways, if there's an answer to be had here in town, my pa, he'd be the one to find it.

Can you be back, say nine o'clock tomorrow? No, make it ten. It may take some thinkin'."

America struggled with her thoughts. It would be so easy to hand her problem over to this big handsome person who was only three years older than she, but it was her problem, not his. Then again, she had to do something…she had come here. Well, either way, she had to get better control of herself before she tried anything else. What was one more day, anyway?

A nod and a smile. An appreciative smile. At least he didn't say he could use her if she was a boy. "We'll be here. You know Homer's barely thirteen…course, he's already taller'n I am. We'll be here at ten o'clock."

The girl had hardly cleared his line of sight when he saw his pa coming toward him. Been over to Argyle, no doubt. He was serious as he listened to the problem. "Been knowin' Emil was alone out there with them youngens, but he didn't ask for help, and we don't go around pushin' help where it ain't been asked. I'll see Bramwell, and Matt Wilson ought'a be there with me, too. I'm takin' your word that she can care for those Clydesdales, but where at you thinkin' on putting her?"

Raymond hadn't figured that one out.

"Son, you're rememberin' she's a girl? That's a special thing out here but it's dangerous, too. Fellows you hire…they gotta be kept away. Puttin' up a place, that'd be no trouble, but she can't be let to stay here by herself at night. Speck she can use a gun, but it'd be bad to come to that."

Raymond again. He had always been good at solving problems, the kind Miss Josie had required of them. "Pa, listen to this. That mill, it's only a quarter mile up the road. If he'd take on the brother, Homer could walk down here at night. I wouldn't reckon a miller'd need anyone at night. And I'd really like to have someone on site with the animals, and it ain't my fault she ain't a fellow. The way she talked, I think that girl means what she says about likin' horses. Otherwise she'd'a got herself a teachin' job like Francine and Rosalie. She passed the same test."

Sam Canfield nodded, chewed his toothpick into a brush of slivers, tossed it away and nodded again. "Reckon I'll run on up to see Bramwell, just to be sure, and then call in Wilson. Mind what I said about that girl, so you just be thinkin'. She ain't to be treated like one of the fellows, no more'n your sisters would be."

"I know, Pa. I could tell right off. First thing I looked at her, I could tell that she wasn't like us. Sort of a blessing, too, wouldn't you say? Wouldn't be surprised if the horses could tell, too, after being treated like bothersome flies by the lot of us."

Sam Canfield leaped astride his tired horse and trotted up to the mill to see the miller. Yeah, it'd work out good, the miller said, especially if he had a place to sleep. Matt Wilson saw right off that he didn't have anything to do with the problem except to make a third voice which was always good. He'd even help on the building if he was needed. And he was!

Poor America thought her heart might just pound its way out of her chest. Those horses! And she could get actual money for taking care of them. Putting out the hay. Brushing them when she had time. Mucking out and piling the waste. The dried-out hunks in the pasture made good cow pats, but the larger quantity in the stables mounted up fast, Raymond told her. When the pile built up high enough, and when someone had the time, they'd drag it out to the pasture and spread it. She wouldn't have to do that, of course.

She turned to him questioningly. "Why not? I could do it if the fellows do. If someone showed me what to do, I'm actually really good with horses. They can tell how much I like 'em."

Raymond smiled at her enthusiasm. He'd have to see how that went. "Now, there won't be a cabin for you for a couple of weeks. That'll give you and Homer time to think things through. Pa says he put up a notice in Argyle that there'd be a place for rent. He and Mr. Wilson thought it'd not be a good thing to let your pa's farm go vacant, the way he worked for it so hard and so long. And the way Homer is growin'. We was thinkin' he should have the chance to make a grownup decision in five or ten years. The rent, it'd make a little extra money for you, too."

As they returned toward the business office, one of the horses took steps toward them, and America stopped, held out her hand, palm up, and the animal stretched his neck toward her.

She took a step closer and rubbed his velvety nose. A snort told her he had sniffed her and found her acceptable. In a low murmur she told him, "Don't you worry, old boy, we're gonna be best buddies. I'll know your name and you'll know my smell. Won't take us no time at all!"

The "hired man" cabin, when it was finished, was standard. Sizeable kitchen/living area, tiny bedroom and ladder to the loft, finished out simply because the space was small up there. In this case, it would be perfect for Homer to spend the night.

America moved in her stove and three chairs…she'd do with a shelf table that could be let down. Saved space. A bed and a bureau for her bedroom, and a feather stuffed ticking for the loft. She didn't need much. When it was all in place, she looked around with satisfaction. Not much to keep clean!

Homer felt bad at first, because he had three meals at the Bramwell's and his sister had to make her own. "Don't think that way," she chided him. "That food is part'a your pay. You're not takin' a thing that isn't yours. Besides, that keeps me from having to figure out what to cook for you. You're still growin' and it'd take more food for you. I'll do fine."

And Mrs. Bramwell asked Homer, "How's your sister makin' out down there with all them black beasts?"

Homer was glad to be truthful. "She loves it, Miz Bramwell. She always has loved horses, and she really likes them down there."

The woman shook her head in disbelief. "I went by there and saw her out in the pasture, lookin' like she was brushin' one of them beasts. Why, her head didn't come up no farther than its stomach…seemed like. Beside her, that animal looked to be about the size'a half the Territory!"

Homer's turn to nod. "She's always been little, like our ma. Pa said she had the brains and I had the muscles. Brains don't need such of a big place to be."

A grin from his employer. "Bein' side by side, I'd rather you had the muscles. Reckon you know that by now, huh!"

Pausing from consuming the boiled pudding with raisins, Homer answered, "All right by me."

Mrs. Bramwell again, "Son, now…I want you to take a bowl'a this puddin' down to your sister. Likely she won't have time to cook, carin' for all them animals. How many she got?"

"Twelve, she says. Course, half of 'em are usually gone workin' of a day. Sometimes at night, too."

Homer carried the covered bowl of pudding the quarter of a mile to the cabin. His sister had just cast a look about the tiny "kitchen." What was handy? She'd had popcorn and peanut butter for lunch. There were eggs and…. Then she saw the pudding.

"Oh, wonderful! Be sure to tell her thanks," his sister instructed between bites.

He must have remembered because it was rare that he did not bring a ham sandwich, a slab of apple cake, or maybe a couple slices of meatloaf. If food was part of her brother's wages, he must be doing very well! Extra special for her was the evening he brought a huge baked sweet potato, still hot in its newspaper wrapping. Swimming in butter, it needed nothing else to make a meal.

Just down the road a few steps and across the street, Pat and Bridie stitched away. Their inventory of hats had increased to the point that they must make a selling trip. They had made a visit to their schoolmate in Shady Ridge and it had carved out a very profitable dint into their back stock.

As it was now, most of the locals who could afford a new hat already had one of the current group. The girls decided they could go south to Enterprise where Eve Adams held her classes. The community of South Bend was close by. It was fun to spend time with school friends, especially those who couldn't go anywhere much because school required them to work every day.

"The pas don't want to make that trip to take us because it messes up two workdays. We could drive and stay over two or three nights. Could make more sales that way."

"If we had a place to keep the horses, that is. Then we'd have to take care of 'em. The fellows are wantin' to drive us...."

"But when? They're workin' such long hours."

"Go in the middle of the night?"

"Maybe real early. Enterprise ain't so far. Then they'd have the horses to ride on back up here and we wouldn't have to mess with 'em."

It took a bit of figuring, and it made a long day, but Johnny Black and Willie Elk ended up going along with the plan. Enthusiastically and willingly. They unhitched the wagon and rode the animals back.

Johnny observed, "This sure makes a long day, but now we know where they are and when they're comin' back. If we let 'em come down here with all these fellows here...and us not knowin'... no tellin' what could happen."

"You're right. We gotta stay needed," his cousin agreed.

The Cookie Jar made a new menu. This place was getting to be a serious stop over for gossiping and checking on the mail hook. People were ready to take a seat on the counter stools or at the cute little tables and have a bite...or a sip. Outings were rare, stuck out in the territory the way they were, so pleasure must be made wherever it could.

The menu expanded. Beans were added, also beans flavored with chile peppers...a popular dish with the hard working fellows. Lunches could be made and packed on request. Generally there was soup, pretty much different every day, but always tasty. It was hot and filling and served with a generous wedge of cornbread.

Sometimes there were fried pies...fruit wrapped in a flaky dough and browned in the skillet. Cookies were a staple. Various kinds. In order to make the supply of cookies last the day, there were mostly leftovers, and the customers really preferred to have them warm and fresh. So, what to do with the leftovers?

As the Irish girls dreamed of hat styles, the McLaughlin sisters often dreamed of food menus. And recipes. The morning sun had not broken through the clouds when Gwinnie shook her sister awake.

"Kristie! Wake up! I know what to do with the leftovers!"

Drowsy and rubbing her eyes, Kristie wondered, "What leftovers?"

"Cookies, sleepy head. I dreamed it. We take all the left-over cookies, crumble 'em, add a quart of applesauce, enough eggs and cinnamon to make a batter and bake 'em in a flat pan. Cut 'em in bars. Call 'em Fruit Bars."

Kristie sat up and considered the recipe. "What if there aren't many leftovers?"

"Fill out with crumbled biscuits and add sugar. Could use cherries or blackberries if we wanted." They're already sweetened.

"Yeah, and we could call 'em Surprise Bars instead'a Fruit Bars, that way they could be different and no one could complain. Good idea! Raise the profit. Now dream of a cheap drink." Kristie settled back on her bed to doze until sunrise.

Over at Canfield Grading and Dirtwork, America… who gradually began to be called Merry…was excitedly getting acquainted with her charges. Looking so much alike, the animals had to have a marking system for identification by those other than Raymond and the Kiowa cousins. Unique, it was.

Branding irons were made at the blacksmith shop using letters of the alphabet. Small letters were shaped out of iron, and a branded print was put in the shoulder and rump of any young foal that would be kept. When a branded horse was sold, as it often was when it became too old for the very heavy work of Canfield's, or when one was lost for other reasons, the letter could be used again. That was why there was a stallion marked "A," which Merry re-named Alfred, or sometimes King Alfred. There was Bob, Mimi, Roughy, Casey and so on.

Just now, the current Lucy was expecting her first foal. The huge animals were most often able to perform this activity without supervision, but due to the value of the beasts, its human attendant was alert.

Merry petted and curried Lucy, bringing her special tidbits and checking for any condition that might be amiss. Everything looked good.

A high shelf had been put in one of the animal cubbies to hold special equipment for treating ailments or assisting in deliveries. It kept the products handy and the stocking of the inventory was more easily done. That room was called the "birthing room" and was somewhat away from the others, the better to quiet and calm the nerves of a skittish animal. Merry had been spending the nights with Lucy all week, just in case she came on early.

It was a night that Raymond had worked late in his office, that he had dozed off from sheer exhaustion. Startling awake, he looked out toward his horse barn and noticed a light shining around the door of the birthing room.

Hmmm. Better take a look. Making his way down the dark path, he stopped at the door. Coming softly through the boards was voice, humming. Then words,

> *"Skip, skip, skip to my loo!*
> *Skip, skip, skip, to my loo!*
> *Skip, skip, skip to my loo!*
> *Skip to my loo my pony!*

> *"I've got a pony prettier'n you!*
> *Lucy girl, what will you do?*
> *You'll have a baby, maybe two*
> *Skip to my loo, my pony!*

Raymond paused, listening. Then followed the old song that was popular during the war between the states. He heard the mournful strains, "My tent is cold tonight, Lorena. The winter snow is here again...."

Next came, "In Dublin's fair city, the girls are so pretty! And that's where I first saw sweet Mollie Malone. She pushes a 'barrow through streets long and narrow, singing 'Cockles, and Muscles, Alive, all alive!'"

Robert eased the door open and located the singer. There, cross-legged on the high shelf, she sat. Her brother's outgrown overalls bunched around her legs and an old shirt draped over her shoulders. She looked like a toy, setting on a store shelf. She couldn't weigh more than ninety points, soaking wet. No wonder the shelf held her up so well.

"What are you doing up there?"

"Waitin'. I think this may be Lucy's night. She stomps and keeps wantin' to turn around. If I sing, she's quieter. I think she likes 'Skip to My Loo' the best. I thought if I got up here she wouldn't step on me accidentally. She wouldn't do it on purpose but she's nervous. She don't know what's happenin', maybe…."

Raymond, standing behind the young animal, agreed. "I think you're right. I see a couple of hoofs."

Merry cringed with excitement. "Oh, goodie. Front hoofs or rear?"

"Front, I think. I guess you've been through this before?"

"Oh, yes! Papa and I used to wait it out together. New babies were very valuable and he didn't want to risk leavin' it all to nature."

Raymond nodded in agreement. Any foal her papa's horse had produced wouldn't be worth a fourth of the value of this one, but that didn't mean a thing to the owner of the animal.

Within the hour, the small animal plunked down onto the straw in a soggy heap. Immediately the pile began to sort out feet and tail and a miniature replica of her mother's face. She would be branded "K" in a couple of weeks. Merry had decided the baby would be Katie or Kurt. At this particular time, Katie was more valuable. Old Wanda had already been put on emergency use because of her age. And she should be replaced. Likely she'd go up for sale to someone with light duties for their animal.

Lucy may not have known about the birthing, but she certainly knew what to do with the baby. Within seconds, she had ripped at the membrane and butted the small animal, who seemed to be all legs, into a standing position. Shaky, but erect. Positioning herself at her daughter's head, she pushed her toward her first meal.

"Good shape, Miss Merry. Go get some sleep. Don't be in a hurry to get up in the morning."

Lifting a defiant chin, she faced her employer. "I'll be up at the regular time. This was just part of my duties!"

It was closing time for the Cookie Jar, the first day after Gwinnie's dream of the Surprise Bars. It looked like there were enough leftovers for a trial, and they had locked the door for the night.

A loud bang, and a voice demanding, "You got any food left?"

"Who…? Does it sound like someone we know…?"

Kristie nodded. "Sounds like that well man…you know, the driller…?"

Gwinnie shouted at the door, "You the well driller?"

"I think so. I'm so tired and hungry I don't really know."

She opened the door a crack, and there in the growing dark was the owner from the business up the road to the north. "Not got much of a choice. End of the day, you know."

"End of my day, too. Them cookies there," pointing toward the sugar cookies they had stamped out with the top of a large coffee mug. "Gimmie a couple. What you got to go in 'em? Any bacon or…?"

Kristie selected to two of the cookies. "Peanut butter. That's the best for these." The expression of her face was as though she sold peanut butter sugar cookies all the time. Confident. Actually she had surprised herself with her own words.

"Fix me up. Make it two. Got leftover tea? I don't care if it's cold. What's the price on these?"

Pouring his tea, she told him, "Free to you, this time. This'll be a new product and we'd appreciate it if you'd mention about them if you like 'em. Price'll be about like biscuit and sausage. We're always looking for something filling for lunches. Somethin' that don't spoil in the heat and ain't overly messy."

The cookie sandwiches disappeared like a rabbit in a brush pile, washed down with a slosh of cold tea. "Make me up one more'a them things. I'll pay," and he sorted out the coins he knew would have bought a biscuit sandwich.

Gwinnie took the coins and poked them through the slot in the money box.

The well driller gulped down the last of tea, grabbed up the final sandwich and opened the door. "Thanks, ladies. Don't think I could'a made it that last mile up to the shop without a bite." And he was gone.

Guinnie, the elected sign maker, calmly told her sister, "I'll make up a sign in the morning. Good thinking on your part."

With a satisfied grin, Kristie sacked up the left-over cookies, sugar, cinnamon, chocolate, peanut and the new one, coconut. There were still enough left to try the Surprise Bars in the morning.

Only one thing left to do to close the day, and that was setting the beans to soak overnight. Tomorrow was another day at the Cookie Jar.

It was not even daylight when the Hats and Hankies shop was jiggling down the rutted road toward Enterprise and their school friend, Eve Adams, the teacher. Eve had told them she had sent a message home with the children and had left the rest of the advertisement to their mothers. She expected a crowd, and wouldn't they have fun on a gabfest all night!

With droopy eyes, the two teenagers looked at each other as they wobbled on the bench. "Was this such a good idea?"

"Yeah, it was. We were forced to. We were gettin' overstocked with hats and now we don't have to take care of the horses." Gwinnie dipped her head toward the two young men on the bench in front of them. "Gonna be a long day for them, too."

"They offered!" Bridie pointed out as she leaned sleepily forward, her face in her hands and elbows on her knees.

Miss Josie chose to spend some time in the Cookie Jar the next morning. Her younger brother and cousin had passed through the last grade of the Prairie Academy, and that was a release for Josie. She had done the best she could for her brother and cousin, and in August next year they would be shipped back to New York and the prep school.

Her father's law partner had been named guardian and had taken over his duties when her parents were lost in the Christmas Eve fire. Josh had been only seven, and she was seventeen. The best plan for them had been to take the train out to the Oklahoma territory to their mother's sister and her family.

What would it seem like with the boys gone? Their cousin, Darrell, was the same age as brother Josh, and Josie had treated them as a unit, alternately partnering them, and then setting them in competition.

She had never pretended to be a teacher, but she had successfully passed on the expensive and thorough education her father had given her and had shared it to the best of her ability. Now it was up to the two-year prep school, and then they could begin reading the law. She could hope and cross her fingers, but she could do nothing more for them except assign a few puzzles or problems during the next few months.

She had married and promptly had two pairs of twin boys. Then a girl. Then another boy. A real handful. And here she was, almost thirty.

Her first "graduating" class had been four girls, three of them now teachers. Better teachers than she had been, she was sure. She reasoned that she had the knowledge to teach but not the heart. These girls have the heart. The next class graduated five girls and one of them now teaches. She heard good reports from Eve Adams.

Another interesting thing, though, was about the girls who were not teachers. Two of them had their hat and hankie business, and seemingly they could make just about anything that could be made with a needle and thread. Then here were the sisters who were busily working right before her eyes. They served breakfast of biscuit sandwiches, lunch of soup or beans or whatever they felt in a notion to cook. In the afternoons there were cookies or popcorn. All four of these girls, her former students, worked and made a profit. She knew that because they insisted on showing her the books. (They had studied profit and loss during their last year.)

Then, right across the road was a boy from the same class. He, with minor help from his father, operated his own earth moving business. He owned a whole herd of the mammoth Clydesdale horses needed to pull the heavy graders and whatever those other things were called.

What would these young people be doing if she had not "interfered" by being tossed into their midst? There was no doubt they would have done well, so had she helped at all?

She sipped tea and enjoyed the solitude of the mid-morning. A rattle and a clatter on the road outside as some sort of rig passed by. There was a "Whoa" and part of the rattle stopped. The door burst open and in stepped a workman…the well driller?

"Young ladies, I just stopped in to report. That thing you made for me was a winner. I didn't need that third one, so I had it for breakfast with coffee. I think it was better after it set. Had an idea for you. That blacksmith shop over catty-corner? Time you see a bunch'a fellers over there, take a plate'a those cookies over there. Cut 'em in half and don't let 'em have a whole one. They always have coffee. Tell 'em you were tryin' somethin' and then leave. See what happens. Right now you can make me up a sausage biscuit for lunch."

Grabbing up the sandwich, he was gone without waiting for a reply.

Miss Josie stared at him and then at the closed door. Then she looked up questioningly at Gwinnie, then at Kristie as both girls grinned.

Gwinnie picked up a pair of fresh-baked sugar cookies, slathered peanut butter on one and slapped the other on the top. "We were about out of food when he came by at quittin' time last night. Settled for cookie sandwiches." She put the sandwich on a plate, deftly cut it in two and set it before their former teacher. "See what you think. Pretend you were a workin' man at the end'a the day."

Just then the door opened again, ladylike. A clean and dressed young lady came in. Hardly even five feet tall. Blue and white striped scarf on her head.

"Oh, Miss Josie! It's been so long since I've seen you!"

"America, my dear, would you sit down with me and share my breakfast? I'm sure I couldn't eat this whole thing."

"Thanks, Miss Josie. I'm thinkin' I'll have no trouble eatin'. I really work up an appetite some days." She sat across from her teacher and helped herself.

"America, dear, I was so sorry to hear about your father. It must have been a shock, but I'm so proud of you. I understand you and your brother both have jobs."

"Yes, ma'am. Thank you. We were lucky, Homer and me. Course, our papa told us God helps us be lucky when we really need it. I went lookin' for a job with animals and Mr. Bramwell at the mill said I wasn't big enough, but it seems like Homer is. He loves it and he gets three meals a day as part of his pay. That's really good because he eats a lot and I don't have much time to cook. I'm the lucky one, though. I have the best job in the whole world. I get to take care of Raymond Canfield's work horses, and he has twelve of them. And there's a couple that don't work anymore."

"You really like that job? It isn't too hard for you?"

"Oh, no. I get to curry them, check for skin nicks and scratches, talk to them and make sure their hay nets are full. You know that horses have to have hay, no matter how much grain they get? The hay is like their bread and helps keep them from the bellyache. But you knew that, of course. I'm just excited."

Miss Josie shook her head. "I surely didn't know that. I'm sure you know a lot of things I don't know about horses. They keep you really busy?"

With a grin, Merry admitted, "Well, I make up some of the 'busy.' Some girls like dogs and cats, but I like horses. Even the mucking out, but I make sure I clean up before I get around anyone."

"What is 'mucking out'?"

"Oh, that's when…well it's really…what it is…is poop! It has to be taken out of their stalls and piled up to start it decaying. Then it gets spread over the back field for fertilizer. Raymond says I can't operate the spreader, but I'll convince him I can. I think it's part of my job, and I'll tell him that. Oh, say! We had a baby. Our Lucy, she's just old enough and this is her first foal. A little girl and I named her Katie. I just love the babies. She tries to suck on my clothes or my fingers. Oh, please excuse me. I just rattle on and on...."

"America, the truth is, I just love to hear you 'rattle on.' I heard about your loss and wanted to help but I know there isn't much anyone can do to make you feel better. I was seventeen when I lost both parents in a fire on Christmas Eve. My brother was younger as you know. I did what I had to do for myself and him, and that's what you did. We may have a lot in common, you and I. For the first year there wasn't a day that I didn't think about how I missed my parents, and then I told myself that they would not want it that way. They would want me to get myself together and go on.

"I've thought a lot about you over the last couple of months but you've done more to help yourself than anyone could do for you. I know you will be a success. Already, you have the best job in the world, and apparently Raymond needed someone. I'm glad he had the courage to hire you, even though you seem too small for the job."

America ducked her head at the compliment. "Thank you, Miss Josie. I was lucky to get to go to school for two years and learn so much from you. I don't think of myself as being small, except on the outside. Inside, I want to be as big as anyone. Mr. Bramwell likes Homer so much, I think he may have a job as long as he likes it. You know, the Bramwells only have girls and their daddy says it takes a fellow to work in the mill with all the liftin'. Homer says it isn't all that much work. I'm just happy we got to stay here in town where we're known. Oh, here I sit talkin', and I need to get to work. Thanks for the cookie. I'm so glad to see you again. Bye Kristie and Gwinnie!"

"Goodbye, America. Stay happy!"

Miss Josie watched the girl go. A shiver of pleasure moved down her arms. So different, she and America, but both had instinctively used whatever assets they had for what they considered was the best for their brother first, then for themselves.

Then to Kristie, "Thank you for letting me test the cookie. Very tasty and filling. I think it might be a bit heavy for some, but good for working men. I might make a suggestion. Sometime you might want to try grinding your own home-grown peanuts and mix with churned butter and a little honey. Or maybe soft goat cheese instead of the butter because it wouldn't melt and run out so easily. Just a thought."

Gwinnie, with a grin, "We'll try that. Maybe we'll name it after you!"

Then Kristie, "Miss Josie, is it gossip to tell something you think is a compliment?"

After a pause for thought, "Kristie, that could go either way. You'll have to decide."

"All right, I decided. Did you know that Merry, I mean America, could sell her property for quite a bit of money but she won't do it. She thinks she should keep it until her brother gets older, because maybe he'll want it. If she had the money, she wouldn't have to work…at least where she's working."

The teacher took a deep breath as the image of herself deciding to teach instead of what she might have done. She had put her brother's needs first…just like America had.

Then, "I think America is doing the right thing about the farm. This way she'll never wish she hadn't let it go, and Homer is still too young to make a decision. Also, I think she likes her job."

With a fast shake of the head both girls stood firm. "She couldn't like it, Miss Josie!" and, "She has to shovel horse poop!"

With a twinkle and a small smile, the teacher arose to leave. "I think she said it was only bad after a long rain because it got gooey! But it works out alright because she has gum boots."

She left behind her two thoughtful stares. Could what she said really be true?

Francine Canfield, brother to Raymond the Canfield Grading operation, graduated one year ahead of the Cookie Jar sisters. She had always been fascinated by rhyming words, and when in school she was introduced to poetry, her thoughts took a turn and formed themselves into rhymes truly without help from her.

It was a Saturday and Francine was at home for the weekend, passing time in the Cookie Jar, as usual, when it happened. When someone else came in, a huge orange and yellow stripped tom cat wriggled his way through the door.

Striding with firm feet and tail straight and high, he marched toward the counter with a huge dead mole held firmly with his strong teeth.

Gwinnie met the cat as though he was a regular customer. "Hello there, Otis. Did you come to buy a fruit pie?"

Soberly she stooped and took the mole by its stubby tail, then stepped behind her counter. She returned with a half a fruit fried pie which she gave to the cat.

Otis, the cat, took the gift as though it was an expected reward and settled under the last ice cream table to enjoy it. When the final crumb had been licked up, he curled tail and long legs into a ball under the chair, careful to be out of the way of human feet, and closed his eyes to rest.

Francine looked from Gwinnie to the cat and back toward Gwinnie. "Now what was all that about?"

"You mean Otis? Oh, a couple of months back we had a rat in here that not only made a mess, he gnawed us awake at night. I tried everything, and even traps, but that rat knew how to trip the catch. Then one day, Otis wiggled himself in here, saw the rat and caught it in one leap. A snap of the jaws and it was dead. I'd been trying for two months to catch that thing!

"But then, he didn't even want to eat it. He leaped up on the counter, left the rat and grabbed a fried pie. I thought it was a good swap, so I let 'im eat it. Thing was, he's in here two or three times a week with an offering. I think he thinks he's buying a pie or a cookie, and the cost is a rat! America says he belongs to the old man with a shack on the land back'a Raymond's place."

Francine again. "But did you notice that wasn't a rat, it was a mole?"

Gwinnie answered with a grin and a shrug. "I know. Otis hasn't got his currency straight yet, but I let him get away with it. That way he'll keep watch. Sometimes we get rats around the back door. Maybe smell the food. Most times he actually has a rat or a mouse, and wherever he gets them, I'm glad to see them gone. Seems worth a bite. He doesn't want meat or egg, though. I think he has a sweet tooth."

The next Saturday Francine handed the girls a sheet of paper, and it was now attached to the wall, right over the mail hooks.

UNCLE EZRA'S CAT

He belongs to Uncle Ezra,
'Old Otis' is his name,
But like his master, Ezra, he's a special kind of cat.

Old Otis ranges near and far.
He stopped off at the Cookie Jar.
Two young ladies there would greet him with a gentle
pat.
He'd been there several times before
He'd crouch down just outside the door
And scoot inside with sneaky speed known only to a cat.

The Cookie Jar smelled nice and sweet
But no one offered him, to eat,
One of those things that humans eat that always
makes them smile.
So Otis crawled beneath a chair,
While no one knew a cat was there,
He'd crouch and sniff the sweetness and just rest a
little while.

So now inside, he waited there
With tail tucked in beneath the chair.
That's when he saw the rat peep out around the
counter's side.
He launched himself without a thought
And instantly that rat was caught
Even if it saw the cat, there was no place within the
shop to hide.

A howl that only he could make,
A leap, a snap, a vicious shake
His sharp teeth caught that rat right in behind his
ugly eyes.
Head clenched in teeth, with dragging tail
Old Otis leaped the counter rail

*And laid that rat beside one of Miss Kristie's Cookie
Pies.*

*Miss Gwinnie squealed with noisy joy!
Just like she'd got a brand new toy.
"That's got to be the rat we couldn't catch with baited
snare!"
He looked Miss Gwinnie in the eye…
With sharp teeth, he then took a pie,
Leaped to the floor and ate the pie right there
beneath the chair.*

*Now, Otis was a clever cat
And he could figure this and that
So now he knew how humans got to eat what tasted
sweet.
It took a swap of this or that.
A Cookie Pie for one dead rat,
Hereafter, he would have the things he really wished
to eat.*

*So every morning after that,
He brought those ladies one dead rat,
But there were times the Cookie Jar had no more rats
to yield.
Otis could take care of that
The hay field always had a rat,
Or maybe there would be one in the mowed-down
barley field.*

*If what it took was one dead rat,
Old Otis could take care of that!*

There it hung above the mail hooks with the notices and
warnings that a lynx had been seen in the neighborhood. The
whole settlement of Corners knew about Uncle Ezra's cat. The old
man walked all over the country, but he never came to the Cookie
Jar. His loss!

Beside Otis' poem was the one presented to the Hats and Hankies girls but the wall space of their traveling showroom had no space for display. Neither did it get the foot traffic that the Cookie Jar enjoyed.

MA STANFIELD'S BONNET

When old Ma Stanfield leaves her bed
Her lacy bonnet leaves her head.
A daytime bonnet will be donned instead.

A soft one made of rosy fleece
With wrinkled tie and spattered grease
Because that bacon always will release.

Now there's a washing to be done
A stripped bonnet is the one
To hide from wind and shade her from the sun.

But when a neighbor stops for tea
Choose lacy edging, flowing free
All neat and proper prairie ladies would agree.

When she needs to gather eggs
In hay-filled nests, 'neath chicken legs,
A straw cap for her head, she always begs.

Prayer meeting needs another hat.
A box in closet holds one that
Is good for prayer, or equally a friendly quiet chat.

Ma Stanfield needs these hats because
Of all the many jobs she does.
And that's the way the life upon the prairie was.

Dark time falls and family's fed
And when it's finally time for bed,
Again the soft and lacy night cap hugs the lady's
head.

CHAPTER 3

It was the year that Homer turned fourteen that Bernice Bramwell turned nine. Now Bernice, called Neecie, had a fetching smile, a charmingly freckled nose and skillful fingers.

She carefully explained to Homer how she had gathered the nuts, cracked them and chopped them fine, because she wanted to make the cinnamon rolls even more delicious. She studied them on the plate and selected the one she felt was the gooiest with sugar and spice, and had the most nuts, and she set it beside Homer's plate at the beginning of the meal. She pointed out that she did it so that her little sisters would not get it. They would not appreciate it fully, and she was sure Homer would. She was right.

She watched him from afar, when she had time, because she was forbidden to come anywhere near the shiny gears of the mechanism that turned the mill. She peeked through the slats in the barn wall when he piled the hay and grain before the small working animals after their day of walking circles in the dust.

Homer was treated alternately like a creature provided for the amusement of the three girls, an appreciated hired hand, and a beloved nephew who was visiting. It almost seemed they treated him as a son. Neecie's adoration was not missed by her parents, and they projected what could happen if it continued and became mutual.

As a miller who had only daughters…well, one did the best one could. Anyway, Homer was an agreeably hard worker and seemed to perform his assigned duties with ease. He would never know that he had inherited strength from a direct line of Vikings who successfully rode the waves by sheer strength and vision. Or that his Viking ancestors stopped over in Holland where their solid, hardworking bodies were a plus.

A Forrester, he was, while not knowing that his forbears dealt in the massive forest logs that build ships and many other things, or that they transported the building material to England. He hardly knew how hard his papa, Emil Forrester had worked in England, in Virginia or by the Mississippi on his way to the Territory.

Nor did he care. He was kept so busy that the loss of a caring father was felt less, and that was a blessing.

Today, the miller had bought a half ton of shelled corn. The women who could afford the luxury, preferred the fine ground meal from the grist wheel, above the coarser product from their own hand grinder. They also preferred to avoid the tiresome time spent on the hand grinder.

Homer adjusted the gears as he had been trained to and poured the golden grains where they would fall at a specified rate to be funneled under the grinding plate, and finally to work themselves through the sifter and out into the hopper as fine-ground meal.

Picking up a ten-pound sack, his employer handed it to him and told him to fill it with corn meal and take it to his sister. Just another of the little gifts of food he was sent home with. He knew without being told that the miller would expect his sister to empty the meal into another container and send back the sack. Sacks were an expense, and the customers who wished a better price brought their own cloth bags. The miller was good about these things, and it made his product more affordable.

It was becoming dusky dark when the boy headed home, because the fall days were getting shorter. He passed the long barn of Canfield Grading and heard a strange sound and huffing and mild complaints from the animals within.

Breaking into a quiet run, he reached the cabin of the hired help, set the cornmeal on the table and grabbed up the gun. He wished it had been the six shooter, but that was only one of the things lost in the mysterious disaster that took his father.

Shouldering the rifle, always kept loaded, he moved quietly along the board wall of the barn. At the far end was the pen that held the latest two foals, securely locked up for the night. Even the foals were valuable, and if someone was stealing them, Homer would put a stop to that.

The next noise he heard was a snarl and growl at his feet. Stumbling to his knees he felt the fangs pierce his calf muscles just as his reflex flung the rifle around in a circle cracking into something he hardly saw. The clamped teeth loosened from his calf, a yelp sounded and Homer was rolled over.

Again shouldering the weapon, he got off a shot, and saw a furry form rise and float over the board fence of the corral. Shucks! Why couldn't he have killed that thieving beast? Blood ran warm down his leg and into his boot, but he stepped with weight on the injured leg and it held him. Not broken. The house was close, so he'd just go on, and that's when he tripped over an object that should not have been there.

Slipping down to his knees again, he felt the warm body of a wolf, fat and fully furred for the winter. He'd got one! Well, that was better than total failure because a dead wolf carcass tied to the fence was a good deterrent for weeks or maybe even all winter.

Stumbling on to the house, he met his sister running from the well where she had been checking on water for the animals that would work tomorrow.

"HOMER! HOMER! WHERE ARE YOU...I HEARD SHOTS!"

"I'm all right. I'm at the house."

Merry stared in horror at the blood-soaked pant leg.

Her brother attempted reassurance. "It's not as bad as it seems. He didn't get a good bite because'a my boots. But there's a dead one out there and I don't want to let something happen to it. Let's take the lantern and bring it in."

His sister commanded, "You stay here! I'll get it."

"No, you need me. There was another one and we're not goin' out there without a freshly loaded gun and two shooters."

The gun was not needed, however, and as his sister carried the lantern, and he held the gun over his shoulder, they dragged the animal by the paws into the mud room of their cabin and locked the door behind it.

America Forrester stared down at the carcass of the animal and told the dead body. "I'm gonna skin you and make a bedroom rug. I'll stomp on you every morning just for the fun of it. You bit my brother and tried to steal my babies. I hate you."

Having vented her true feelings, she pushed Homer into the kitchen and washed the wound. Truly it wasn't as bad as it could be, because it COULD HAVE BEEN a rabid animal, and it clearly wasn't. He would have a sore leg for a while, but his employer would be doubly proud of him for his bravery.

That was just one more thing that made the miller stroke his chin and watch the young man. It might yet be possible to have a son at, say…eighteen years? Maybe nineteen. A girl shouldn't be permitted to marry before age fourteen, that being age Mrs. Bramwell had been.

The Irish girls were dutifully collected from their selling trip to Enterprise. The two-day visit had been a lot of fun with much giggling and eating to be done. Eva's soldier husband had agreeably made himself absent while the ladies made popcorn, peanut candy and laughed a lot. Eva was still happy with her classes, now in their new building, and her visitors were happy not to have classes. In any building. They did, however, still have more inventory than they had planned. Apparently there had been a problem with availability of funds at Enterprise. Not surprising.

Clearly, something else must be done. Quickly. It was absolutely necessary as there was no more hanging space in the traveling showroom. A nod between the girls, and Bridie began, "You fellows gonna be workin' on next Saturday?"

Johnny and Willie glanced meaningfully at each other. There was obviously a reason for this question, as the girls were seldom concerned as to where the fellows were when they were not around them. For that reason, Johnny Black skipped answering the question and went straight for the reason for the question. "Why, you got somethin' goin'?"

Pat's turn at this tag-team match. "No, 'spect not. Leastwise we won't be sewin'."

Willie could play the game as well as anyone. "Why? You got rich all of a sudden?"

Bridie again. "Nope. Got sore fingers."

Short pause. Then Johnny. "Fingers too sore to lift a spoon to eat ice cream?"

Another pause. "Might be well by Saturday."

Expected response. "Buggy or travelin' van?"

"Van."

Next a long, decision-evoking sigh. Canfield Grading was not particularly dependable with its schedules. "Depends on if an emergency happens."

Knowing that emergencies could not be planned for in advance, Pat summed up, "Sounds fine. Plan for noon?"

"Sounds good. Unless you girls need time for shoppin'."

Bridie's turn. "Let's try for eleven. Your horses."

That taken care of, the girls turned toward what they would be taking. The little dress shop in Argyle was usually a good market for hats, so, of course, the girls would take them all. Hankies hardly took up any room, and dresses were not a good seller for them. However, shawls crocheted or knitted from fancy New York yarn did really well.

The girls could make them quickly, but seldom bothered. Their moms were expert, and it was a good way to make points at home for the moms who had no other good outlet for their product. It took no effort to take the shawls. The moms packed them carefully in boxes, along with lavender sachets or rose petal packets.

It had been a big thing when the Argyle Sweet Shop installed the ice cream making equipment. The engine that ran the ice cream machine was turned on every Friday, Saturday and Sunday, and on any other time that a sale of a certain total value had been pre-arranged.

Equal to the ice cream was the outing to be planned for with special friends, the trip there and back providing sights and other incidents to discuss later.

Miss Josie went occasionally. She enjoyed the occasion, but not so much as the younger set did. Ice cream had been a common thing in New York City at the time she had left. For the young people here, it was a new thing. Ordinarily, ice cream was only made when the snow was deep enough, and that was always in the winter. Ice cream was meant for summer. Clearly!

With a small smile, Miss Josie noted for another of the many times that outings such as that seemed to encourage the young people to wait longer for marriage. The Cookie Jar sisters and the Hats and Hankies girls could very well have been married by now, instead of owning and running their own business. Same for the girls who were teaching. Even Johnny, Willie and Raymond might have entered marriage for the sake of staking out and obtaining one of the scarce girls. As it was, they were choosing to wait, earning money that bought special things they wanted. Money that their own hands and brains had earned, and over which they had total control.

It must be a heady and exciting concept for a territory girl. Miss Josie had heard Gwinnie and Kristie negotiating with their father over the purchase of supplies.

"But, Papa," Kristie pointed out. "You don't like to grow peanuts and we need a lot of them. That's why we put the notice up over the mail hooks."

"It ain't that, really. I just don't have time to pull the nuts off those roots and clean off the sand."

The girls locked glances, and Gwinnie offered, "We could do it. We might have the time, but if we did, we'd have to change the notice so other men could price them either way. Why don't you see what you could grow them for? And let us know."

Kristie softened the words. "You'll be able to do the popcorn, won't you? I know you don't like the tiny ears, but the grains come off a lot easier than field corn. I'll bet your estimate will be the lowest."

Then Gwinnie nodded agreeably. "I'll bet it will. But if it isn't, you still have Mr. Bramwell at the grist wantin' to buy the field corn."

A few customers came in, and Mr. McLaughlin settled back in his chair with a small smile and a sigh. Pouring his hot coffee from his saucer back into the mug and glancing at Miss Josie.

"All this here is your fault, Miss Josie. I should'a been able to tell these girls what to do and what to think until they got 'em a man to take over."

Josie returned the jest. "I'm guilty. And to think, look at all the money it cost for you to totally lose control."

The man nodded, cheerfully. "I 'speck you've noted the size'a Raymond's business? Got 'em six fellows working. Not all the time, but he keeps busy. Pretty much."

Then Miss Josie. "It looks as though Miss Forrester is making him a good hired hand. I know for certain that she thinks she's got a dream job. Her words, that is."

An agreeable nod. "Yeah. You know, I had a little doubt when he talked about puttin' her on. It was plain he was needin' help with those horses, but there's problems in putting a pretty girl in amongst a lotta young fellows."

"Has it worked out all right?"

"Seems too. I've talked with him and I talk with her occasionally. It seems to me those two haven't taken a look at each other, both of 'em bein' intent on what they're doin'. That Raymond, he thinks he's got what he wants. Wanted them horses when he wasn't even 10 years old, and if that girl wasn't the best to be had on takin' care of 'em, she'd be gone, I assure you."

Nodding her head appreciatively, Josie commented, "Sometimes things work out right, don't they?"

The man drained the last of his drink and stood, "Yeah, but it wouldn't'a without you bein' here, givin' 'em somethin' to think on while their brains was settin' in."

"Mr. McLaughlin, I thank you very much for your kind words."

"Don't need thanks. Just the truth." And with a grin, he was gone.

When Josie was alone in the Cookie Jar, Kristie came to join her. "What'da'ya think of our cottonwood grove out front. Leafin' out good, huh? We'd never have thought of it if Mr. Digby hadn't suggested it."

Josie nodded, agreeably. "He likes to be kept busy, and he loves to furnish an answer to those who might not yet know the question."

The crippled miner had certainly been an answer to her. He was an old man with no family. Josie had been a seventeen-year-old who had just lost her parents in the tragic Christmas Eve fire. They filled a need in each other, and Josie became the daughter/granddaughter that he had never taken time for arrange for himself, and he was the guiding parent/grandparent in a situation where her blood father would have been helpless to assist. Sometimes things work out right.

Kristie continued, "We've ordered cute little lanterns to put on the limbs and the evenings are getting longer, lettin' people come by and sit outside. With so many of our friends stoppin' by, we were using a lot of popcorn, bein' the cheapest thing we have, and them not always havin' money." Leaning closer, she confided conspiratorially, "It's a temptation to let 'em have it free, but we talked ourselves out of that. Who knows where it'd stop and this IS a business, as our teacher explained to us during that last tough year of school! I remember you telling us that whatever we did, we couldn't give away what we were trying to sell. So we just lowered the price. And bought more. Folks can get water, mail hook service and a notice board for free, but everything else has to cost somethin' so we can make a profit. Else there'd be no Cookie Jar."

Gwinnie joined them in time to hear the last several sentences. Pulling up a chair, she shared, "Some fellow came by and wanted to know if we sold something called a burrito...said it was a pet name for a little donkey. Just dough with spiced meat filling and browned in the skillet or oven. We just about gave up, because the dough kept fallin' apart till Carlotta told us her mother-in-law made them, and they had to be started with yeast dough. 'Course, the fellow didn't know that. He just thought it was dough.

"But you know what? It makes a way to use left-over beans! We start fresh on cookin' beans every mornin', and every evening we use up what was left over to make up the "donkeys". That way we have 'em ready for breakfast. Fellows like 'em better'n the girls do, but they generally got more money!"

Kristie again. "Oh, I forgot! We need to put beans on our list for prices. Pa likes growin' beans. He may make us the best price on them. Another thing, you suggested we put our own ground peanuts in the cookie sandwiches, and they ARE a lot better. The goat cheese doesn't melt in the fellow's lunch boxes. Thanks for the idea."

"You're most welcome, and now I must get back to whatever it was I was putting off until tomorrow. Later, girls." And she was gone.

Days passed and the fall weather now had a chill. Merry Forester shivered a bit and slipped into her fuzzy robe. The house was cooling down and it was time for her to be in bed. It had been a long day and her muscles ached.

A "norther" was coming in, for sure. Black clouds heaped in the northwest and the south wind was kicking up. She had felt it coming on that morning and decided to muck out the stalls even though they were not in bad shape. If a storm came in, it could get awfully messy, so she'd just take care of it now.

One thing after another, but now the day was over and she needed to get to bed. Homer had climbed to his loft a couple of hours ago, saying he had a heavy day as well, and had brought her a slice of chocolate layered cake with coconut frosting. Yesterday it had been sausage meatloaf with sundried tomatoes. Came in handy. They were so lucky Homer got such good food.

Kicking off her warm slippers, she stepped onto the wolf skin rug by her bed, remembering to stomp on it for what that animal did to her brother! The wolf hide was stiff, and not soft and cozy as the way Mrs. Gray Owl's rugs were, but it worked. And it was big.

In spite of the cloud bank, a full moon lit the corral and sparkled off the skiffen of snows that had fallen during the evening. About a half an inch, now. Horses were cozy and settled, and she was grateful to be slipping under the warm quilts. A good time of the day, and she dozed off to sleep in minutes.

The next sound was a rattle and a clink, and she startled awake, feeling for the rifle that was by her bed. No more sound. She settled back in the warmth of the feather ticking.

A bang and another clink. Dashing to the window she searched the corral with anxious eyes. Something was wrong.

Flinging her robe over her shoulders, she grabbed up the rifle and slipped out the door. At that moment, a crash of a barn door, a clamor of feet and an angry whinny. King Alfred!

The black silhouette came dashing out of the barn, the rider laying low over the stallion's back. The animal's front feet cleared the gate, landed, then a head reared and front quarters turned again toward the barn.

Head again jerked forward. Nose lifted and another angry whinny as Merry shouldered the rifle. Bracing the barrel on a fence post, she fired. A scream…another whinny…whirling feet and flying tail. Front quarters rearing and hoofs slashing through the air like daggers.

She aimed again, but the animal was now riderless and was fast returning toward her and the gate of the corral. In the moonlight over the whiteness of the snow, she saw a dark form running…getting smaller in the distance.

Lowering the gun, she called, "Come on, boy! King Alfred, good fellow!" Whirling again, seeming to try to get his bearings, he came toward her voice. Merry sang out, "Skip. Skip. Skip to my loo! Skip. Skip. Skip to…" and finished the ditty.

The commotion aroused Homer and he was in his boots and running from the house, door banging behind him. He saw the monster horse meekly following the tiny figure whose hand reached up to his flowing mane, just to give him confidence.

Homer entered the stall just after the black hooves and hind quarters and the nervously switching tail. His sister was in the dark of the stall…somewhere. "Sis? Where are you?"

"I'm here, I'm fine," called a voice from the direction of the hay net.

He couldn't help chiding, "I wish you'd'a called me, 'stead'a takin' this on by yourself."

Lifting the lantern off its shelf, she struck a match to the wick. Beams of light filled the stall. "I would'a, but there wasn't time. But thanks. Homer, someone was tryin' to steal King Alfred! Right outta his stall! I got 'im, though. Didn't kill 'im cause I saw 'im runnin'. Scairt 'im off, good and proper."

"...Runnin' away? You're sure?"

"Positive. If he hadn't, he'd be dead!" Raising her voice, she declared to the interior rafters of the barn, "HE WAS TRYIN' TO STEAL KING ALFRED!" The four-hoofed subject of the conversation whickered a murmur from his rubbery, velvet lips. The huge head butted softly against America's robe.

"It's all right, fellow. Bein' a choice between you and him, I choose you. Every time! He gets the bullet and you get the stall."

Homer surveyed the scene in the light of the lantern. "Sis! You're barefooted! You're walking in the snow barefooted. You gotta get in the house right now or neither me nor King Alfred nor no one else is gonna have you...you bein' dead!"

"Barefooted?" She looked down at her feet, wet and mucky up through her bare toes. "Hmmm, I'll come on in." With one last hug and affectionate pat, she caressed the lowered head. "You'll be all right till morning, King. Then we'll talk about this."

With a conversational whicker and grumble, the animal watched her leave, just as though he knew exactly what she said. Chances are, he did.

In the house, Homer drew still-warm water from the stove reservoir and filled a deep bucket. "Sit down and get your feet in here while I build up the fire. We're both gonna get warm."

The girl looked up at her tall, bossy brother. New experience... him ordering her around! *About time*, she decided! And there was no more sound from the corral or the barn that night.

"Shot 'im with a rifle in the middle of the night? What on earth were you thinkin'?" Her wide-eyed employer demanded an answer.

"Sure I did. I wasn't thinkin' nothin'. I knew for sure HE WAS TRYIN' TO STEAL KING ALFRED!"

"Barefooted...?"

"Wasn't no time for shoes! Lucky I got 'im close, he was. If he'd been farther on out, I might not've missed him. I'd'a killed 'im for sure, before I let him steal Alfred."

"You know for sure you missed 'im? That blood on Alfred's back...and all?"

"Saw 'im a'runnin'. Could'a took another shot at 'im, but I didn't."

She was right. Horse hooves dug into the soft dirt through the gate, small barefoot footprints following. A scramble of dirt where Alfred fought the rider and tried to come back...deep prints where he reared. Disturbed snow where the person had landed on the ground, and running boot prints toward the back of the quarter section, veering toward State Highway. No other sign of him.

Before the week was out, the Forrester cabin was furnished with a new six-shooter and the gatepost had a heavier chain and lock. Also, Raymond's hired man got a raise.

At the Cookie Jar, Merry Forrester was asked, "Weren't you just scared to death?"

"No. I was mad, and there wasn't any room or time for scared." And she added as though it was the total answer. "He was tryin' to steal my horse! He would'a if I hadn't shot 'im. The King knew it was all wrong and he called me to come help 'im. He knew what to do, and I knew what to do. Now it's over. Could I get coffee and cornbread? Lots of butter."

When Miss Josie was hearing the story, she pictured a scared girl of seventeen pulling her ten-year-old brother from his bed and pushing him out a second story window just ahead of the flame. She had no time to call for help if her brother was to be saved, and she was also barefooted. Shaking her head with wonder, she knew that no one in the community could identify with America more than herself.

Mr. Elwood, who had rented the farm belonging to Merry and Homer, brought his rent money to her, along with the gift of a leg of venison, salted and dried into what was essentially a huge jerky of meat. Shaking his head depreciatingly, Mr. Elwood explained, "You'd never believe the activity of deer we had this year.

Had so much meat, Mrs. Elwood said the smoke house was too full, so get rid of this on those young people."

With a smile of thanks, she took it. But what does one do with it? It did not occur to her to ask the neighbors, or even Mrs. Bramwell. The dried haunch was much too hard to slice and fry like steak. It was more like salted leather, unless sliced sliver thin. And even the slivers just sat there in the iron skillet, scorching on the bottom.

So she dumped in a half a cup of water. After the steaming and sizzling settled, the water began to soak up the meat slivers, settling them down into a soft, tasty pile. The jerky had almost no fat, so it took a dab of butter to keep them from sticking. Sandwich? She piled it into a biscuit but slivers kept falling out.

Dumping the meat slivers back into the hot skillet, she broke an egg on top and stirred it. Almost instantly it turned into a moldable heap, stuck together with the egg. Lifting it out again, she tried it in the biscuit. It stayed. The inch-thick pile of tasty concoction bit easily and chewed even better.

Quite filling, it was, too. Really, really filling! She cut the biscuit into what would have been half, and finished eating, putting the cut off part in the warming oven.

By supper time, the fire had gone out, and the warming oven was more like an ice box.

Weariness and hunger influencing her, she lifted out the half sandwich and took a bite. *Hey! Not bad!* Settling down with a cup of milk, she finished the sandwich and went to bed.

As she settled under her quilts with a satisfied tummy, she told herself, *I've got to remember to tell the Cookie Jar. That sandwich was just as good cold as hot.* With a smile, she drifted off to sleep. All in all, she was pretty pleased with herself.

Stuart Campbell had itchy heels. At least that's what the graybeards of the family called it. First he was here, and then he was somewhere else. It was like he was trying on locations in the way one tried on shoes to find one that fit, and like so many others of his ilk, he headed west.

The boundaries of St. Louis and Memphis seemed constricting to young men and it could have been that they were constantly dealing with people, or barges, or ocean going sailing ships that were either coming from some mysterious place, or going out into the great unknown. Consequently, many were restless.

Stuart had been harboring the thought of checking out another location when he saw the advertisement. Young men could find work out west constructing roads in the country and laying bricks on the streets of the towns. Now, what could be difficult about either job? Nothing, actually.

The west wasn't so mysterious. The *Santa Fe* made regular trips there and back and furnished a variety of occupancy comfort. One could pay the fare and sit in the cars, or one could hide in one of the boxcars, tucked in among the crates and barrels, riding free. Or there was the other way, and it actually offered more freedom.

When it left the station, the longer the train was and the more cars it pulled, the slower it was to really pick up speed. Stuart had heard tales of those who waited on the overpass until a suitable conveyance came by slowly enough. Then he had only to drop himself down on the top of a selected car. Now, he was told that the bump was rather hard, and he must immediately find a handhold, but there were many of them on the tops of the boxcars...but not the Pullman cars with the soft seats inside.

He was also told that a thick jacket was required, with long-handle underwear, if possible. It seemed that no matter the warmth of the day, when night came on, it would be cold on the top of that moving car. Also it was told to him by experts that one must carry a small rope to attach oneself to one of the many hooks on the tops of the cars, or one might fall asleep and roll off.

Stuart collected these bits of advice and mulled over them in the dark of the night. He would do this, of course, and now all that was left was just the selection of the time. Summer, of course, would be best.

As he lifted crates and bails on the wharf, his mind was elsewhere. He loaded the barges because the wages were the first step to once more get to satisfy his itching heels. There needed to be enough coins to buy a really good horse.

One thing about jumping the train cars had not been told him. The overpass that was the most convenient was closely watched by the law. The uniformed officers took exception to loafers hanging about, waiting for a chance to endanger their lives. Stuart had learned this while he was checking out the location preparing to endanger his own life.

Just an innocent passerby, he seemed to be, and saw ragtag fellows being hauled off the overpass by the ear...so to speak. He, of course, would not be ragtag. He would be a well-dressed young man, simply passing the time of day.

In the meantime, he worked. The loaded barge before him was attached to the tug and it pulled away. Another took its place. It appeared that there were three more to load for this particular job. All in a day's work. No thought required. Do what they told you to do.

It was early spring when Stuart decided the time was now right. Well-padded with coat and underwear, a stout cord in his hand and a pleasant jungle of coins in his pockets, he ambled along the thoroughfare with the wagons, buggies and other foot traffic. In the distance was the puffing and blowing of a loaded engine, the shrill tooting of the whistle and then the iron horse was on its way.

Stuart was a great believer in omens, as were his forebears from the Scottish hills. He was not absolutely certain that the "little people" had anything to do with the affairs of humans, but it didn't hurt to hope for their help.

As it happened, a loaded wagon pulled by tired mules pulled through the area over the tracks, and Stuart knew he would not get a better chance. Seating himself on the edge of the overpass, he swung his feet over just as the black smoke from the engine welled up around him. He would let two cars pass to avoid the smoke, and then drop.

He did. The fall was hard, and the momentum of the boxcar rolled him precariously close to the edge, but, as he was told, there were a lot of hooks. Grabbing one, he held on as the train gathered speed. *Hey, man!* What was so hard about this?

Pulling himself up to the center of the car, he found he was not alone. Ragged coat, grizzled whiskers, tattered shoes. *Oh, well....*

Stuart spent the night on the boxcar, glad of the advice to take along a rope. The monotony of the sway and the grind of the drivers from the engine three cars ahead, lulled him into sleep and he could have fallen off but for the tug at his wrist. Morning was trying to break in the east as the train finally slowed, huffing huge swishes of air from its brakes.

His companion, silent until now, advised, "Be ready to jump off, soon as ya can. They can be hard on a fellow here."

Being so warned, he was ready. Pull in shoulders, make a ball of his body and roll. Down the slope of the grade built up for the track, he whirled. When he looked around, he was alone. The other fellow? Who cared. Stuart was well on the way to scratching the itch on his heels.

He found himself in some little town in Kansas. Joining himself to gatherings of fellows about his age, Stuart learned that the action was farther south, down in something called the Territory, or sometimes called Oklahoma. Well, he could manage that, but this was the time to get a horse. If he jumped the train again, he might be carried farther than he wanted to be.

He could buy a horse, all right, but he quickly found that people here really loved their horses because of what they cost. To buy one that he liked would leave him penniless, and he liked to eat more so than he liked a fancy mount, so he bought an animal with more experience than strength, but no matter....

Heading south, he saw a lot of country. Interesting, but only to pass through. The raw frontier town of Guthrie was good for a week, and then he set out again. Oklahoma City was good for a week and a half, but the heels still itched.

Jogging along on the plodding hooves of the scruffy animal, he did a lot of thinking. He needed a job to replace his dwindling supply of coins, and there was no end of the opportunities. He decided to be choosy. He passed through a place called Argyle and stayed a day. Interesting. He could come back to this place, but first he'd look around.

Allowing his mount to have his fill of grass in the bar-ditch, he took stock. Not a bad place. Certainly different from St Louis or Memphis.

Moving on again, he did, wonder of wonders, find a diner of sorts. Cookie Jar! Caddy-corner from the diner was the blacksmith shop. Sauntering up to a group of men, he casually asked if there would be the chance of employment around here. If so, where was the best place to go?

"Well, stranger, if'n it was me, I'd stroll over to Canfield's. Young feller over there, he'd know of something if there was anything goin' on."

Stuart bought a sandwich and sat at an outdoor table to eat it. While he sat, a man on a big, beautiful black horse trotted by and turned in at the drive of Canfield Grading and Dirt Work. Brushing off the crumbs, Stuart followed, leading his tired horse.

Raymond looked the fellow up and down. Looked strong. "Well, now I don't need anyone on the road right now, but there's another job I got. You ever build any fences?"

"Sure thing, mister. Lots of times." It bothered him none that he did not even know fences were built. He rather supposed they grew up out of the ground wherever they were needed.

"Well, quick as you get situated, come on in and we'll talk."

Assuring the fellow that he was ready now, he was told that he would need to cut down cottonwood trees and trim up posts. (What trees were cottonwood? They all looked like tree wood to him.)

Then he would take the post hole digger (the what...?) and set the posts good and solid. The fence would be a half a mile long and barbed wire would be strung in five strands, strong enough to keep in a herd of Clydesdales. (What was a Clydesdale?) Now did he think he could handle that?

"Sure thing, mister."

Raymond was a bit doubtful but was ready to give him a try. Demonstrating the operation of a post hole digger, a new piece of equipment for the area, and indicating the size of cottonwoods to come down, he left him on the job.

Stuart shortly realized that his mouth may have gotten him where he really didn't want to be, but he picked up the ax. Before he struck the first blow, he looked around, appreciating the scenery as several more of the big horses munched on the new grass. Rounded and shiny, long tails swishing. Stunning animals. *Wonder what one costs?*

Merry Forrester saw the man and heard his request. She looked him up and down. Strong enough looking, well dressed. Good boots. She turned her attention to the animal tied at the front gate. Sorry animal and should be put out to final pasture. Her next thought, any fellow who could dress like this one, did not seem to be one who would chop down trees, or ride an ancient animal. Something was not quite right.

Not her problem, however. Her own problem was Olivia, the sassy lady with the "O" branded on her shoulder and rump. She had somehow caught a briar into the fringe of hair that bushed around the hoof of a Clydesdale. The wound had bled and glued the hair into a scabby wad so Merry would need to bind the leg in a soapy bandage to soften the scab enough to get to the injury to treat it.

While she had been winding the bandage, she sang to the horse to reassure her. Softly worded, "Ama...zing grace. How... sweet the sound! That...sav...ed a wretch like me!...." Olivia whickered softly and turned to watch her beloved keeper. To better see her, the animal took a sideways step, and placed her foot solidly on the hem of a lace trimmed pettislip. Accidentally, of course.

Patting the bandage into shape, Merry poured a cup of warm water over it to be sure it was soaked. There! Standing up she heard the whisper of ripping cloth and stared with dismay at the lace trimming of the pettislip held firmly beneath the injured lady's solid hoof. Encouraging the animal to lift her foot, she retrieved the torn edge of her garment.

Heaving a resigned sigh, she patted the animal and headed toward the house. She had known this was bound to happen, and that she should not have come to the barn in a dress. But she was only going to stay a minute, and then go over to the Cookie Jar for a spell while the soaking happened. Oh, well. It was time to see Pat and Bridie anyway, so she ripped off the rest of the lace strip and headed to her house. There was enough of the pettislip left to protect her modesty for just a small walk across the road.

A knock on the door at Hats and Hankies produced no response, so she went on to the Cookie Jar. There, at an ice cream table sat Pat and Bridie, with Gwinnie standing close, discussing something or other. They motioned her over. "The fellow over at your place. Raymond give 'im a job, did he?"

"Uh…I don't know. I just saw 'im. Didn't look like he was dressed for what has to be done, but I got another problem. I need some new clothes."

With the utterance of the last word, two rosy Irish faces turned toward her with eyes lit up like a little girl's when seeing a brand-new Christmas doll. "A new dress…?" Pattie asked hopefully, as hats and hankies were becoming boring, but dresses, now, that was a fun challenge, but it took an order from someone with money.

"Maybe three dresses and a new pettislip. What fit me at thirteen is getting too tight. In places."

Pat and Bridie exchanged looks and nods. Pat offered, "We won't have a thing already made that'll fit you. I'll go over and get our pattern book." And she was gone.

Bridie happily followed up on her favorite subject, looking Merry up and down as though she was seeing her for the first time. "What sort of dresses did you have in mind?"

"I don't know. Thought I'd talk with you before I tried to pin down an idea."

The happy look on Bridie's face could have outshone that on the face of a restless baby receiving a cookie. "Oh, don't worry. We show you some things."

The pattern book open before them, Pat began, "I'm thinking of a navy blue double dotted Swiss for summer. Full skirted. Do you think it'd lay right, her bein' so short?"

Bridie, after a pause. "It would if we double roll the hem. Or better, make a lace trimmed ruffle. That'd add weight. White shirtwaist. Will you need a bonnet? We've got one that's just precious and it's all fixed."

Before she could answer, Pat again. "Bri...you remember that gold sateen with the tan check, and the bouquets of pink and yellow roses?"

Bridie, excitedly..."And the shiny gold ribbons! Perfect with her hair!"

Kristie strolled over, wiping her hands on her apron. "I think she'd look good in pink. Double sided lace in up-and-down stripes on the skirt and sleeves. White bonnet. Perfect for summer."

Merry looked from one to the other and decided to retrieve the conversation. "That pettislip...I was bandaging Olivia's foot and she stepped on the lace. I stood up and...r...i...p!"

Pat turned quickly. "Did you save the lace?"

"Well, I...."

"Don't worry if it's stained. Bring it over. It'll work on something. We never let lace get away."

Then, after a moment of thought. "What do you mean... Olivia stepped on it?"

"Well, she didn't mean to. She was just wantin' to see what I...."

"How did she.... Who is she...?"

"She's the one with little Paul, that'll have to be sold. She got caught on a thorn bush."

"Paul...sold? What are you...?"

Gwinnie squealed in true Gwinnie fashion and tossed up both hands. "Girls, she's talking about a horse! For goodness sake, remember who we're talking with!"

Merry, still trying to retrieve the conversation and inject a bit of accuracy. "Well, actually she's a mare. Little Paul is a colt and we're only keeping fillies right now."

CHAPTER 4

Silence as the three stared at her, not registering a word she said. "I just knew I'd better get some dresses because I know it takes a while to make 'em. I'm thinkin' I'd best just let you make what you want to. I don't think I can grow any taller this month, so you'd know what was best."

Smiles again. Back on safe territory. "We could use that shirtwaist pattern Francine liked. It's easy to cut down and it's summer cool. One shirtwaist…?"

Merry nodded. "To start with. I've actually got nothin' that fits anymore, and I mostly live in overalls. If I'd'a changed before I fixed Olivia, I wouldn't'a tore my pettislip…but it was too short, anyway."

Pat to Bridie. "Remember that pattern with sleeves gathered on and loose at the edge? That would look good." Taking Merry's arm, she indicated a position just above the elbows. "About here. Fine lace on the edge. She'd like that, don't you think…?"

"Or we could edge it in prairie points. They're dainty and still heavier than lace, and they'd let it hang nice."

"You're right. Prairie points made out of the same material. Takes more time but costs less. We need to show her what they look like. My mom might make 'em. She likes to do 'em."

"Yeah, and hers are tiny and that'd be the best for Merry. Do you want to see the cloth we're talkin' about?"

"Well, if you think I should. To tell you the truth, I don't have any idea what you're talkin' about. You always look good so you can just make me look good! How's that?"

Grins and dimples. Then Bridie, "I'll go get the tape measure."

Pattie, then. "Don't bother. I brought it along."

Merry hadn't had so much attention since she had fallen out of the barn loft at age five, when she had been trying to toss hay to the horse.

The Irish girls disappeared with a list of her measurements and a lot of chatter, and she was left with the Cookie Jar staff. "I keep wanting to tell you about a new sandwich." She suddenly had their undivided attention.

After telling them about her discovery of a venison sandwich that was just as good cold after setting for hours, she added, "I'm thinkin' Johnny and Willie would like it. It stayed so tender and flavorful, and they work so hard. Make them wait till lunch for it, though. Tell them it won't be good until then. They eat just about anything."

Kristie nodded. "Does Raymond like it?"

A pause. "Well, I don't know. I'm never around him when he eats. I don't really know what he likes." Then, with a chuckle, "He was a smart fellow when he didn't hire me to cook! I'd'a been gone a long time ago. I know horses a lot better. And speakin' of horses, I need to get back and tend to Olivia's cut. It should be soaked up now so I can see how bad it is. Incidentally, the Elwoods that rented Papa's farm have a lot of dried venison on hand. He said the deer were drivin' him nuts, eatin' the garden. They got more deer meat than they need. Likely get it for a good price, too."

With the comforting sense of having gotten something done, she strolled back across the road. Her natural glance would be toward the pasture, checking to see who were out there. Alfred was working, also Lucy, and.... Well, there was Olivia, her halter still on. They were much easier to lead with the halter in place, and she would have to bring the mare back to the barn for treatment.

Where was Harry? He was grazing beside Olivia when she left them. Hmmm, she'd just change her clothes and.... But at that moment, she saw a dark figure moving at the back of the lot... too far away to see the brand, but there was someone on his back. Where was that new fellow with the high dollar boots? His horse was still tied by the road.

NO! she shouted to herself and ran to her cabin, unbuttoning her dress as she ran. Skinning out of it and into overalls, grabbing up the new six shooter and slamming out the door. Running at her fastest speed, she jumped onto Olivia. "Sorry, girl! You're the only one with a halter, and I need one."

Steering her head toward the horseback figure at a distance, she kept her eye beaded on it until it disappeared in the brush a quarter of a mile away. Digging her heel into the mare's flanks, as best she could, she yelled encouragement. "Come on, we can catch 'im! Good girl! Come on, let's go." And Olivia went.

Clydesdales were known more for strength and not speed, but, after all, Harry was also a Clydesdale so the race could be fairly even. She reached the section of the fence that had been cut, barbed wires flaying out in both directions.

Carefully guiding the mare through, she again clicked her to full speed. Looking down at the bar-ditch for hoof prints, she saw the direction Harry went. Depth of prints indicated a full gallop.

"Come on, girl! We can catch 'im." She yelled with more confidence than she felt. Hoofs pounding, they climbed the shallow rise of the road and at the peak, she could see the thief up ahead. He had at least a quarter of a mile lead.

"Stop, thief!" Merry shouted at the retreating figure, and raising the new weapon, she fired a shot up into the air. She really hated to waste the bullet, but it was a desperate decision. At the shot, the rider turned to look…his mistake. Harry, having no bridle for being guided, turned his head at the movement of the hand off his mane.

Lost seconds, only. The thief was an experienced rider and soon had Harry straightened out and galloping again. Lucy was pounding her hooves gamely, gaining slightly on the race before her.

Merry shouted out, "Stop, thief. I'm a bad shot and if you don't stop I may hit you. I promise you I won't hit the horse." Still he pounded on, ignoring her demand.

A big sigh, a deep breath, and Merry shouted out a familiar cry. "In the sweet…bye and bye…. We shall meet on the beautiful shore." Maintaining the same tune, she sang new words, "If you don't stop…I'll aim high. And I'll blow out your brains with one shot!"

Harry, recognizing a beloved voice and a familiar tune, reared and danced on his hind hooves, pawing the air with the front ones. He sounded off with an angry whinny and a whirl. Catching his rider off balance, he reared again, sliding the thief back over his flowing tail. Dancing around in circles, he presented such a dangerous prance of hooves, the man struggled and twisted, finally rolling toward the protection of the ditch.

By now, Olivia had reached him. Merry pointed the gun toward the figure she saw ducking away and took aim. Her shot took off the high, fancy hat. Shouting again, she told him, "Sorry! Aimed too high. Told you I was a bad shot! Hands in the air and turn around."

The hands went up.

"Turn around and head back down the road. Don't go to the ditch or I'll try my luck at shooting lower."

His hands still in the air, she walked him back to the blacksmith shop, singing at the top of her voice. "When the roll… is called up yon…der! When the roll is called up yonder I'll be there!" Then starting at the second verse, she intoned, "On a bright and cloudless morning, when the dead in Christ shall rise…."

As she started on the third verse, she had reached the corner and a congregation of at least a dozen men were watching the proceedings. Among them was Samuel Canfield.

Staring, someone commented, "Wouldn't that be one'a Raymond's horses?" Of course it was! Most of the huge black horses with the white foot fringes were Raymond's. Sam Canfield followed on with, "…and that'd be his hired man with the new gun he got her. God bless America! Hold 'im, girl, while I get a rope."

When the would-be thief was disabled, arms tied to his side, Harry had edged up beside Merry, belly to belly against Olivia. Merry Forrester, being small and Olivia being huge, sat with her knees far apart and feet extended out rather than hanging down.

There followed a small conference as to what to do with him, and Merry had refused to leave. If they were taking him to Argyle, she should go along. After all, she had risked Olivia's health to run him down, and she was determined he would not get away.

Sam Canfield shook his head. "I don't think you should go along, Merry. I'm hopin' to get 'im there alive, and I know how you feel about 'im. Now, if you'll just go back and get his hat, I'll get 'im mounted onto 'H' and meet you at the shop." In minutes the world-be thief was on "H" for Harry and being led away.

If one could have read what was in his mind as Stuart Campbell rode, head hanging low, they would have learned an interesting thing. *That girl,* he thought, *I don't know her name, but I'd bet there is a McDonald in her background. Those sneaky McDonalds fought dirty, with yelling and slinging things with sharp edges. The old folks talk of all the Campbells that were sent on to their reward on account'a them rascals. But who would'a thought...a girl the size'a that one...!*

With a deep breath and racing pulse, Merry agreed it was likely best she not go, and she headed back up the road to retrieve the expensive straw hat. On the return trip, she guided the mare back through the clipped wires to note the damage. It would have to be repaired immediately, and the animals would have to stay in the corral until that happened.

There were four others not taken to work today, and as she passed them, she sang, "Oh, Beulah land, sweet Beulah land! As on the highest mount I stand...and look away...across the sea... where a mansion...is prepared for me! I view the shining...."

Behind her in a line were Jenny, Dollie, George and Nancy. Necks extended and fond eyes on the rider aboard Olivia. Her anger still fierce, Merry glared at the thief as he was put on his own horse, his arms still bound. Brad Cullen, Miss Josie's husband, was saddled up and Jeff Wilson, his cousin would help. The last she saw of the thief, he was the center of a trio marching up the middle of the road on the five mile trek to Argyle and the law.

She turned Olivia back toward the barn, and realized she still held the thief's hat. The crown of the hat had straw fanned out where the bullet went through. Finally, she permitted herself a slight grin as she realized why Mr. Canfield had sent her after the hat. He was afraid, mad as she was, that she would shoot the thief anyway, maybe even after he was tied.

Olivia had weathered the chase quite well. It was hard to get a good Clydesdale down, and the cut had not had time to infect. She removed the moist bandage and the clot had dissolved as well. With a special comb, she straightened the hairs of the spat. One huge difference Clydesdales had, beside their size, was a sensitive leg vulnerability.

Back in their Scottish heritage, the animals had conveniently developed a thin fringe of longer hair, called feathers, that grew down from their hock to their hoof. Like the fringes on leather apparel, the "feathers" helped to drain away moisture from the legs into a brush of longer hair extending out over the hoof. This brush of hair must not be allowed to be continuously damp, as it would breed infection.

Olivia, however, looked good. The scabby blood was gone and a fine, two-inch-long brier scratch was now visible. A day or two of treatment and a close watch on her should take care of it.

Then there was the broken fence. Well, she couldn't fix the fence wires. The stretcher was too heavy and besides, it took two men, and she was only one!

Hunger descended over her like a spring shower. Oatmeal. Steaming hot and butter rich! That slice of cherry pie from Mrs. Bramwell, and maybe even a SMALL dried-venison sandwich. A pot of strong tea…no, she'd make it coffee. Today was special. She had driven off a thief.

Then maybe she'd sit and try to imagine what Pat and Bridie would come up with. But then, she remembered the wobble in Nancy's gait as she had come to the corral. In her condition, this could be the night. The thing to do would be to have a big meal, and then go out and check. Whoever it was inside her, making her wobble, would be either Isaac or Ina. New babies were such fun!

After an examination, she was sure Nancy had another couple of days, so she crawled into her bed and was instantly asleep in spite of the coffee. And the dream! She seldom remembered dreams, and she smiled a bit as she ate her breakfast. She had dreamed that little Isaac was born, and her employer had gathered the colt along with Paul and the other two small ones and taken them to the sale barn. He had taken her along with them and seemingly had not noticed that she was not one of the animals. She remembered standing there with the auctioneer shouting his song, and the buyers looking her over and not seeing she was a human. Very funny, actually! Especially when a prospective buyer had wanted to see her teeth to determine her age!

She related the dream to her brother and elicited a small smile, but it seemed that he was not surprised at the dream. Even she, herself, could imagine herself as one of the herd that occupied the corral.

Pat and Birdie plied scissors and needle, giggling with excitement as they had not for several weeks. Such fun and such a good order. They hadn't had this much fun since they created Francine's wedding dress and a few other necessary garments for her.

It was true that Merry had begun to fill out, here and there, and something needed to be done, but they didn't know they'd get the job. They were aware that she went to Argyle to order shirts and overalls and other things for herself and Homer.

The blue dotted-swiss skirt would be first. The thin-woven, fine fabric, together with Merry's small size, meant some adjustments must be made. Her skirt should not fluff out like it would if she was eleven or twelve. By adding a heavily gathered ruffle that was faced with stiff broadcloth of the same blue shade, they made the skirt hang in soft folds, as it should. Skill in making necessary adjustments was a talent they could not have done without in this business.

Next was the white shirtwaist. It was made with the cut-down pattern used for the garment Francine had burned in the prairie fire that almost took her schoolhouse. Fine, delicate store-bought lace on the portrait collar and on the loose-fitting sleeves. Tiny pin-tucks down the front and back assisted in protecting her modesty, though it was obvious she'd need a pretty camisole.

Why not go ahead and make the camisole…they always sold well if she didn't want it. She surely MUST have enough money… she never spent any except for a cookie or tea at the Cookie Jar.

Finished and on display hangers, the garments looked so beautiful they hated to take them down. Finally they decided that Gwinnie and Kristie should see them, and…hey, why couldn't they leave them hanging above the mail hooks for a day or two? Something this beautiful should be shared! The space, however, must be bargained for.

"We'll help you shell peanuts if you want?" The bargain was struck and a week's hanging equaled a half a gallon of shelled peanuts and a lot of giggling both ways.

The stepped-on lace now decorated a new pettislip. No more stains. Just a glistening white, but it could not be displayed. One did not display fancy unmentionables, but they were such FUN to wear.

While they measured and cut the lovely gold fabric with the pink and yellow roses, they acquired three new orders, and before the week was out, they had two more as fallout from the hanging display. Life was good, and thank you, America. God bless America.

In the year 1906, America was sixteen and the girls across her road were two years older. Homer Forrester was fourteen and Neecie Bramwell was ten. Neecie was two inches taller than last year, and her dimple was more practiced. She was negotiating for small heels on her boots but had not yet won.

Her parents were only concerned with her feet at that age and not her appearances. She still made sure she was close if Homer needed anything, and he was never farther from her sight than she could help. Her parents did not help in this matter, though they nodded their approval. She seemed to be doing well enough by herself.

It was also in the year of 1906 that Oklahoma became a state. Parcels of land on all sides had become states. There was Kansas, Arkansas and Texas and finally the Territory had made it.

The day it happened, the community of the Corners had a party the like of which the settlement had never seen. From habit, the gathering started at the Cookie Jar and spread out from there. Everything edible was served as long as it held out. Tea and coffee by the gallon, and a tea/fruit juice punch followed.

The six school-type tables with bench attached stayed filled with rotating groups. The inside of the diner was crammed to capacity, and others wandered joyously about…into the road and around the Hats and Hankies van. "Rah! Rah! And no one can stop us now! We are a state and it's about time!"

Help from young girls was solicited, and seven-, eight- and nine-year-olds carried refreshments and mopped up spills. Ten-, eleven- and twelve-year-olds popped corn continuously, one kettle-full after the other.

As the evening dark fell, the lanterns in the trees had their wicks trimmed and their fuel tanks topped off. Little girls sang songs and little boys marched, though no one knew quite why. And didn't care!

Sheet after sheet of cookies were baked and sold while too hot to eat! Babies went to sleep on spread quilts, oblivious to the noise around them and the dawn broke before the party did.

The Cookie Jar girls persuaded Johnny and Willie to make a trip into Argyle to replenish depleted supplies, and the Irish girls went along to find the right gold thread for Merry's dress, and also, just for the thing of it!

When Kristie and Gwinnie finally found time to count their money they wondered if anyone in the town had anything left in their pockets. The girls made more on one day than they had during the total last year, but now, of course, they were out of supplies. They had learned during Miss Josie's last teaching year that money received in a business was not necessarily profit. Inventory must be replenished, but even then, it was a huge day.

The Hats and Hankies van also had a summer's supply of orders. Who knew why? Just a thing that happened! But Merry's outfits would be first, because the girls were so eager to see them on her.

Also in 1906, the Reverend Armstrong and his family came to the Corners.

A vacancy had occurred. The old circuit rider preacher had finally worn out and had been called up higher to receive his reward. He would no longer travel through the rain and the scorching heat of the Territory of Oklahoma or try to remove a gravel that was causing his horse to limp. He no longer had to try to speak in an outside arbor against the constant prairie wind.

He had been found by his son, looking as though he was asleep. His precious, valuable King James Bible was open over his chest. His gnarled, arthritic finger was pointed to Psalm 23. "…He maketh me to lie down in green pasture. He leadeth me beside the still water…." Yes, he was now being led beside the still water, and certainly his soul was being restored!

Records of his ministry indicated the interest was greatest at the country community called The Corners, so it was there that the Reverend Armstrong would be sent. He would look about for, maybe, a site for a permanent building. He would test the interest of the community, cast about for a suitable house to rent…that sort of thing.

He had older children, grown and married, and then he had had Phillip, who had a job in Oklahoma City. The son was a builder, and if a church was to be constructed, they could count on his help. It took about three hours for the community of Corners to learn all there was to know about the preacher, and by the next day, Enterprise and Shady Ridge were also totally informed. One more day and South Bend and Sentinel Rock would have the news. A real preacher at the Corners! Looking for a place to be permanent!

Imagine! The Territory was now a state, and a permanent preacher was looking to settle! What could possibly be next for the Corners?

What was next was Phillip Armstrong appearing at the gate of Canfield Grading. He'd like to have seen a fellow there to talk to, but there was a girl. Maybe she'd know. All he needed was a job for a little while until his folks settled whatever it was that God had sent them into. No, he'd just wait until the man was there. The girl looked busy and certainly didn't need him bothering her.

Edward Morison picked up another two bricks in his calloused hands. He set them carefully in the herringbone pattern designated by the designer of the street. The city of Memphis had found that they had more red clay than money so they fired bricks rather than producing asphalt. Most residents agreed with the decision but their reason was because they looked nicer and did not require the smoky, sticky, smelly asphalt.

To Edward Morrison, it mattered none. Bricks…asphalt… one was the same as the other to him. He was paid by the hour if he could keep up and paid a premium if he could outpace. The effort he put forth turned into coins at the end of the week. A lot of ideas for the money took their turn in his mind. Laying bricks made for a lot of time to think.

Now, some small business of his own…? But which one? Maybe a piece of land, but how would he use it? That would likely depend on where the land was located. Tennessee was a good state but he really had no ties to it. He just happened to be here…and this job presented itself so he took it. The fishing boats were always busy. Maybe he should buy a boat? Maybe he could live on the boat? Some people did. But if he met THE girl, would she like it? And if he was on the boat all day, how would he meet THE girl?

When he had explored each avenue, he returned to the first. A business? But which? And that was yesterday. Today he had the letter, its white envelope tucked in the large rear pocket of his work coveralls. Words from Aunt Sybil's blocky handwriting printed themselves in his mind as he stood to wipe the sweat out of his eyes.

As a small boy, he had liked Aunt Sybil…and he probably still would. She had no children and had seemed to like him. Then she and Uncle Clarence had done that land race thing in the Territory of Oklahoma, and wonder of wonders, they had won a piece of land. On occasions since then, he had considered going out there, just for an adventure, but one thing after another turned him aside.

His aunt and uncle were somewhat older than his parents and they eventually seemed to lose touch. The city of Knoxville was several miles east from Memphis, and he could go back there. His two brothers and sister were there starting their families. He could go back…but somehow he didn't.

Then the letter.

> *…Edward, honey, we wouldn't want to put any burden or obligation on you, but we felt you should be notified of our current plans. We are getting to the age that we must slow down.*
>
> *Here's what we have planned. We are going to put an advertisement in the paper for a young man, or a young couple to come and live on the property to care for it without salary, and when we pass on, the land would pass on to them. In actuality, we are looking for an heir.*
>
> *We realize that all your family are in Tennessee, and when you settle down, you will likely want to be near them. We felt, however, that we should first write to you. We will not do anything until fall, and there would be time during the summer to see if you liked it here. It's really a nice little community and now it even has a school.*
>
> *Clarence says it has good cotton soil, and there seems to be a good market for cotton right now. Or even wool. There is a bit of sheep raising hereabouts. A cartage company established a route for freighting the wool by wagon and trailer from the gathering point in Hydro to the shipper at Lokeba. That is two of our local towns.*
>
> *We think of you a lot, and remember when you were a little tyke, getting into everything! Your mother would likely not appreciate my writing this, but we thought it was only fair to you. If we were going to offer this deal to a stranger, it should be passed by a nephew first. So, if it seems interesting, send us a letter addressed to Argyle, in care of the Corners, or just come on out. If we don't hear by the end of summer, we'll go on with*

our plans. Here's hoping the best for you and whatever you decide to do.

Your loving aunt and uncle.

His left hand picked up two more bricks and his right hand placed them, working them down into the sandy base. Powdered concrete would come later by someone else, and then another person would bring the roller. Next, the water. Good system. Good roads.

Oklahoma Territory. The plus would be a quarter section of his own, and a pair of relatives who liked him. Or used to like him. The minuses were…huh…well, would they let him do what he wanted? Remembering back, he nodded to himself. Aunt Sybil always gave him what he wanted, even if she had to sneak it to him.

He had money. There really wasn't something that he wanted badly enough to spend the money on. He could just run on out there for a "visit" to thank them for the offer. That was only right… wasn't it? Today was Wednesday, so he'd think it over for two more days. Maybe draw his pay and go. The Santa Fe was making regular runs now. Straight through Kansas…south to Oklahoma City. Why not?

That's how twenty-one-year-old Edward Morrison found himself at the blacksmith shop just cross-cornered from a place called the Cookie Jar. Served a decent cup of coffee, that place did. A lot better than the stuff he was currently drinking, only because the cup had been thrust in his hand.

"The Morrisons? Now, isn't that where…Sam, you know about the Morrisons?"

Sam broke off his current conversation. "The Morrisons? Well, now, son, if you come down from Argyle, you passed it about a mile and a half back. Old couple? No family hereabouts?"

At Edward's nod, he became more specific. "Yes, siree. Old Clarence used to come down here time and agin, but he's on a cane, now. Could be he's not up to it like he used to be. So, if you'd just turn that animal around and go on up past Canfield Grading, and Bramwell's grist mill, and keep on goin', it'll be the next house. Sets off the road a mite."

Edward put on his smile, tossed aside the last of the evil brew in the coffee mug, saluted in a friendly way and announced "So long!" The agreeable horse amiably turned north and broke into a trot.

He'd have known Aunt Sybil anywhere in spite of the additional wrinkles. And the familiar old white-haired fellow approached with a remembered grin. Two teeth missing. Hand extended. "You made it!"

His aunt had trouble with her eyes and mopped them dry with the hem of her apron. "Oh, son! Little Edward…and you got so big and handsome! Just look at 'im, Clarence. You ever see anything so handsome? Oh, you must be hungry. I'll get something right on. I was aimin' to make dumplings, so I'll just hurry 'em up!"

She approached him with open arms, hugging him like he was six years old again. "You just sit down there and talk with Clarence. Talk loud so's I can hear you in the kitchen."

While his uncle listened and demanded details of everything that happened in the last fifteen years, Edward entertained the most attentive audience he had known in recent memory.

Later, he was literally pushed out the back door with instructions to look over the place. Clarence couldn't go along. He'd just slow him up, Aunt Sybil advised. One hundred sixty acres of mostly flat land. A few trees here and there. A cow and about three goats, apparently needing to be milked in two or three hours. Chickens all over, and a few cottontail rabbits. Beside him trotted a Collie mix, his tail a plume of cream and tan wagging encouragement. Likely hadn't had someone to walk with for months. Maybe longer.

Good supper ending in butterscotch pudding and topped off with coffee… almost as good as that at the Cookie Jar. He grinned at the thought that, though his aunt looked good as she served him the coffee, she didn't match up to the lass with the honey-colored hair and friendly smile.

The words were good, though. "Now, son, I know you haven't had time to plan, but we thought we would say right off. We're not lookin' for someone to take care'a us. The Lord's been good, and we have enough put by. We was just thinkin' it'd be best, us out here all alone from the family, if there was someone close by to notify the rest'a the folks we'd gone on when our time came. Then again, if we had anything of value, we'd like it kept in the family if there was a person to be able to use it. That's how come us to write to you. You're not to feel any obligation, and we're so glad to see you. It'd be pleasure if you could spend the summer, whatever you decide."

Same old Aunt Sybil. Always on the giving side, so why did he think they might have changed? So now, there was a lot of thinking to do and tomorrow was another day.

On the next morning, he remembered that, while he was sipping the good coffee at the Cookie Jar, he had looked across the road and seen the most marvelous horses. Dark, trimmed in snow white spats on each foot, shiny and well fed. Must be a place that sold animals, because they had such a massive barn, generous corral and no house that Edward could see.

Back at the Cookie Jar, he asked, "You know who owns those horses over there?" Indicating Canfield Grading with his elbow.

Nodding, the owner of the honey-colored hair told him, "That'd be Raymond Canfield but he's harder to catch than a cool breeze, sometimes. On the job all the time. But the hired man is there, the one that takes care of the horses. He's a girl about this high, and she'll be there somewhere." Kristie indicated a height just under her chin. "She could know when he'll be there, but probably not. Those fellows have long hours but she can leave 'im a note. She'll bring the answer over here so you can get it in a couple'a days."

Hmmm. Couple'a days. That'd be a serious and unavoidable reason to come back and take another look at this girl. Likely belongs to some fellow already, but that don't hurt her looks none. Kristie, they called her.

Edward stopped at the gate and watched. Presently the "hired man" came out of the "hired man" house and crossed toward the barn. "Uh…Miss? Do you have a minute?"

Merry Forrester stopped and waited. "Raymond'll be here sometime before midnight. Leave me a name and what you want to ask, and I give it to 'im. If he wants to answer, I'll take it over to the Cookie Jar."

He handed over the information, and she nodded a dismissal. She obviously had things to do.

Edward headed on back to his relatives and was told, "Oh, that'd be America Forrester! Her pa met with disaster and left her and her brother alone. Both of 'em doin' well. The boy's helpin' out at the grist mill and the girl, she takes care'a the horses."

"That little thing? Why, she's hardly up to those horses' withers. Wouldn't weigh ninety pounds, soakin' wet!"

"Yeah, son. That's what it looks like, but I wouldn't be thinkin' 'a payin' undue attention to those animals. She's already took a well-placed shot at two different attempts at thievin' one of them horses. So far she's managed to miss, but the pa of the owner, he hopes the word gets around. He'd afraid the next one'll get that girl so mad she'll not be able to miss the fellow with her six shooter. His son said it wasn't that he'd hated to have the fellow shot, he'd worry most about who'd take care'a the animals while the law was sortin' it all out."

"The girl is not his?"

"Not that I hear. She's a schoolmate, and when she lost her pa, he gave her a job. Been there about two years."

"How about the girls at the diner?"

"Diner...?"

"Uh...the Cookie Jar, I mean."

"Oh, the McLaughlin girls. Pa is Scottish and ma is Welsh. They run that place all by themselves. Have since they was twelve and thirteen, seems like. Names are Gwendollyn and Kristallyn. Hard to tell them girls apart."

Edward digested that information. The one he met must have been Kristallyn. "Thought I might see the owner about makin' a deal for a pair'a those horses. Need somethin' strong if we put the back forty in cotton."

His aunt and uncle exchanged excited glances. Uncle Clarence nodded at him. "They're good animals that Raymond's got, and he knows it. Sets a high price on what he sells, and they are either young foals or older animals, past their prime for pullin' his machinery. Works those horses hard, but they've been took good care of when he lets 'em go. Still good for plowin' or wagon pullin'. Course, we've got that one out in the pasture, and him teamed up with the one you rode in with…that'd be a start…maybe?"

"Good idea. Uncle, you got some friend around here that'd give me some advice on cotton growin'? I'm getting' too old to make stupid mistakes, and all I know about cotton is that it's fluffy and white."

Aunt chimed in, "Yeah, but before it's fluffy and white, it's stickery and brown. Tricky as Old Lucifer himself to get at, without getting' bloody fingers."

"Hmmm. Would something else be better?"

"Don't know, but you'd get a lot of advice down at the blacksmith shop. Some of it you might use, and a lot you couldn't use. It's a thought."

Edward put that together with his other thoughts and left to look around once more.

Merry Forrester had dreams. She'd had several dreams about her father, and mostly they had sent her to the hayloft to sob her loneliness into the pile of horse blankets. It was just the suddenness, she told herself. It had been hard to lose her mother, but she had been younger and she still had Pa. Pa was the one who talked to her and Homer, who read to them from the Bible Story Book (where was that book, packed up in the loft?) and he read from his precious King James Bible. She knew exactly where that was, it was in the drawer tucked in with her linens. Every book was precious here in the territory.

There was that story in a book called Malachi. That's how she knew that wherever heaven was, it had windows. God was able to open them and toss out stuff that He wanted people on the earth to have. How did that story go? Maybe she'd get that book out this evening…something was bugging her that she thought she should remember but didn't.

It was time to bring home her new skirt. It had hung for two weeks in the Cookie Jar and Pat and Bridie had profited by it.

Easiest favor she ever did for them, that had cost her nothing. But now she wanted it.

Tapping on the door of the Hats and Hankies van, she was ushered into the crowded space. "I was thinkin'," she began, "about a shawl. A crocheted or knitted one in white."

Pat and Bridie exchanged glances and nodded. They certainly had those.

Merry continued, "What I thought of had little shell-like designs...sort of. And lots of holes to see through."

Slight frowns, and Bridie decided, "You think she's talking about the pineapple pattern?"

"Maybe. Got one right here." Well, it wasn't right here, but it was in the third box from the bottom on the second row. Sliding out the box, she lifted the lid. The aroma of rose petals whiffed into the small space. Pattie slid her hand carefully under the paper-enclosed bundle and pulled back the sheets. There, in an orderly fold, was the snow-white lacy garment meant for looks but was actually warm enough for a spring evening. Lifting out the shawl, she draped it over Bridie's shoulders, and the model turned so Merry could see how it draped.

With a wink, Pattie stage-whispered to Bridie, "I know why she wants this? She's set her cap for that new fellow up the road."

Bridie whispered back, "Yeah, but he don't know he better not look at them horses if he wants to keep his head!"

Eyes crinkled with laughter, they giggled at the color rising in Merry's fair neck and cheeks. "You girls cut that out, if you want to sell this shawl. I need two more shirtwaists for summer. And another skirt out of heavier material...maybe two. When you have time."

Pattie nodded. "Well, we'll put you next. Your gold dress is finished, and the pink one almost. While you're here, you can try 'em on."

"And figure my bill."

"Ah, not yet. Just wait till we're through and see if you want anything else."

Merry walked away with a small grin. Smart business girls. She was thinking one more dress should just about do it. Maybe light gray and shiny…with blue trimming? Or maybe she'd just let the girls decide. Yeah, she'd do that, and now she wanted to look at that story in Malachi. The one about windows in heaven.

Phillip Armstrong had decisions to make. How was he to know when God would make His wishes known? But the certain fact was that the old couple really were his parents. AND HE DID KNOW FOR SURE THAT God expected him to honor them

When that little community called the Corners lost their circuit preacher, the Board had come to his father, hat in hand (so to speak) and asked him to fill in for just a little while. Philip had a job in Oklahoma City. Not a good one, truly, but…. Well, he could let it go and see what could be found to do in Corners.

He had never graded a road, and horses were not his first choice of an animal, but the place called Canfield Grading and Dirt Work seemed to be a going business. Might have some kind of a job? Wouldn't know till he asked.

The young lady (girl?) couldn't tell him much. Did say something about a fence to be built but the last fellow that wanted the job tried to steal one of those horses. Like to'a got hisself shot. Did he know how to build a fence?

Well, now, how hard could that be? "Did the fellow get it started?"

A shrug of the shoulders. "I'd say he got the digger and the ax down there, but I didn't see any fence."

"Digger? You mean a post hole digger? And he was supposed to make the posts? I'd really like to talk to whoever makes the decision. I know all about posts and hole diggers."

Merry looked him over from head to foot. Ordinary hat. Shirt sleeves partly rolled. Top button open. Solid shoes with leather laces. Said the right words. Looked right. Maybe….

"Tell you what. You leave your name and I'll pass it on. I know he wants a fence a half a mile long. Wants to plant alfalfa for the horses."

"Smart idea. I'm Philip Armstrong, and I can…."

"Oh, you belong to the preacher? I heard he was doin' some lookin' for a place for a church. Sure hope he finds it."

"I don't really know, that being his business and God's. Not mine. But he talked with someone named Elwood and they...."

"You mean the Elwoods a mile over and a half a mile south?"

"Yeah. Pa has his wagon settin' in front of their house. I'm figurin' he'll be needin' me later, if he has some buildin' to do. In the meantime, I just need a temporary job. I'd sure like to build that fence."

"Tell you what...I'm hard to find, sometimes, and I make no decisions. I'm just the 'hired man' that takes care'a the horses. I'll ask Raymond Canfield and take a note over to the Cookie Jar if he wants to see you. The girls there are always working. Just ask for a message for Philip and they'll have it."

Merry went on to the barn, her thought racing each other around in her head. *The preacher is talking to the Elwoods. I wonder what they're tellin' 'im.*

There were three precious fillies in the baby pen. They were so cute with their long slim legs and fluffy white socks. Reminded her of little girls in new summer white shoes and the short white socks called anklets.

She hummed the tune of "Skip to My Loo" and the little animals crowded around her, nibbling at her elbows and trying to whicker and snort like their mamas. She had cut a turnip into three small pieces and fed it to them. Horses like these must be kept tame. They grew much too big to be allowed to be mean.

Raymond listened to Philip's request. He really wanted that fence done, but after that last one.... "What if he tries to steal a horse...or steal you, maybe? I'd hate to have someone killed and have you in the pokey. Do you really think he's safe?" He waited.

"I know that it's his pa that's looking for a place for a church. The fellow says he can only work temporary because if his pa finds place to build, he'll be needed to help 'im get set up. Maybe build the church house. He looks like he knows what he's a'doin' and he was glad you had a post hole digger."

CHAPTER 5

That did it for Raymond. Only fellows who knew what a digger was, were the fellows who had used one. "Tell 'im to see me Saturday morning." And he was gone.

Both crews came in and loosed their dusty, sweaty, thirsty horses. Suddenly she had four beasts in her care, and they followed her to the water trough below the windmill, blade busily drawing up their water. Six young men walked away from their animals, utterly and eternally grateful for Merry. Before she was hired, the duties at the horse trough would have been theirs, and one of them would be staying overnight in the hayloft. A weary sigh and a grateful shake of the head. God bless America.

Merry had a water pail and a brush, and by plying the brush as high as she could reach, swabbed the dust off their backs and down their legs, feeling as she did so for any sores, bruises or strains.

Cleaned and refreshed, having drank their fill of water, they were led to the stalls for grain. Horses that worked as hard as these really needed their grain and they hungrily licked up every last bit that was given them. Back to the pasture for the night they went, walking to the tune of "Amazing Grace," following Merry like four big puppies. The air was so mild, they would graze a while, then doze in the field until morning.

Mrs. Bramwell had sent down her special braised ribs with tomato sauce. She used peppers and special herbs and it was even better heated up the second day. And this was the second day. The turnips that had been left in the ground were now sending up pale green tops. These were picked and wilted down with bacon grease, topped with a sliced onion. Perfect.

Cup of tea and the King James Bible. Malachi. Here it was in the third chapter. The windows of heaven where good things would be tossed out faster than the people could use them. All they had to do was bring a tenth of what they had to the church because it belonged to God. But what if they didn't have a church!

A tenth. One dollar out of ten. Not bad. She remembered her father going into depth about the importance of doing this. Where did he send his tenth? There was no church. If she could only ask him! The scary part of the chapter was that if they did what they were told, they would have what was thrown out the windows of heaven. If they didn't, they would be punished by not having as much for themselves. It looked like God was going to get His part one way or the other.

Nodding with satisfaction, she closed the Book and put it back in her drawer. She agreed with herself that what she had just read was what Papa had talked about. Such a long time ago, and she wished she could remember all he said.

This would take some thinking about. Homer wouldn't be any help; he had been a lot littler than she was. She'd have to figure this out by herself.

Philip was there early on Saturday, and Raymond appeared shortly after. Together they walked to the back of the section.

"Now, I need you to back up this way for about a hundred fifty feet from the back fence and stretch five strands of barbed wire from one end to the other. I'll decide later where I want the gate."

Philip nodded. "You want the posts outta the trees back'a the fence? That'll clear it out except for the roots. Could dig them out later. You wouldn't have a stretcher, would you? That makes a lot better fence. Tighter, with these big animals of yours, they may try to do a little fence leaning once that alfalfa came on."

"We have stretchers. We just don't have help to operate them."

"That's all right. I can do it alone. It just takes a little longer. Stretcher makes a lot better fence. I can do you a really good job. By myself, it'll likely take about a month. Like I told the lady, I can't take on too much on account of my father may need me for a while. Old as he is, he needs help and I'm all he has." His tone was apologetic.

"Just do what you can. As is it, I have no fence, and sooner or later I will have one. Wantin' to get it plowed up over the winter and planted with alfalfa next spring."

"That'd work good. Have you thought that if you're looking for horse feed, you could sow wheat in the fall and have spring grazin'. The sprouted wheat'll help crack the ground for the alfalfa. Help keep moisture in."

"Sounds good, friend! Maybe you'll have more time here and there.Anyway, you have a hard month ahead of you and if you have trouble, tell my hired man and she'll pass it on. Seems like she sorta runs things here, anyway. See you later."

And he was gone.

A distance-eating stride took Philip to the back of the section with his measuring cord. He picked up the ax and had a dozen of the two-inch diameter cottonwoods on the ground and trimmed before Raymond cleared the front gate.

Dusk was falling before the young man left his job. During the afternoon he had come to a decision. If the "hired man" was in charge, he should ask her first. It only made sense.

Edward Morrison was still in a quandary. The quarter section of land belonging to his aunt and uncle was strong on his mind. Cotton had stickers and must be picked. The same applied to beans. And corn. A herd of registered cattle would be expensive, and he certainly wanted to be sure before he parted with his coins. There were sheep, and they required shearing…but only once a year. There were goats and they required milking. Twice daily.

Uncle was old and might be some help, sometimes, but he mustn't count on it. What he decided on must be something that he could manage by himself. An orchard? Then again, it took several years for trees to be productive and he didn't know a thing about fruit trees. *Keep thinking.*

Maybe two different things. That would make a variety of duties…and concerns. What two things? Popcorn? It certainly seems to be popular down at the Cookie Jar. Quick to fix, inexpensive? Not messy…right filling for the bottomless stomachs of young people? Was there a variety of seed that was especially good…?

Maybe there was a wholesale market in Oklahoma City. From what he remembered, the stalks were smaller and could be put closer together. One horse with a muzzle should be able to till it, or two animals at the outside. Likely one of those Clydesdales his neighbor had…the ones he only sold when they were babies, or old folks.

All right. Popcorn was a possiblility. *What else*. Hey! He had it! Bees. They found their own food and would share it with humans if they knew how to get it away from them. He'd learn.

Edward was a collector of information. Not consciously, but it was just that he was most always interested in how something was done, and eventually one accumulated a lot of information. So bees ate flowers. What kind of flowers? Were they very picky? The obvious place to go was the blacksmith shop.

If the fellows there didn't know something, they would be glad to refer him off to some who did…or at least could refer him further. The blacksmith shop was only a mile and a half south… just a good walk for a fellow who was still thinking.

As he passed the Cookie Jar, he felt a distinct longing for the little wire ice cream chairs that looked fragile but weren't and the tiny tables. Refreshments and pleasant scenery.

He decided, however, to tend to business first. After he consumed a polite amount of the stuff they called coffee, and had put forth his question, he would treat himself. The sun was pleasantly warm. When he had gone about a mile, he began to hear the click-click-click of the windmill at Canfield Grading. He spent a quarter of a mile or so thinking of the water it would take to fill up those beasts on a hot day, and the small size of the "hired man" whose job it would be. As it was, the whirling blades brought up water in little rushes and splashes, and when the trough was full, the blades were unhooked to ride free in the wind until more water was needed.

As he got closer, he glanced over toward the mill, and a small figure with a blue scarf around her head was seated on the edge of the water trough, appearing to have her feet in the water. Good day for it!

Next corner was the blacksmith shop. Seven fellows were lounging around, probably re-telling jokes they couldn't remember having heard yesterday. Good place to be! The men looked up to greet him and steer him toward the re-boiled coffee.

After the obligatory two sentences of weather observation, he was free to ask, "Any of you fellows know where I can find out about raising bees?"

One old codger nodded. "Yeah, I know a fellow that tried it. Thought it was a money maker but he got stung." Old joke. Polite chuckles followed, then a silence.

"They's a feller down towards Enterprise that collects wild ones. Sometimes sells 'em by the hive. He'd know something, I reckon."

One elderly fellow, crippled in the foot, offered more. "I might know a bit to get you started thinkin'. I don't know anything about what they call tame bees. How'd a body do that? But the wild ones like persimmon blooms in the spring. Get so thick in them trees, one don't dare to get close. The thing about persimmon trees is, if you got a lot of bees, it makes a good persimmon crop, and the women folks like the ripe persimmon for the sugar. Use it in candy and cakes.

"Nuther thing is that new plant called alfalfa. Has little blue blossoms and the blooms lasts a good long time. If'n it was me, I'd think on plantin' a strip'a alfalfa and puttin' a row of 'simmon trees down the middle. Then I'd look for somethin' else to come on later in the summer. Fellow down south, he'd be knowin' what'd be good, I'd think. Havin' food close'd keep the bees from usin' time and energy, lookin'."

The fellow sitting enthroned on an upturned nail keg, spit a brown stream and readjusted his cud to the other side of his mouth. "Young feller, you come to take care'a the old folks up there on the Morrison place?"

Suddenly Edward had all eyes turned on him. Undoubtedly, it was a question that been on all minds, and he was expected to answer it. Edward shrugged, noncommittally. "Not really. They seems to be doin' just fine. The thing is, they're my folks and I came on a visit. Looked around and took a likin' to the land here. I'm thinkin' they'd let me do somethin' to keep myself outta trouble while I'm here. Thinkin' bees might do it. Believe I'll amble on down to Enterprise sometimes this week. Thanks for the coffee. Later." And he took his leave.

Edward turned and left. He had no idea where Enterprise was, but he did know where to get good coffee. Seven pairs of eyes watched as he left and grinned to each other as their guess was legitimized. There were nods as they saw him turn in toward the Cookie Jar and open the door.

"Speck one of them McLaughlin girls is about to get took?"

"I'd say it was about time. They're past sixteen, ain't they?"

"I'd say eighteen, maybe nineteen. Leastwise, that oldest one."

"Them girls have their own business. They don't need no man to take care'a them. It just ain't right for girls to be let to grow up that'a'way."

"Reckon McLaughlin had his reasons."

"Part of it was needin' someone to take care'a the mail hooks. It was all right for old Miz Carlile, but girls need to get somethin' outta it."

"Yeah, but I'd say it wasn't no different than those two in that travelin' van. They're close on to the same age."

"Well, if we're talkin' on that, think on Raymond Canfield's hired man. Can't see how it'd be right for a girl child to get so good with a six shooter. Goes agin nature. You saw how she shot at a person without no second thought. Seemingly."

The man with the crippled foot shifted to a more comfortable position and placed his walking cane across his knees. "If'n she hadn't been a good shot, she'd'a never been able to miss 'im and keep 'im alive. Thief had reason to be grateful to her. Nuther thing, if she hadn't been a good shot, Canfield's boy would'a lost two'a his high dollar animals."

A pause as the old gentleman with the cud took stock of the group. Then, "Well, I just say there ain't no good in bringin' up girl children to go out and earn money and shoot guns. Purely takes away the pride of a man."

Old, crippled Digby again. "You thinkin' a fellow couldn't be as good? Way I hear it, when a fellow marries, the preacher says 'they two are one.' Seems to me like, all of a sudden when them words is said, that fellow is suddenly a smart business person who may be a crack shot. If they are one, then whatever she is…he is. Wouldn't you say?"

It took a while for anyone to say anything. Digby's logic took some thinking through. The blacksmith, Brad Cullen who was Miss Josie's husband, wore a small, amused smile, and regretted to pound on his red-hot horseshoe because it drowned out the conversation.

"Well, it didn't use to be that'a'way. It seemed like it was good for a man to be a man."

Finally Brad, the blacksmith, could keep quiet no longer. "Fellows? You got any idea how those young ladies got the idea they could take care'a themselves? If it didn't used to happen…and it does now, what was the change?"

Old Digby tried hard to keep a straight face, but it was difficult.

Finally one brave person piped up, "It was that school marm that put learnin' in them girls and it just ain't natural. Goes agin the order'a things, I'd say."

A long, thoughtful pause. Then, "If we don't get some rain soon, that popcorn is going to pop right out there on the stalk."

Several sighs of relief. "Heard there was a shower over to Westridge. Shore didn't get any of it here."

Edward Morrison could only imagine the conversation after he left, but he didn't care. Good coffee…a spicy cookie…and lovely scenery. Only a step away. Honey-colored skin…butter and honey-streaked hair. He even liked the way those fragile-looking wire chairs felt.

The more he thought of growing popcorn, the better it sounded. Shorter stalks, long green shiny leaves. Seemed like he heard of the little gadget that you poke the ears into and the kernels all scrape off. He'd have to check that out in Oklahoma City.

And the bees. That alfalfa and persimmon tree combination sounded good. There'd be the sugar from the trees and the bees would for certain pollinate the alfalfa. Along with the popcorn, of course.

The big thing he needed was a fence. Saw Canfield Grading getting a new fence. Maybe he could talk to that fellow. There had to be more to it than it looked like. But he'd figure it out.

Philip Armstrong mopped his sleeve across his sweaty face. If he took his lunch sandwich up to the windmill he could get a fresh drink. He was so parched he felt like he was 'a'spittin' sand hills.

He saw the "hired man" at the mill, and if he went toward her with his hands visible and no horse under him; surely she wouldn't shoot. "Miss, I got kind of a question. The boss said for me to run it by you. I see a comfortable hay loft in the barn, here. I'm thinking if I could get permission to sleep up there, I could work longer hours and get more done. Another thing, it'd be a lot more comfortable than the floor of the crowded wagon where my parents are staying."

Merry swung her bare toes back and forth in the cool water. And thought. This fellow actually worked. He was a son of the new preacher who wanted to stay here, and he was going to help them when they found a place. This wouldn't cost Raymond a thing. Why not?

"Sir…Philip, I can't answer for Raymond, but I'll pass your question along. You might bring a sheet or something to sleep on with you tomorrow just in case. Come get a drink and cool your face. We got that big oak back there with good shade while you eat…or even to take a nap."

Thus dismissed, he did as she said. He'd purely like to get this job done before his pa needed him and staying in the barn would help. Somehow, when he was with his parents, he was suddenly a little boy and got sucked into their problems while he had enough concerns of his own. And the pure fact was, they considered him such a child that his advice to them was not readily taken. Until they needed him…like now.

This little community sure was a nice place and he had to live somewhere…didn't he? That place across the street, the Cookie Jar? He knew they sold breakfast, and it looked like other things were available. He'd see after tomorrow. Well, back to work.…

As it happened, Raymond made an immediate decision to allow his hired man to make the decision. "You're thinkin' he knows what he'd doin' and won't steal a horse? Or you?"

A pause and a tilt of the head. "Well, he's the son of the preacher that wants to settle here, and he is planning to put up his church house when his pa decided. You know all that. Why would he try to steal a horse?"

"I don't know. I just don't want you to do anything that'll get you put in the pokey. I got no one else to take over here."

Nodding, she advised him, "You can be sure I'll not take a shot at anyone who doesn't have one of your horses under him."

So Philip took up sleeping arrangements in the loft.

It was also in the year of 1906 that Pat and Bridie acquired an itch that they had trouble deciding on a way to scratch.

Among the books received from Aunt Sharon in New York were pictures of the current styles, and also patterns that could be ordered. The two girls on the Territory valued these books because they were so talented they could copy many of the styles, at least those that would be acceptable out on their prairie.

Among the styles were other advertisements, most of which were merely interesting to look at and conjecture about. One, however, stood out in their minds.

It seemed that the maker of machinery that created ready-made clothing had developed a smaller version of the machine that could be operated with foot pedals, and they were eager to send one anywhere in the United States. All that was required was money.

That was where the itch became difficult. One thing they had learned in their last year at Miss Josie's school was that a person in business does not ever spend their last cent unless (1) they knew exactly what they were buying. (2) They knew the item could increase their bottom-line profit. (3) They knew for sure that, if the item proved to be a disappointment, they were prepared to take the monetary risk and continue business without it.

The girls of the Hats and Hankies were not sure of any of the three. It was just that they wanted one of those machines even though they had not actually seen one. Almost daily, they forced the idea from their minds, but the next day it popped right back in.

"We could ask Aunt Sharon if she could find a better price...?"

"I hate to be a bother. What if we become a pest and she doesn't send us anything else for free?"

Nodding, Bridie agreed. "That would be a catastrophe. Not even that, we don't know how much it would cost to ship it, and for certain it'd need a crate. We couldn't ask her to do that."

"Do you suppose someone in Oklahoma City has one? Maybe that we could look at?"

"That's an idea! But...well, consider the going and coming, we would lose two whole days of work, and there would be the expense of a room for the night and food. All that added together.... And I'm not sure we should go alone."

"Yeah, it'd cost at least half as much as the machine...maybe. But look how fast it can sew! I know for a fact that Johnny and Willie couldn't go. Raymond keeps them on the road all day and half the night."

"I guess. I wish I could see it work before we paid money. Do you think anyone would object that the garment was not handmade? And what happens at the end of a seam? We always tack a stitch-back to firm the seam. Would we just tie the two threads?"

"Hmmm...I don't know. I'd think the ladies wouldn't care... if the work could be done faster and a little bit cheaper. The cost keeps a lot of the younger ladies from buying what they'd like."

"That's true. Doesn't seem to bother Merry, though."

"Hey! We haven't made up her bill, and she keeps asking. We keep thinkin' there'll be something else she wants and she won't buy it if she pays up."

"How much is her bill? I hope it won't be too much of a shock when she gets it."

Pattie shook her head. "Merry wouldn't order what she can't pay for. Miss Josie taught her, too. She works as hard as we do, and she knows what it is to make money. But she's so much fun to sew for."

"Yeah, and she looks so cute in what we make, she's bound to be an advertisement. And it IS fun, almost like making doll clothes!"

So went today's conversation…similar to what went on daily. The party on state day had given them a lot of orders, many of which had been prompted by Merry's new outfits.

They worked quietly until Pattie squealed excitedly. Bridie reacted instantly. "Did you cut yourself?"

"No, but I got an idea! If that sewing machine is advertised in the style catalogs, it'll be in the Montgomery Wards Catalog over in Argyle. Might be cheaper, and it would come already crated without bothering Aunt Sharon."

Bridie put down the shirtwaist and the buttonholes she was making. They were tedious anyway, and her eyes were beginning to cross. "You know…it just might be in the catalog, and the fellows might be able to make that size of a trip. It's got to be terribly heavy and we might need help with it."

"Yeah, but if they can't go for a while, we could get my pa's buggy and go alone. Someone there would help load it when it came in, and anyway, all we need on the first trip is money."

"Do you think we'll have enough right now?"

Pattie shook her head. "I wouldn't think so without giving Merry her bill."

"I guess we have to. Say, do you remember that new thing we looked at, the dress that hangs all the way from the shoulders to the hem, and has an elastic waist and a belt. We wondered who could wear something that simple but we didn't think of Merry. She could. I'm thinking it'd be perfect."

"It wouldn't make her look like a candle…slim as she is?"

"No, we'd trim it up. Think about white with blue embroidery and a blue sash. Maybe a blue shawl to match the belt. It seems like she's wanting some dress up things."

"True. The fact is, folks may not recognize her out of her brother's overalls. We could show her that picture when we give her the bill. If we took the time to make the trip, we should be ready to buy if it looks good. And there's another thing about Montgomery Ward. If something doesn't work, they take it back. I'd hate to do that to Aunt Sharon."

Bridie was thumbing hurriedly through the style book. "Here it is. Picture that on Merry, and maybe with a big velvet bow and a tiny tulle veil instead of a hat? 'Member how we saw it in that book?"

Pattie contemplated the idea. "She'd need white shoes. 'Course, if we did black instead of blue, her black ones would work. Maybe with a black bow and veil hat."

Bridie pictured the change and nodded. "Black would be better, and she doesn't have anything that color…leastwise, anything that still fits."

The Hats and Hankies staff saw Merry as she made her way to the Cookie Jar. America Forrester was glad to get the bill. She hated to owe anyone, and at the moment, she was becoming painfully concerned that she owed something to God, but she couldn't decide how she could pay Him. Taking the clothing bill she told the girls, "I wanted one more thing and I didn't want to decide until I asked you what you had."

Bright eyes and smiles were exchanged as Pattie opened the book she had under her arm. "We were just thinking about you when we saw this dress. Not very many people could wear this, but it would be perfect on you."

Then Pattie. "Picture it in your mind with black embroidery and sash. And black shoes. What do you think?"

With an apologetic half smile, the hired man faced the girls. "I regret that my mind doesn't make pictures the way yours does. That's why I pay you to think for me. If you think it's right, I'll take it, and I'll bring your money tomorrow…unless you want it sooner."

"Oh, tomorrow's fine. We'll likely be gone the next day. Is there anything you need from Argyle?"

"Sure is. I need stockings. I'll bring the money right over."

Philip Armstrong, the fence builder, showed up with his quilt to sleep on, assuming the hired man would have everything fixed up with the boss. If he stayed over in the hayloft, his food would have to come from the Cookie Jar. Certainly, no problem there.

He also brought his metal lunch box and he'd see what they had at breakfast that would work for lunch. That would save time as well, and he wouldn't need to clean up and try to look presentable. Fence building was a messy, sweaty job, and no way around it

The hired man wandered out to where Philip was working. "Your pa find him a place for his church yet?"

"No, afraid not. He really likes where the Elwoods live, but they say they're just renting. He was wanting a place close for people to reach, but not like here on the Corner."

"You're sayin' he really likes the Elwood's place?"

"Seems to. The way it's flat up by the road and has the trees in the back. The Elwoods said they'd sell a corner to the church if it was theirs and they said they were lucky to get that place. They're just renting, they said, and the rent was really reasonable. Said they hadn't ever thought'a just rentin', but it was workin' out for them."

With that explanation, he picked up the post hold digger and holding it poised over the beginning of a hole, let it drop of its own weight. Separating the handles and lifting, he made the jaws of the digger pick up a clod of dirt. He was very efficient with the gadget and was making good time, she noticed.

"I've got to leave. I hope your pa finds a place. We sure could use a preacher full time, 'stead'a once a month when the weather permitts."

Pattie looked at Bridie. "We don't have to wait another day. We've got the money now. With what we have, it's got to be enough…maybe. Leastwise, this way we'll know, and can be savin' for it. I keep on thinkin' it's the answer, and not just my wantin'."

Bridie nodded. It was her sentiments exactly.

The rooster on the corral gate post aroused the sleeper in the loft. He had had a good night. Quiet and soft beneath his quilt, and a breeze like he certainly didn't have on the floor of his folks' wagon. After inspecting for straw in his hair, red-brown and very curly from his Irish ancestors, and washing up at the water trough, he made his way over to the Cookie Jar, tempted by the aroma of their coffee.

"For the lunchbox…?" Gwinnie asked, responding to his question.

"Yeah, I was thinkin' I'd see what you had that'd keep."

With a toss of her butter and honey hair, a wide smile displaying her dimples, she assured him, "Got just the thing. It's popular with the well drillers and the fellows over at the Grading. It's a special sandwich, and I'll make you one. If you don't like it, you don't have to pay for it."

Philip thought he couldn't hardly beat a deal like that, and Gwinnie was released to shave thin chips off the dried venison they had purchased from the Elwoods. Thin…thin…almost so a body could read through it. Gathering the prescribed amount of chips, she tossed them into the hot skillet with a half a cup of water and a tight lid.

In two minutes, the water had either been absorbed or had sizzled away, and she tossed in a small hunk of butter. A fast stir with a fork, and an egg was broken on top. Stir again. With her spatula she pulled the pile together to fit an oversized biscuit and patted it flat. One minute to brown lightly, flip it over and another minute. Then she slid it on a plate to cool a bit before putting it in the metal lunch box.

All of this she did while setting another pot of tea to steep, removing a tray of fresh-baked sugar cookies and sliding another pan of cookies into the oven, then pouring a cup of coffee that Kristie took to Philip, along with the sausage and scrambled egg he had ordered for breakfast.

In fifteen minutes Philip walked away with food in his stomach and food in the lunch box. *Efficiency. Extraordinary young ladies. Wonder what their husbands do?*

It was a really long day. Just as he was quitting, the sun had already fallen below the trees in the west, and his employer was making his way out toward him. He paused and waited.

"Phillip, I've been thinking. I believe I'll have you cut back toward the back fence, before you go any farther. That way, if you have to stop, one field will be done. Also, I might want to turn the animals in on one side and not the other."

"I can do that," Philip was quick to say. It made a lot of sense.

Raymond tested the posts for wobble. There was none. "You're about ready for the stretcher, aren't you? I'll have to see who I can spare to help."

"Well, I might say this again. I really don't need any help if you don't mind my being a bit longer. I've learned how to attach the stretcher to a post instead of it being held. I think it'd depend on which you needed the most, the grading or the fence."

"Friend, I like the way you talk. I'll be glad to let you do it by yourself. How did you do in the loft?"

"Just perfect. 'Course, I was promised by your hired man that I would be safe as long as I was not on a horse. It sounds as though humans are expendable, but not your horses."

With a chuckle, Raymond agreed. "That's about the way I see it. I'll set the stretchers out by the gate and you can get them when you need them. Good luck." And he was gone.

Back in the hired man's house, it was the night of the dream. Well, it really wasn't a dream as one would describe it, but a sudden awaking in the night that had Merry sitting upright in her bed. The answer. She now had the answer.

Of course the Elwoods could not sell part of their land to the preacher (actually, God) but she could. Actually, what she could do was measure off a tenth and GIVE it because it was part of what she owed to God, and she purely hated to owe anyone. Especially God.

Someday, she hoped at least, she would know where her father had sent his tenth. It had to be somewhere, because she could now remember it almost like it was yesterday. It had drifted from her mind as she was growing up, and as she had worked toward taking care of herself and her brother. She remembered sitting of an evening in the lamplight with her mother rocking and mending... or something. Her father would read from his beloved King James Bible that had cost so much because the whole book had not been readily available until recently.

She could picture Homer on the floor with some kind of toy. She had a distinct picture of him squatting on his knees... that were always skinned. He would be arranging his toy wooden animals and attempting impossible things like trying to make his chicken stand on the back of a horse...or piling his tiny wagon so full of animals that they were laying on their sides. He was always "inventive."

The one time she remembered well was when her pa was talking about God's money that he let us spend for Him. *If we spent it the way He wanted us to, He would make sure we had enough. If we decided to spend it all on ourselves, we would be punished in some way. He was clear about it when he said that "God did not like to be robbed."* It said so in Malachi chapter 4 verse 8. "Will a man rob God?" Pretty scary, when one thought about it.

Now, sitting upright in her bed, Merry felt her scalp tingle. If she could GIVE the land to the church (Philip's pa), that would pay her tenth on that land. Likely hers and Homer's, both.

For a fact, they would never live there, at least together. She had this wonderful job, and the way she saw it, Raymond would always have horses, so she would always have a job. Even better was the way the Bramwells treated her brother, and how well he seemed to fit in with their family. They even bought him some special coveralls so his clothes would not get dirty or torn, and they even washed them for him. It would be easy for Homer to see how they were being paid by God for the way their father had lived.

But now, it was time they were on their own. That would take some thinking, and she had mucking out to do. Mucking was good for thinking. Shovel a scoop of poop and put it on the pile. Big horses really made a lot of it, but it was spread on the pasture and made very good grass. Raymond was even letting her operate the "spreader" which was actually a dirt scoop used in the road building. It just required to be hitched up backward to spread instead of dump.

She'd have to see to making the gift to the church legal and that meant having it surveyed. She would want to make sure that God wouldn't think she might want it back. The nine-tenths that was left was a big lot of land, and no matter what Homer might eventually want to do, there would be plenty left.

Philip mopped his sweaty face and thought of lunch. He had no idea that one of his concerns was rapidly melting away with no effort from him…. It was actually dissolving in the conscientious mind of the hired man.

When the sun was overhead, he cooled off at the windmill and settled under the oak tree with a bottle of water and his lunch box. *Hmmm, sandwich nice and thick. And cold.* And he was very hungry. One big bite, and the tender meat fell apart as he chewed, flavorful and moist. It couldn't have tasted better if it was hot and actually, as hot as the weather was, it seemed better cold. Along with the fresh pumped water from the windmill…just perfect.

He wanted more than anything to lean back on the grass, but he didn't. The way he felt, so tired and now with a comfortably full stomach, he might not wake up until morning. Rather, he leaned against the trunk of the tree and thought. His pa was really too old to do the job he was given, but with his experience, the church board just couldn't resist calling on him. It was hard for a pioneer preacher to retire.

There were three separate times that Rev. Armstrong had started from nothing and built up a congregation, arranging for a church to hold the services. Three times he had stayed with it, being available to his congregation at all hours. Sleeping when he could. Teaching, loving and burying. Finally handing it over to another. And now he was old…and tired. And he still just couldn't say "no."

Another thing was, now he needed his son and had pulled him in and away from a job. Not the best job, Phillip admitted, but he was working toward it. He didn't want to leave it, but, just like his father, he couldn't say "no" to duty. Well, at least he had a temporary job now, and was able to earn a little money. Truth be told, he liked this one better than the last one, but that was neither here nor there.

His eyes closed and his head nodded. The jerk woke him up and he rubbed his eyes, drank the last of his water, and headed back to the fence building.

Hunger again attacked him as the sun was lowering behind the trees. One thing for certain, he didn't want to let that place across the road close for the night before he had food. He imagined he smelled savory beans cooked with meat and spices, but, of course, it could be his imagination. He was almost a half a mile away.

Gathering his tools, he headed for the barn. He'd need the wire and the stretchers tomorrow and hoped for a horse to sled them out. Maybe the hired man would help with the horse, so she could see he wasn't stealing it. Also, he thought she had the horses trained to do anything she wanted them to do, if only she sang hymns to them.

It WAS beans. Other things were prepared, of course, but only beans would do. They came aromatic and steaming. Alongside them was what looked like a dough package...about six inches long and browned. Gwinnie explained, "I don't know if you're acquainted with burritos. Some folks aren't but a lot of our fellows like them in lunch boxes. We can make it hot, but this is cold because we wanted you to try them...no charge for this one. They're popular with some fellows because their mom made them when they were little. I'll bring your coffee."

Hmmm, that little wrapped thing was quite tasty, and if he ever got tired of the egg and venison, he'd try it. *Hey, maybe hot for breakfast!* A thought, anyway.

It was late when Pat and Bridie pulled the buggy into the O'Day's yard. It had been quite a day at Argyle, ending, as usual, at the Sweet Shoppe for ice cream. And a lot of talk. The sewing machine was expensive, but not as much as they'd expected, considering the weight of it and the expense of the crate. It would be offloaded in Argyle, and they'd have to get it on home, but they had three weeks to plan that.

It would be a long three weeks of waiting for the order. They had thread, pins and a package of needles, just for safety. One couldn't sew without needles…unless they had a machine, and even it took needles. Special ones. They had ordered an extra package. The three pairs of stockings for Merry, one white and two tan, were sacked and stuck in with the thread.

Bridie waved goodbye and headed down the road to her house, and Pattie took herself into her room and stretched out on the bed. Spending such hard-earned money was frightening, exciting and exhausting. Almost as tiring as decision making. She dozed off to sleep with a vision of the white dress they would make tomorrow. No fancy cutting and fitting. Straight and dignified with its shiny black satin sash, cross-stitch embroidery on the hem and the sides split up for about eight inches…maybe only six.

Anyway, as slim as it would be made, the splits were necessary for easy walking. Six inches would likely take it almost up to her knees. It would be certain to show a peek of pettislip lace. Merry might considered the slit indecent, but still…the scene in her mind told her that the slit must be at least six inches.

It was dark when her mother shook her awake. "I know you don't want to sleep in that dress, and you need to come and eat. I don't want you to starve to death in bed, and us havin' to do something with the body." Pattie grinned. That was one of her mom's most favorite sayings. Food was very important to her mother.

Reverend Armstrong would have been getting concerned if he had been a less wise man. Sometimes it seemed that God took an uncommonly long time to send down an answer, but he knew, by now, that his heavenly Boss acted in His own time. But what should he do now…just stay parked in the Elwood's yard where he felt most comfortable? Or tell Philip he could go back to his job in

Oklahoma City until he was needed…if, indeed, he still had the job? He decided to take a stroll around the property to perhaps ease his tension. Waiting was so much harder than doing.

A pink hollyhock tree was in full bloom. He walked over to it, marveling at the multitude of blossoms. Yes, he knew it was actually an Althea tree, but that sounded like a girl's name, and his mother had called it a hollyhock tree because of the blossom shape.

Bees were buzzing in and out, making use of every scrap of nectar. This was such a lovely lay of land. Slopes and knolls, tall trees and bushes. The people who owned the place must have loved it from the way they placed the buildings, and the few expensive blossoming shrubs. Tomorrow was again Sunday. *Lord, is there something I don't know about what I should do? Perhaps if I let people know, they would meet…here? Or what, Lord?*

Merry Forrester and her brother slept late that Sunday morning. Neither had anything special to do, and the Cookie Jar would not be open until later, and then for only a couple of hours.

When she heard Homer begin to stir in his loft bedroom overhead, she stepped out onto the wolf skin rug, remembering to stomp on it, reminding it what it did to her brother.

Start breakfast. The oatmeal bubbled and plopped with rich goodness. Biscuits rose up and browned, just as they were meant to do. A jar of Mrs. Bramwell's jelly graced the table.

"Homer, do you remember anything at all of when Papa was talking about money?"

Her brother buttered his biscuit and considered. "No. I know you think I should because I was there, but I really don't remember."

"No, Homer. I really don't think that, but I'm about to say something I think is important. I know that money earned and money given is something God considers part His. If He does not get His money, He promises to do something that will make us remember what we should do. If we do what He says, He will make things good for us.

CHAPTER 6

Just think about you and me. There is no way I could have arranged for us to have what we have. I just happened to go to the Bramwells at a time when they needed someone...but not me. Now, you have a good job you like for people who couldn't like you better if you were their own son. You have someone to cook for you, even better than our mom and they're even nice to your sister. On top of all that, you have Neecie following you around like a big-eyed puppy, just hoping for a smile or a good word."

That brought on a grin. "Aw, sis...."

She continued. "And look what I have! My very most favorite job in the world, and who would have thought that a fellow as smart as Raymond would actually hire a girl to take care of his horses."

Homer, with another grin. "Are you sure he knows you're a girl...the way you run around in my overalls? With that blue thing on your head?"

Merry ignored him in true sisterly fashion. "The thing is, we have that quarter section down on Cedar Bush Road. The Elwoods are so good and bring me the dried venison, and the rent, but the thing is, that land is something that was given to us. Or, maybe not ALL of it. It was really bought with money Pa earned. Philip Armstrong says that his pa, the preacher, says that would be the perfect place for a church."

Merry watched her brother scoop up a spoonful of the oatmeal with brown sugar. He really did look like he was listening. Then he lay down his spoon and looked at her.

"Sis, if God doesn't like it when people know what to do and don't do it, then why are you and I doing so well? I have a good job, you have a good job. If what you read is what you think, why isn't God punishing us? Or other people who don't do what they should?"

Deep breath. She expected this. "I don't know about others, but I didn't think about this until a couple of weeks ago. I think it was the timing that was important. Philip talked with me about his pa, and I don't think the preacher would have thought to look for me, and the Elwoods had no say in the matter. But about what's happened, I think you and I are doing well because of what Papa did, and we belonged to him at one time. Now we don't.

"Here's what I think. We should mark off at least a tenth of that quarter section and give it to God for a church and trust the preacher to see that God gets it. What do you think?"

Homer didn't miss a bite. "Sis, you're the one who figured it out. Do what you think we ought to do, because I certainly don't want anything to happen to my job at the mill. Mr. Bramwell lets me do almost everything now. Another thing, I've been savin' up for a buggy of my own, and later a horse to replace ours that died. I think I may have enough money already. In only two years I saved enough, and I thought I'd have to work a lot longer for both."

Merry nodded. Just one more thing to ask him. She wanted to make sure. "You don't really need or especially want anything from the property? I don't want to sell it, until you're at least twenty-five or more, but I know what we can do with it right now. Buggies and wagons gotta be parked somewhere. In a few years you might think it would be handy to have a church in your yard, maybe. Or you could always sell it later. We'd likely get even more for it if we wait."

Homer nodded and repeated, "I want you to do what you think we should do. You're the one who remembers what Papa said. I only remember how much fun he was when we went shooting, or fishing, or when he told stories about England. I think I'll head on down the road and see if there's anybody around to talk with."

With a wave, he was gone. Merry stepped into the worn overalls and tied the blue and white striped shawl over her head. It kept a lot of dirt out of her hair even if it did, maybe, keep her from looking like a girl!

Everybody was out in the pasture pulling wads of grass with their teeth and looking around while they chewed. King Alfred took a few steps toward her, and she began to sing, "In the sweet... bye and bye...we shall meet on that beautiful shore! In the sweet..." and by now the King was beside her, whickering with his soft, lips like he was trying to help her sing.

Lucy came for her share of the patting. Even shy Rosie came up behind her and nudged her elbow. America Forrester looked around her and nodded in agreement with herself. She could never, on her own, have found a place to stay that was so wonderful as this, and so close to Homer where they could keep track of each other. And she'd have to say, for a brother, it would be hard to beat Homer for being easy to get along with. If Neecie Bramwell just hung in there, she might be the lucky one to get him!

Just one thing...if she just knew where Papa sent the money that was God's, she would send hers there and everything would be perfect. She was certainly going to be careful about God's money and save it for Him, because she really liked the way He was helping her, so far. Was that being selfish? She hoped not.

Everyone in the pasture got their share of the petting, and their hooves got a quickie inspection. No one was limping and no one had infected fly bites. She broke out in singing, "Skip to my loo, my darling..." and left them. She had all kinds of washing up she needed to do, and a couple of magazines from the Cookie Jar to look at. The ones that came from Aunt Sharon in New York and had not yet fallen apart from use. They were always fun to look at, and the horses wouldn't need her until evening.

On Monday morning Merry noted when Philip walked through the gate returning from breakfast. She was eager to get his help on what she needed to tell his pa. "Phillip, could you do something for me? Would you tell your father I'd really like to see him as soon as he can spare the time? It's something really important."

The fence builder brushed back his red-brown curls with his shirt sleeve while he considered the request. "I know my pa, and if you, or anyone for that matter, need to see him, he'd want me to come and tell him immediately. He always has time for someone who needs him."

"Oh, no, it can wait...."

"Nope. I'm going to tell him right now." And he turned around to walk away.

"Well, you could at least take a horse...."

Looking her full in the face, he told her, "Now, that's something that I absolutely will not do. There is no way I would be caught on one of your horses. My pa does not want to bury me before I help him get his church going." Then he added, "Really, thanks, but it's not far and I can be there and back by the time we saddled up. See you later."

A half an hour passed and a pair of horses trotted up into the Canfield Grading yard. Philip dismounted and headed for the fence. "Brought 'im. He's all yours."

"So pleased to meet you, miss. My son said you had need of my services."

"Uh...yes. It's just that I hadn't expected him to bring you immediately. I'm hardly fit to talk with anyone, but this is the way I work...."

"Think nothing of it. Let's hear how I can help you. I just learned from the Elwoods that you and your brother own the place down on Cedar Bush. Lovely place."

"Yes, sir...Reverend. That's what I want to talk about. My brother and I owe something to God, and we want to get it paid as soon as we can. We want to deed a part of our quarter section to God, and we don't really know how to do it. You're the closest to God that we know and wondered if...."

A nod and a smile. "You're saying you want to donate property to the church? How kind of you! That must be why I couldn't seem to get interested in any other location."

"No, sir. We aren't being kind. It isn't ours to give. We know that God expects a tenth of it, and our papa would want it done. We didn't even think about it until now. But we want it done as soon as possible. When we get a surveyor, you can tell us what to do...can't you?"

110

"I surely…uh, yes, I can help you deed the land to the church. It wouldn't be to me, of course, but I can help."

"Thank you, and we think you should expect to have the northwest corner, with a 200-foot frontage and about five hundred feet back. We'll check that for sure to get the right amount. Go ahead and start the building if you want to. I think you were going to need Philip when you did and we'll miss him. He sure can work fast. I appreciate you coming, and I've got to get to work." With a grin, she added, "I'm the hired man here."

The preacher, being thus dismissed, was now on his own. He strolled out to the fencing just as Philip was pounding the last of the staples to the barbed wire onto the posts.

"Well, son, it looks like you'll be having another job for a while…."

The more that Edward Morrison walked around the Corners, the better he liked it. Here it was, only two weeks that he had been here, and already the fellows were shouting "hey" to him as he passed and discussing the weather when they met. Everybody was friendly and seemed as comfortable as an old shoe.

He had just about settled on what he wanted, and discussed his plans with his uncle, who assured him, "Now, son, you just do whatever you want to do. Take your time. We don't want to be pinnin' you down, but your Aunt Sybil is havin' herself a time, getting' to do things for you, and have someone to cook for that eats like a workin' man. That's interestin' about the bees. Wouldn't'a thought of it, myself."

Edward nodded. "The same with me. Someone had to help with ideas. I only made arrangements for one hive, and that not until fall. This seems to be the big time'a the year for bees not to be moved. Seems like everything that has a bud on it has popped out in bloom. Now, about that popcorn patch…you ever put a plow to that land in the back?"

"Can't say as I did. Mostly just worked a garden place, but I'll warn you. It's like they say out here, there ain't been a plow in the ground since God created dirt. Won't be no easy job."

"Figured that. I'm wantin' to make a deal for one of them horses down the road, but ain't had a chance. That fellow's harder to catch than a greased snake. I'd like two of 'em, but I want to make my cash last. There's sure to be things to get that I haven't thought of, yet."

His uncle nodded. "Son, one of them horses'll out-do you. When it comes to plowin' with it, you'll be the first to give up. Not that monster of an animal. You might want'a look over that plow I got out there in the shed, chance you get a minute'a time."

"I'll do that, and thanks."

The Hats and Hankies girls were tying off the last stitches of the white dress. They were purely eager to see it modeled, and they had slipped Merry's order ahead of the line of those waiting, being certain they wouldn't need more than two days to finish it. As it turned out, it was only a day and a half.

"Don't look like too much on the hanger, does it?"

Bridie tipped her head to get a better perspective. "No, but that's on account'a the elastic in the waist. Pulls it together in a wad. It'll look good on her, and she's about the only one. Watch some bigger woman to want one, thinkin' it'll make her look like Merry!"

Pattie giggled at the thought. "I'll let you explain to her why she can't have it!"

"I don't know! They're easy to make, maybe she'll like it and not know the difference, and then, again, maybe we're wrong. 'Course we haven't been wrong yet." "Maybe Merry'll come by on her way to the Cookie Jar. She can get it, then."

It was late Wednesday that Philip found a minute to come over to the Cookie Jar to get away from the shovel for a while. Nothing would stop his pa from marking out the shape of the footing and beginning to level it.

The thing was, though, that his father hated so badly to have to dig up the hollycock tree that he just couldn't seem to get started on it. He finally realized that it was the only way to go, and he had Philip dig another place for the bush so it could be planted out of the way. Maybe it would live. He had said it was hard to kill a hollyhock tree. Maybe he knew.

By then it was late afternoon, and that other thing occurred, so he said he'd just come and tell Miss Forrester what happened. It was wonderful to get away from Cedar Bush Road. Actually, no one loved his father more than Philip did, and he would do anything to help him.

The bottom line of it was that they were so totally different, they couldn't seem to get anything done when they worked together. If his pa had tried to help him with the fence, he wouldn't be half through yet. If only he could just get pa to tell him what he wanted, and then go away and let him do it. Not much chance of that, at Pa's age.

He stopped in at the Cookie Jar on the way. Great little place those girls had. Stepping inside and blinking from the sun in his eyes, he saw Merry sitting at one of the little tables. He was making a move to set at the next one, when she offered the seat at her table.

"Might as well leave a table for someone else. I'm just over here wasting time. This is the only table that lets me watch the driveway to see if someone goes in."

"You're on guard, huh!"

"Yeah, I'm thinkin' Raymond'll be stopping' by, and someone left 'im a note. If I don't say somethin', he'll likely miss the note. I don't want someone comin' by and blamin' me that he didn't get back to them."

Just at that moment Raymond stepped through the door to the Cookie Jar. He had a lot to catch up on, and he'd have to miss being home for supper. Needed to get something to tide him over.

Stepping in and blinking at the dimness after the sun's glare, he saw several people, including his fence builder who promised to come back as soon as his father released him. He'd know him anywhere. With that mop of curly, dark red hair, he sort'a stood out in a crowd.

Someone with him. New girl. Long, wavy light brown hair that curled on the end. White dress. Must be his girlfriend. He saw the girl reach over toward Philip and pick a piece of straw from his hair. Just like a girlfriend! Oh, well, a fellow had a right to have a girlfriend. Just so he remembered to get back to the fence. Picking up a couple of cold burritos, Raymond paid and left. Too much to do.

But then when later he saw a girl with pretty hair and a white dress come into the equipment shed with a note, it struck him. THAT must have been his hired man he saw with Philip! Would you believe it…he hadn't realized that she must have hair. Of course, she hadn't been born with that blue and white stripped scarf on her head but that was all he ever saw. Well…well….

It was shortly after that when Phillip appeared again at Canfield Grading. Merry was in the corral bent over a huge hoof that was lifted and extended back. The beast was turning to look at her, his eyes glistening brightly under the long, thick lashes. Phillip had a quick supposition that those thick lashes must help to keep the blowing sand from his eyes.

Merry had some sort of pliers in her hand and she was intent on the sole of a hoof. Huge, beautiful beast. That must be King Alfred, the one she sang to in the pasture so many times. He watched intently and silently until she released the foot and then the beast set his foot on the ground.

She moved up to the animal's head, petting his face and stroking his ears. "Now we got that old rock out of your foot. You'll feel a lot better." The horse blew his breath onto her arm and whickered softly. One could imagine he was thanking her for whatever it was that she did. When the horse looked up at Philip, Merry turned toward him.

"Oh, hi! I didn't know you were there."

"I was quiet. I didn't want to disturb the doctor in the midst of an operation. I also didn't want him to put that hoof down on one of your feet."

"Aw, he wouldn't do that. He just told me he had a gravel stuck in his hoof. He's got a red spot where the gravel cut him. I'll have to clean and treat it. Were you here to see Raymond?"

"No, I'm here to see you. We've started leveling for the foundation on the church and we came across something that my pa wanted you and your brother to see."

"What is it?"

"I can't say. They want you and your brother there because it was your land, and they're not sure about it."

"And you can't say…. Did someone get hurt…or something?"

"Not that. Is just…."

"…that you can't tell me. I'm afraid I can't come until evening if it's not an emergency. And Homer's usually pretty busy. Would that work?"

"I'll go tell 'em. Good luck with your operation."

Waving, he was gone.

It was mid-afternoon that a horse and buggy pulled into the drive. Out stepped her brother with a smile that seemed to want to split his face.

"My new buggy," he announced. "I've been sayin' I needed to start lookin' and Mr. Bramwell was up in Argyle when folks came by with a wagon and this buggy, sayin' they had a problem and needed to sell the buggy for quick cash. Mr. Bramwell knew it was a bargain, so he went ahead and paid for it, then came home and got me. He said he knew he could resell it if I didn't want it, but it's just exactly what I wanted. Almost new."

Merry looked the vehicle over from shafts, to wheels, to the little luggage boot in the back. "Looks like a courtin' buggy, to me," she observed with a grin. "Good timing. You'd better get busy and find a girlfriend or Neecie'll have you yet."

"Yeah, she's already wantin' a ride."

"Speakin' of a ride, you and I need to go down to Cedar Bush after you get through today. Something's happened down there that we need to see. Philip was just here."

"What was it?"

"He said they didn't want him to say. I can't imagine why they'd need us, but if you'd bring the buggy by, I'll ride with you and tell you if it's good enough for a courtin' buggy. So now, take your new toy and go. I've got a horse hoof to treat."

115

She watched as the shiny black buggy with the ivory wheels ground through the gravel of the driveway. Good stroke of luck. Or was it luck? *Hmmmm.*

When they later rode into the familiar yard of their childhood home, activity was brisk. Philip was attached to the shovel, his mother was raking dead sticks out of the way, and his father was once more checking the measurements with his cord. A couple of neighbors were making themselves useful…maybe.

When they saw who came, work stopped. "Miss Forrester, we needed you here because we didn't know if changes were in order. It happened when we needed to lift the hollyhock tree and reset it. See, over there we have the hole all ready.

"The thing was, when Philip put the shovel down way out here, you know you gotta be careful not to dig too close till you see where the roots are. Wouldn't want to damage important feeder roots. We'd sure like to see it keep on growing.

"Well, anyway, when he put the shovel down, it sounded like he hit a rock. You know there aren't too many rocks in this soil, less'n it's a stone ledge. Not like over in Arkansas where the farmers swear their fields grow rocks. Back in England, they made fences outta what they pulled outta the ground.

"Well, when his shovel made a sound, he dug out around whatever it was, 'cause we'll have a use for every rock we find, and he was thinkin' it might be a big rock."

Merry took a breath to relieve the tension. She glanced over to where Philip leaned against his shovel, grinning as though it was difficult to keep a straight face. His pa loved to talk…maybe that made him a good preacher?

The Reverend continued. "Then we all went to help get the rock up, and it wasn't a rock. It was any wonder he didn't break it with the shovel, you know how fragile glass is. But I dug around with my fingers, you know, the dirt here is so soft and full of loam. It ought'a grow good crops. Anyway, I pulled out whatever it was and broke off the dirt clods. Didn't try to open it 'cause it wasn't mine to open. That's when I sent 'im up to get you two. Reasoned that you didn't know it was here, so it wouldn't'a been something that was given to the church.

"We saw right off that it was a jar, but the lid was rusted into a clump." He finally handed Merry a jar. It was glass, and of the half a gallon size that was prized by large families for canning because they held so much. It was as heavy as a rock and made of the glass that had a blue cast so they really couldn't see what was in the jar, except that it rattled when tipped up.

At this point, Philip took over the words. "I got my knife here, and it'd be no trick to cut through that rusty lid and rip it out. Want me to do it?" He directed the question toward Homer... man to man.

"Sure thing. Go ahead and cut 'er open."

The knife slipped easily through the thin rusted metal, and the wafer of rust that was cut away, fell to the ground. Homer held the heavy jar as the brother and sister looked in.

Coins! It was absolutely full of coins, still bright and shiny. Tucked in among them was a note, somewhat yellowed. Merry carefully pulled out the paper and spread it with her fingers. All eyes followed her in eager expectation.

She read the note, swallowed hard and felt her eyes fill as she recognized her father's writing. She held the note so her brother could read it, and they looked at each other as though they were speaking without words.

Handing the note to Philip, she wiped her eyes with her sleeve. Homer reached toward her with a comforting hand on her shoulder. "Papa's writing? For sure?"

She nodded, retrieved the note and read to the expectant faces. "The note says, 'GOD'S MONEY I am putting it here until God tells me where to send it. He has been so good to us, helping us get to this wonderful country, and giving us America and Oklahoma.'"

Reverend Armstrong nodded knowingly. "Oklahoma is a wonderful place."

Merry sniffed and corrected him. "You don't understand. I'm America and my brother is Oklahoma. They named him when they knew they would come here, and always called him Homer."

Long silence. "I wish Papa could see this. His children finally get to know where to send the money. That bush was his marking place. If there isn't enough here to pay for the church building, then I know it'll at least go a long way." Keeping the note, she handed the jar to the old preacher who had tears streaming down his wrinkled face. For once in his life, he had no words.

The return trip started out in silence except for the hooves of the horse on the gravel, then Homer observed. "Looks like we must'a done the right thing, huh, sis?"

The buggy turned the corner and headed north, just as Raymond came out of the blacksmith shop going toward home. Different horse and buggy…always an interest in the community. There was that white dress on his hired man. She was sitting there beside a broad-shouldered young man who seemed to know how to handle a horse. And that was certainly not the red-haired son of the preacher. Hmmmm.

Homer again. "How much money do you think was in that jar?"

"Don't know. 'Course it really doesn't matter. Papa was always good at counting, so we know for sure he had it right."

"Something to think about, though. I was thinking on the way home with my new buggy, the way it just seemed to fall in my lap. Just what I wanted. And I didn't even know yet about Papa's savings bank!"

Reverend Armstrong sat up most of the night with paper and pencil, planning this way and that. He added to the length of the planned church building, he added to it the cost of benches made with planed wood, and he figured in a starter house for the minister who would take over the church eventually.

In fact, he would begin on the starter house first, as Mrs. Armstrong was a bit old to put up with the hardships of the wagon for another month and likely more. If he'd tack up a note in the blacksmith shop and in that little diner than Philip likes, he'd be sure to attract some help.

Edward Morrison hitched his uncle's horse to the plow he pulled from the shed. He could go ahead and break the ground to get a head start on next year. The way the men folk talked, it'd take more than one turning to get soil he could use.

He needed to see if he could get one of those Clydesdale horses. He'd rather have an old one that couldn't work with the heavy machinery anymore. He didn't relish the thought of rearing up a colt and breaking it to the plow when he had no idea how to do it.

Three weeks passed and the mail order was waiting in Argyle. It would take a wagon and a pair of strong arms, and it made an excited foursome on a Saturday afternoon. However, the sewing machine clearly was the focal factor. The fellows were not happy to be less popular than what was unseen in a crate, but they persevered in good humor and it got loaded.

Ice cream, fun and giggles, but it was evident the girls were eager to see what they had bought. It was reassuring to the fellows, however, to realize the girls could not manage it alone. There was a lot of heavy machinery in that crate. Some muscles would be needed before it was set in place and where else would they get muscles?

Uncrated and bolted to the floor in the rolling showroom, it took up a great lot of space. In fact, it was difficult to edge around it. Clearly, something was going to have to be done. Parents were invited to the unveiling, and the fathers saw, at a glance, what was coming.

A building. It wasn't that they had thought it would not happen, it was just that the girls, being young, could change their minds in a moment. It did not, however, happen that way.

Standing around in the blacksmith shop, the two fathers and the landlord had a conversation that ended in a negotiation. After about five minutes thought, Mr. McLaughlin, property owner and close friend, offered a deal.

"Bein' as how we're friends, and the four girls bein' close here, I can do this. I can't sell the property because it would be a chunk outta the strip I got plans for, but I can give you a lease for as long as your girls want to use it.

"If you fellows can build a building at least twenty feet by thirty feet, and put up a fence, you can have the land with no rent as long as my girls are running the Cookie Jar. I know how those four help each other like on State Day when the community ate up every crumb and they called in all help. That's the deal I make for you, but not for anyone else. I got the Rollin' Five and Dime settin' up next to you."

This was news. "You mean Ralph Carpenter is comin' off the road with his route? Wouldn't'a thought that'd happen. Seems he does good business the way the country is fillin' up."

Mr. McLaughlin nodded knowingly. "Doin' good, all right. Fact is, he's bein' needed at home, and it's his thinking that folks'll come to him, now that they know 'im. 'Nuther thing is, with a building, he can put in a lot more stock. That'll be a big thing with the women folk. He'll be takin' the next lot, right this side'a the Saddle and Tack Shop."

Mr. O'Day and Mr. O'Grady walked away together. Mr. O'Day first. "What do you think? Reckon those girls'll make it profitable and not up and decide to get married?"

Bridie's father stroked his chin thoughtfully. "You know what I'm thinkin'? It seems likely to me that even if they did, those girls're doin' too well and havin' too much fun to just give it up. 'Specially after that new gadget they spent their money on." With a grin, he added, "Besides, the way Raymond keeps those fellows workin', they likely ain't even got time to attend their own weddin'. Can't say I heard talk from Bridie's mom on any plans bein' made."

"My thoughts exactly. Reckon we need to take the gamble. Puttin' up just a shell of a house won't be much of a problem, and we gotta remember those girls been spendin' their own money for nigh onto five years. Doin' good, seems like. 'Course, Patricia never came to me for advice so I don't know what she's doin'. Goes to her teacher. That teacher shore made a difference around here."

Pat and Bridie didn't wait for the new building. They crowded themselves around the new machine, learning the specific track the thread had to follow, how fast or slow to operate the treadle and how to tie off. Didn't take them very long.

The first thing made was a hankie. "Look at that! Finished in two minutes and look how neat! Tiny stitches and all locked down tight. All that worry the ladies was havin' was for nothing!"

"Let's see what we've got in line. If one of us measures and cuts, and the other one pins and sews, look how fast it'll be." In the excitement of it all, they could make a simple dress in less than two days instead of a week or ten days.

Raymond had seen something that deepened the frown on his forehead. He had been fooled by the girl with Philip in the Cookie Jar. Who would have thought that was his "hired man"? Then there was the time he came in and found that new fellow from up north talking with her. And after that, he saw her riding in a strange buggy with a fellow he didn't recognize from where he stood.

Was he in danger of losing her? It could happen! Girls got married, didn't they…? And all of a sudden, maybe…?

He hadn't thought that much when he hired her. He thought for maybe a week, or even a month, but no girl would stay and do what had to be done. He'd just let her get her fill, and then he'd find someone else. A fellow.

He had been needing someone for quite a while. His fellows really hated taking care of the horses after they had put in a day of work. There was that mess of griping and complaining when it was their turn to stay over. He thought that sometimes they waited for him to leave so they could go on home…or that they were so tired they crawled in the hayloft and went to sleep. Now, they could just pull into the yard, and park the machinery. That girl could unhitch the animals as well as they could, and it gave her a chance to inspect them for wear and tear. No way would they want to take over that job again.

He had noticed that the horses did not have infected insect bites. The hair of their spats was trimmed and they always had clean hay at night when they were in their stalls. The muck was never piled up in the corner of a stall. Fresh water was drawn up in the water trough, and when the wind became brisk, the windmill was unhooked. A strong gust of wind could bend the blades, but it didn't happen with his hired man aboard.

The hay nets were always full in the winter. He'd finally stopped checking to make sure. Pulled leg muscles were always bound in liniment rags, and there were almost no lost days. Something like this was easy to get used to, and he'd long ago quit thinking about the horses and concentrated on keeping the fellows busy.

What would it take to assure that she would stay? If she wanted to get married, she could certainly have a choice of fellows, even in her brother's overalls and that blue and white thing she wore on her head. He'd raised her pay, and she'd thanked him, but she didn't act as though she thought it was particularly important.

And that singing! Those mammoth beasts followed her like puppies when she sang. He had a mental picture of the many times he had seen her practically sitting under those animals working a burr or gravel out of their hoofs. They stood motionless on three legs, with necks bent so they could watch her with adoring eyes.

Holding up a foot like that, why, if the horse over-balanced and took a step, he could break her in two!

And blankets. If the wind was cold, she let them out to pasture all buckled into their blankets. Saved body heat and strength, of course, but she could hardly reach over their backs without something to stand on.

Then, there was the really big thing. She had saved him two horses, at least, and seemed to think it was nothing. Said that was what she was hired to do. Was it? *Hmmm....*

It seemed to Raymond Canfield that he had been born a businessman, and even the thoughts of his resting moments were spent on profit and loss. He had been hardly in his teens when he had seen the potential of the massive Clydesdale horses...then new to the territory. It was then that he had persuaded his father that they were worthy of investment with some of his inheritance from his grandmother. At that time he had no idea of what could actually be done with them.

Now, as he looked around at the quarter section of prairie land, also from his inheritance, and saw the standing pieces of heavy equipment designed for shaping dirt into roads, terraces, and farm ponds. Machinery for building the necessary cellars for preservation of summer food. For leveling pastureland.

He looked around and knew the beginning of it all was the strong, heavy bodies of the Clydesdales, along with his own energy and dreams. His dreams. Here he was barely over twenty, and he made contracts, hired help and created a profit. That's what kept it all running…the profit.

He had always been careful of his assets. He could well afford to build himself a home of his own, one that he would undoubtedly need later, but he still stayed in his childhood rooms. Food prepared, clothing taken care of. No effort on his part. Time saved.

And his assets. It was surprising how some of his best assets had come about. The incidental appearance of the Clydesdales into the territory. His inheritance. And the chance acquaintance of Miss America Forrester.

He had never meant the association to last for years. Maybe weeks, or at least until she got tired of the cold, the heat, the smell, the tending of scratches and sores, and the constant presence of the muck. Especially muck, the massive amount of waste produced by the animals.

However, it was now two years later, and the fifteen-year-old former school mate had turned into an attractive seventeen-year-old, definitely old enough to marry. And there were those who knew it. There was the new fellow who was making him a fence. The new preacher's son. Handsome fellow with curly, red hair.

He had seen Phillip stop in on a lot of occasions to chat with his "hired hand." Merry never stopped her work to talk with him, but it seemed they had a lot in common to discuss. How long would it be before Phillip decided to save her from a life of drudgery? A fellow with his skills and ambition would have no trouble supporting a wife here in the work-filled territory.

How long indeed. And that was not all. There was the old Morrison couple who enticed their nephew to come live with them with the hope of his being permanent. It seemed they succeeded because he was making motions to turn their quarter section into a profitable spot of land. Why would he spend time chatting with Merry Forrester?

Raymond sighed and stroked his chin. He was not equipped to dealing with circumstances he did not understand. Merry Forrester had stayed long enough to make herself indispensable to him, and, for the life of him, he could not determine what would keep her around much longer.

He could pay her more for her services. She accepted what he gave, did what he asked and took impressive care of his animals. Of course, there was the property left by her parents, but it seemed to mean nothing to her and her brother. The unworldly pair had handed portions of it over to the new preacher for a church.

Not only that, she and her brother had fenced off the back two thirds of the quarter section and rented it to a sheep farmer. His rent was turned over to the preacher for his use. How did one deal with that?

It wasn't that Raymond did not know about girls. He had two sisters, for goodness' sake. Maybe he'd have to smother his pride and ask them for help. How did one keep an employee who needed nothing from him?

The thing that actually brought the matter to a head was a recent stopover at the Cookie Jar for a sandwich. He saw his hired hand seated at a tiny ice cream table with both Phillip and Edward across the table, chatting away. She always looked so different when he saw her there that he didn't always recognize her.

For work, there was those old overalls and shirt outgrown by her brother. Over her hair she always tied an old blue and white scarf. She could pass for a homeless hobo if she was not so small. He hadn't thought so much until he saw her chatting in a friendly way with the two fellows and she was dressed in attractive clothes with her honey-colored hair curling below her shoulders. Now, tell me, how long could that last before she was snatched away?

It was on a weekend when his younger sister, Francine, was home from her teaching job in Shady Ridge, that he finally put aside his pride and asked her the question. What should he do to get the attention of a girl?

Francine struggled to keep from smiling smugly. She could see this was VERY serious, or her brother would not have come to her with the question. Now Francine, like her brother, gave matters her best thought. Offhand, she told him that he must find out what the girl wanted more than what she already had. When she saw that the answer did not impress him, she begged for a week to think about it.

While he waited the week, he wandered around the barn and corral and thought. She did not seem to be in view at the moment. Then he heard sounds from the hayloft and the scratching of something…tines of a pitchfork?

Climbing the ladder he saw he was right. Clad in the baggy overalls and the much-too-big shirt, his hired hand was scooping the remains of the winter hay to one side. When she saw him, she stopped and looked his way, leaning her chin attentively on the pitchfork handle.

When no command came to her, she explained, "I thought I'd just shove this old hay over so it would be easier to get it down for bedding. That way the new hay can be pushed to the back by whoever brings it in. I like the horses to have the freshest hay we have."

Raymond nodded. He hadn't thought to have someone do that. So, what did he say next? She waited…he nodded and turned to go back down the ladder.

"Should I be doing something else?" she called after him.

What could he say except, "Oh, no. That's just fine."

Francine thought the matter over, and confided in her sister, Rosalie. "What do you think has gotten into Raymond? Could he have something on his mind besides dirt, contracts and horse drawn equipment?"

Rosalie didn't know. She saw her brother more often than did Francine, but she was concerned with her own life and the teaching of the children at the local Prairie Academy. Hmmm, well, Raymond was past twenty and certainly had a right to think on something else. Certainly he could afford a girlfriend. Why, he could afford more than that. So what did he have in mind?

"Francy, do you think he might be thinking of America? She's been there for two years, and he should know her well enough to know what she wants. Even with his tunnel vision, he should know that."

Nodding, Francine added, "With her right there under his nose, you'd think he would, but he asked me, and that was a big step for him. He couldn't be thinking of Gwinnie or Kristie. Or Pat or Bridie. Who else is there around here except little girls?"

Rosie agreed. "It's got to be Merry. She's been coming over to the Cookie Jar a lot, and she has some brand-new clothes. Pat and Bridie just love to sew for her. Say it's like making doll clothes. Attracts attention, too. Phillip, the preacher's son, likes her and I've seen Edward Morrison with her. Do you think Raymond's jealous?"

"Maybe…but somehow that doesn't sound like him. He's always seemed to get what he wants, and when he has questions, he asks Papa. This has to be serious. I told him to give me a week. Maybe one of us will think up an answer. Meanwhile, I think I'll make a little trip to the Cookie Jar and see what I can learn."

Francine changed to her walking shoes and added a shady, wide-brimmed hat. She had a lot of hats, all made by Pat and Bridie. They liked making hats for her because she was such a good advertisement for them. She was tall, walked properly and she lifted her handsome chin just the way the pictures in the magazines showed the New York ladies did.

The trouble with the wide brimmed hats, however, was the territorial wind. One didn't want to always walk with one hand on one's head to keep the hat in place, and there was no way to use enough hatpins without lacerating one's scalp. Today, there was a quiet breeze, and wide brimmed hats were such fun because so many things could be put on them for decoration.

The Cookie Jar girls came over to chat with her when customers permitted, which was not often on a Saturday afternoon. No, they hadn't seen Raymond except to step in to grab up a snack and leave. He seemed to be like usual, all business.

CHAPTER 7

That was no help at all. Francine left the Cookie Jar and walked across the road. As usual, her brother was not there, but there was the overall clad figure adjusting the windmill to pull up fresh water for the horses.

Glad for company, Merry took Francine to her cabin for… what? Well, she had some raisin cookies sent by Mrs. Bramwell, or she had popcorn. The popcorn was really her favorite and she was a bit hungry.

Francine nibbled a cookie while she waited for the popcorn. She looked around the house, accessing it critically. The answer to Raymond's problem had to be centered here. It had to be, because he didn't go anywhere else.

Merry's tiny living quarters contained only necessities…just like her own tiny room at the Shady Ridge Academy. "Hmmmm, I believe you have just about the same amount of room as I have in the schoolhouse. That is, not counting the loft. But your brother has that, hasn't he?"

"Yeah, Homer is only here at night, though. All his eating and clothes washing is done by Mrs. Bramwell." With a grin, she added, "Or maybe Neecie Bramwell. She seems to consider Homer to be her own private property to be petted and groomed for her own pleasure."

"Has her cap set for him, has she?"

Nodding. "She even asked his advice about staying at school for another year. It seems Rosalie is encouraging her to do that and take the Certification Test like we did."

"What did he tell her?"

"He said he didn't know, because he didn't know what her mama thought, but later he told her he thought she should do it if her folks let her. She has a lot to do at home, he said."

Francine helped herself to the popcorn and asked, "Do you ever wish you had decided to teach? You made a good score, and you could, you know."

Merry looked her with surprised eyes. "And leave here? Oh, I couldn't do that! I have the very best job in the world. I get to take care of the horses and do everything just the way I want to. I even mentioned to Raymond that if he had some goats out in the pasture they would help take care of the horses. Goats are protective, you know, and they'd set up a racket if a stranger came in the pasture with them. That'd give me time to get the gun."

"Hmmm, I didn't know that. Goats are watchdogs."

"Better than watchdogs. They are attuned to other animals and dogs are mainly attuned to people. If someone made friends with a dog, he might just let them take a horse. Goats wouldn't want any of the horses to be taken away at night. Raymond has some goats located, and quick as Phillip gets back to the fence building, he'll bring them here."

"Do you know Phillip very well?"

"Pretty well. He stops by to talk when his papa drives him crazy. His papa needs him to work on the church building, because Phillip knows so much, and then he wants to tell him how to do it." She grinned at the interesting situation. "He comes here to talk with someone who has some sense, he says. The thing is, he's very fond of his parents and is so glad they're building here. Says he may stay here, even though he had a good job in Oklahoma City."

"What all does he do?"

"Most everything. He repaired the privy at the Cookie Jar and made a hit with Gwinnie. She was afraid to go in there with it leaning from the last windstorm."

"Do you think there might be more than friendship there?"

"I hope so. Phillip is a really good friend, and so is Gwinnie. They'd make a good couple."

Francine reached for the popcorn. Well, there goes the friendship with Phillip. He's obviously not after Merry...or at least she isn't after him. She watched as Merry opened a large jar of peanut butter and scooped some into a saucer. Then she offered the jar to Francine.

"I just hate to cook. Turns out I like to eat peanut butter with a spoon with my popcorn. Makes a perfect lunch. I don't blame you for not wanting any. Most people don't. I just don't like to cook."

"Yeah, that is a bit of a problem. I have it good because Mrs. Brown makes my meals. Girls get married, they seem to get married to that job as well. I don't really mind cooking, but it's not my favorite thing to do."

Merry scooped a bit of the butter on a spoon. "I really hate to think of cooking. Homer brings things home for me from the Bramwells. I think they feel they have to take care of me, too, because they like him so much. That's fine with me."

The conversation moved on to fashions and the latest magazines Miss Josie's Aunt Sharon sent from New York.

"It looks like you have a lot of new clothes. Aren't Pat and Bridie getting really good at what they do? And that machine they bought makes it so much faster. How do you like the machine?"

"I like it. Seams stay in a lot better and gathers come out flatter and don't make me look like I have a wad of fabric at my waist. And look at this," Merry invited, as she took a pink flowered item off the wall peg. "They made this for me as a joke, but I just love it."

Francine took the piece of cloth and spread it out into the triangle that it was, looking questioningly at Merry.

"It's a scarf! I think they're tired of seeing me in this blue and white one of my mother's. Besides, it's just about to wear out. Maybe I needed a new one. But just look at the tiny hem and all those tight stitches. It would have taken them an hour, at least, to hem that, and they certainly wouldn't be making it up as a joke. They'd use their time for something they got paid for. But they gave me this for a laugh."

Merry set the triangle on top of her head and pulled the points back under her hair and on her neck. Tying it into a quick knot, she had a new look. Masses of pink flowers instead of the boring blue and white stripes. Honey colored hair billowed out below the flowery pointed tail at the back of her head

"Merry! That looks good! You need to wear that all the time, and maybe have them make you more of them. It even covers your hair better than the other one, and I know that helps keep your hair clean."

But Merry, with a proud smile, just folded the pink flowered triangle and set it aside. Her actions said she would be wearing the blue and white scarf as usual, and maybe the pink one to go over to the Cookie Jar.

She returned the lid to the peanut butter jar and the popcorn dish was empty. It seemed time for Francine to leave.

"It's been fun to see you again. Now don't let my brother work you too hard."

Merry tossed her head and retorted, "Oh, he never tells me what to do. That's one reason why I like this job so much."

"You really do like it don't you?" Francine couldn't help asking.

Merry tipped her head to give emphasis to her answer, "Yes. I really, really do and especially compared to what a lot of girls do in kitchens and over washboards, and for no money at all...?" Shaking her head, she added, "I surely wouldn't trade with them. And speaking of that, how would you feel if you were required to give up the job you're so good at?"

With a sigh and a smile, Francine was forced to admit, "America, you are exactly right. It would be very hard for me to do."

With a wave she was gone.

A quick stop back at the Cookie Jar and she saw Phillip with his long legs tucked up under the tiny ice cream table, elbows planted firmly and eyes gazing intently into the hazel eyed gaze of Gwinnie McLaughlin. And from the look on Gwinnie's face, she wasn't minding it at all. Hmmm....

Francine gave a lot of thought to her day, but did not speak to her sister, Rosie, until late on Sunday afternoon. Before she hitched her little chocolate pony to her tiny chocolate colored buggy to return to her job, she and her sister took their lemonade out to the double porch swing that was attached to the lower limb of the giant elm in the yard.

She began, "I don't really have this all figured out, but I think America must be mixed in it somewhere. I don't think Raymond needs to worry about Phillip, he seems to have eyes for Gwinnie.

"And I'm not so much of a mind that he's liking Merry, as it is that he's afraid of loosing a 'hired man.' I could be wrong. But if I'm right, he has no worry there, either. America Forrester does not want to keep house, even with the benefit of a marriage. Apparently Raymond pays her well, and she has very little use for money. Have you been in that little cabin he built for the 'hired man'?"

Rosalie shook her head. "Likely I should have, but I haven't. It would only be neighborly to do that, but I'm so centered on the school, I don't even think of what might be a friendly thing to do. I should, especially if Merry is going to be connected with the family…even as a hired man."

A sip of the cool fruit drink. "You know, Rosie, she had not one picture on the wall. Mrs. Bramwell, where her brother works, sends leftovers, it seems like, and if there's nothing else she either eats at the Cookie Jar or she eats popcorn for lunch, spooning peanut butter from a jar. Likes it, she says."

The whispery squeal of the swing chain on the limb competed with the early spring crickets.

Francine again. "Merry is not doing what she has to do. She is doing what she really, really wants to do and she's happy she gets to do it. If someone thinks she has her cap set for Raymond and his successful business, they're wasting their thoughts. He is her employer and she treats him with the friendly respect that she might treat old Digby or Mrs. Gray Owl. Her attention is centered on the frilly hairs around the horses' hooves and their tendency to get infected. She gives thought to the safety of the horses and has suggested Raymond get goats because they're good 'watchdogs' and they would set up a holler giving her time to get her gun. You remember, she's already saved him the theft of two of those giant beasts."

Then Rosie. "Well, what are you going to tell Raymond? I'm glad he asked you and not me."

With a sly smile, her sister replied, "I think I may tell him what my student, Isabel, told me when I gave them a problem fragment. She said, 'You ain't give us enough facts. There ain't no answer to that problem.' So I'd say let's let it rest a week, and if we don't have an answer, we'll ask for more 'facts,' and incidentally, the reason he asked me and not you was that I was in his line of vision at the time he wanted an answer. You know Raymond. His mind can be elsewhere."

Rosie agreed. "It might help if we knew Merry better. She likely knows Raymond better than we do. You remember she was not only two years behind us in school, she had just moved here. We weren't little girls together with her. And there is the way Miss Josie worked all of us…well, you remember! No time to be friendly."

"Yeah, and about all we saw of Raymond those days was the top of his head across the table while he got his own homework done."

It was during the next week that a something or other on the grader broke a very necessary chain, and he had no spare. He reassigned the workman and headed for Argyle for another chain.

He started to take the buggy, but actually took the wagon. It seemed useless to take a large vehicle for a small item, except that the chain was quite heavy and the wagon was handier at the moment.

It was midafternoon when he reached Mac's store. Outside the building a crowd had gathered around something of obvious interest. Shouts of encouragement, exclamations and a few metallic bangings were heard. Curious, Raymond worked himself into the crowd.

There, right in front of the hitching rail, was a brand new, shiny tin lizzie. Some were calling it a horseless carriage but tin lizzie fit it much better. Green, it was, with black trimming around the doors and the windshield. The top was folded back in shiny ripples of oiled canvas.

A fellow in a bowler hat, wide suspenders and ivory spats over his shoes was staring red-faced and perspiring at the vehicle.

Someone in the gathering shouted at him to "kick it again," whereupon the dressed up dude, lifted a foot, drew it back and then pounded it into the tire of the car. The force of the blow left the fenders jangling and the man grabbing his injured toe. He bellowed with pain as he hopped around on one foot.

A crescendo of laughter arose around him, causing him to turn to the crowd and scream, "If I had a chance, I'd trade this blankety-blank thing for a wagon and team this instant. It's more contrary than a female and not near as pretty. Whoever invented this thing needs to go back to the nether region where he came from."

In stunned silence, the crowd moved back. Anyone this angry was likely to do most anything, and it was time to put a distance between them and him.

The man turned and looked into the sober face of Raymond Canfield. "Well, what…?" he demanded ungraciously.

Raymond, the steady. Raymond, the unflappable, just repeated, "Mister if you really mean that, I'll trade with you. I got my wagon right over here, and a couple of strong horses are attached to it."

Mr. Fancy Dresser turned and looked. Good solid wagon. Huge, beautiful horses. Shiny black animals, trimmed in white socks. They stood switching their well-kept, brushed out tails at the flies that had gathered around. Occasionally stomping their hooves, sending the white ruffle of hair to ripple attractively.

To the exasperated man, the animals and rig were sheer beauty. "You really mean that, Mister?"

In a totally un-Raymond-like way, the answer came. "I surely do. I'll trade even-steven." Then his business experience appeared. "I'll need a signed paper from you. Then you can drive away with them. Their names are Charlie and James. See the 'C' and the 'J'?"

Required papers signed and witnessed, the man drove away and the crowd now gathered around Raymond. He was very well known and was considered a calm businessman. It would be fun to see how he got the "blankety-blank" machine going.

Raymond stalked into Mac's store and asked. "Mac, I need the loan of a horse to bring back my team and get this thing home."

Trotting down the road toward the Corners, Raymond seemed to come to his senses, and treated himself to a wry smile. "What, in the name of everything sensible, have you done, Raymond Canfield?" But Raymond had no answer for himself.

He explained to America that, having no one else who was not out on the jobs, he would need her to go with him to bring something home. Her only comment was, "You let James and Charlie go?" It was not exactly an accusation, but she needed to know about her charges. His nod satisfied her.

He took the buggy from under its cover, hitched Lucy and Minnie to it and headed back to Argyle. For, after all, he still needed the chain for the grader.

There remained a few gawkers around the machine. Mostly youngish men knowing it might be a long time before they again had a chance to inspect a machine like this. Besides that, they were curious as to how Mr. Canfield would get the thing home since the former owner had so much frustration.

They were only slightly disappointed when he secured the front bumper of the tin lizzie to the boot of the buggy. While he did so, America Forrester was pouring over the machine, front to back. She read the little metal tag, DETROITER 1913. She punched her fingers against the tufted leather of the seats. Hmmm, firm and smooth. She turned the steering wheel this away and that, leaning out to see its reaction on the front wheels. She opened the door and slid inside. She took the key from the ignition and put it back. She opened the glove compartment and saw the book that also said DETROITER 1913.

She clasped the gearshift stick and felt the tightness. Pressing a pedal, she felt the stick jiggle in its location as though it wanted to move, not that it was broken. She pulled a knob and was delighted as small rubber-trimmed sticks swiped the accumulated dust from the windshield.

Raymond was getting a bit hot and sweaty, a bit irritated with the chains and beginning to be full of doubts about the wisdom of his purchase, but there was no way he would let on in front of the still assembled group of young men. Testing the chains, he deemed them strong enough to get the thing home. It seemed no heavier than the buggy and the air in the tires would make it roll well.

Nodding with satisfaction, he indicated Merry should climb in the buggy and was surprised when she shook her head. Stepping out, she indicated the way the steering wheel turned the front wheels. "I'm thinkin' I need to stay back here and keep the wheel straight. Otherwise it could maybe head for the ditch."

"Hmmm, well, you know these horses, I could stay...."

"No, it needs to be me. We don't know what those girls you hitched on up there will do. They've never pulled a Detroiter 1913 home before and might need a firm hand. All I gotta do here is keep the wheel straight...don't you think?"

On further consideration, she had a point. Though his being able to control the horses better than she did...that just didn't figure. Anyway, if she wanted to ride back there...why not?

In full view of the gathering, he clicked the "girls" into action and they lifted their aristocratic hooves, leaned lightly into the harness and the buggy began to move, pulling the machine behind it. Merry gently turned the wheel toward the road and the Detroiter obediently climbed from the ditch and docilely followed the buggy.

The caravan headed south toward the Corners to the shouts of "Bravo!", "Hurrah!" and "Atta-boy!".

During five miles of the trip, America Forrester met her First Love.

Introduction...courtship...and honeymoon! All in one neat package! Her employer, she knew well. This was not a desired trinket he had purchased for his pleasure. This had clearly been an un-thought-out offer, and he had, in his business-like way, been obliged to follow through. Be that as it may, she saw the future and knew it was hers!

Raymond looked back only a couple of times out of curiosity. He was not concerned for her safety. He knew she was well able to provide for that.

Leaving the girls in their harnesses, he took out the new grader chain, poked it into a tow sack and laid over the shoulders of Nellie. Without a word he trotted out the gate to go to wherever the current work stoppage had occurred.

Merry lifted the hinged sheets of tin that exposed the little boxes, springs, gears and flexible belts. She unscrewed the cap on the radiator and looked in. Water! All right, how about his other one. She took off the cap and drew back, startled. Ha! The fuel. Not kerosene…maybe, gas?

Sliding in behind the wheel once more, she tested the pedal. If she pressed lightly, the gear shift stick moved. If she pressed hard, something else tightened. What? It was going to take some experimenting.

Snapping open the little box that she would learn was a glove compartment, she took out the little book and opened it with a happy sigh. Here's where she would find out what was what.

Just then Minnie let out a snort of impatience. Oh, my! The girls were still hitched up. How awful. Sliding out of the car, she took the hitching chains from the buggy and returned the conveyance to its cover. Removing the harness from the girls, she led them to the pasture, apologizing all the time. Whatever was she thinking! Letting herself get so distracted! *Would you believe…!!*

The next big excitement was when Homer came home. He brought a still warm bowl of Venison dumplings, but it was ignored as the new machine was gone over, stem to stern. Her brother's excitement was almost as great as hers, as he knew he now had hands-on access to a real working tin lizzie. Well, it would be working just as soon as his sister figured out how to do it.

With Homer's help, she pushed the machine into a shed, covering it over with a tarp. She wasn't sure how to get the top up, but even then, the barn and corral were dusty. In the light of the kerosene lamp, the brother and sister delved into the wonders of the machine, looking over each other's shoulders at the little guidebook.

A mile and a half down the road, it occurred to Raymond that he had not taken the animals from the buggy and put it away, but he immediately remembered, his hired man could do it as well as he could, and she would. He turned his mind to the length of time it would take to repair the damage to the grader, and then send someone home with that item, while the rest of the crew did…well, he'd see how far along they were.

It was past midnight before the brother and sister gave it up and went to bed, because after all, they had jobs. During her breakfast, Merry glued four shiny quarters to a piece of stiff cardboard and put it in an envelope. Sending it to the address in the book, she asked if there were any other papers they could send her? About how to drive and that sort of thing?

In two weeks she received another booklet and the note that said since she had the manual, she would know which parts to order if she had trouble, and the book they enclosed was general instructions on how to operate an AUTOMOBILE. Ah, that was what she needed. By that time she had learned the names of everything under the "bonnet" as it was called, by matching them up to the drawings in the book. She was still a bit hazy about how the movement actually occurred, but obviously it did move. That was enough for now. Certainly, she'd need more gas soon, but there seemed to be enough to get the motor started…after a lot of coughing, gagging and hiccoughing from under the bonnet.

Pushing the pedal to the floor, she tried to move the stick into reverse but it stuck frustratingly where it was. When she let up on the pedal, it slipped into place. Oh! There were two positions to the pedal. One said the stick could move and the other position said that the wheels WOULDN'T move. *Hmmm. Good to know.*

It was about a month later that Raymond was bringing his crew home at the end of the day, and he met a shiny green DETROITER 1913 in the driveway. The driver was SO tempted to toot the horn, but she feared for the reaction of the horses.

The automobile obligingly stopped to let the boss and the crew into the yard, then it put-putted into the road and down past the Cookie Jar, by the Blacksmith shop and turned in at the Prairie Academy School. Miss Josie no longer taught, actually, but she was often on the premises and this was one time she was there.

Strange sound? She pushed back the curtain behind the desk she used to occupy but was now occupied by Rosie McLaughlin and her own cousin, Carmelita Wilson. An automobile! Coming into the yard! How exciting.

Hurrying out toward it, she saw it skid slightly as the brakes were applied. A low cloud of dust had been kicked up, but was now settling. The put-put of the motor stopped and the door opened, letting the smiling and proud America Forrester step out. Neither lady could think of anything to say for looking at the fancy new toy that everyone agreed would never replace the horse, no matter how much fun it was.

Miss Josie had heard about the machine, of course. Nothing much missed the gossip lines. She did, however, know Raymond Canfield and his dedicated singleness of purpose. It just didn't sound like him to bring the tin lizzie home, and it CERTAINLY did not sound like him to spend the time from his business to get it to run.

During the three years she had taught Raymond, she thought often that here in the territory was the kind of boy who would do well in New York. So solid and conscientious, though he pretended he wasn't. He seemed almost embarrassed at times that he knew his lessons so well. He would never, for the world, have let his classmates know how he used long hours under the lamplight to so "easily" go through his assignments.

This tiny scrap of a girl who moved to the territory in her third-grade year was something else again. What America liked, she did with exemplary care. She was active and free-spirited, and her free work was always something entirely different from what a teacher would expect of a girl of nine, ten, and eleven. She had treated her teacher's Certification in the same free-spirited way, making a score that was good, but not excellent, simply because that was not important to her. Miss Josie would have been very surprised if she had chosen to teach but was not as surprised as some when she so quickly found her footing after losing her parents. She had found her brother's footing as well, it seemed.

So, here she was, beaming with pride. She had been given a challenge, she met it and succeeded. The news of this little trip down to see her teacher would be heralded from the west end to east end of the county. The news would be formed, re-formed and embellished and some of it would even be the actual truth. The girl finally found words.

"Oh, Miss Josie! This was the most fun I ever had in my life. Raymond traded for it because it wouldn't run, but I read the book with both eyes, just like you told us to do, and figured out what was wrong. It was the thing-a-ma-what hooked on to that there," and she whipped up the folding sheet tin of the bonnet. "I looked at the picture of how things were supposed to look, and that thing wasn't in place. Must'a bounced off on the rough road. I don't know why the man didn't know that. He drove all the way out from Oklahoma City, and he didn't know how to fix it. You'd think he'd be sure he knew how to get home.

"Anyway, I've never had so much fun in my life. I can't drive very far, though, because there isn't much gas. I'll have to take a horse in to Argyle and get some. Mac sells it in five-gallon cans, like the kerosene. Now I can just drive into Argyle when Raymond needs something and be back in less than an hour. Isn't it wonderful?

"When I get more gas, I want to come and take you for a ride. Do you think Mr. Brad will let you go? I know some husbands wouldn't let their wives ride in something like this, but its such FUN!" Then she thoughtfully added, "Raymond traded James and Charlie off, and I miss them...."

"James and Charlie...?"

"Oh, that was two of the older horses. He was going to sell them to Edward Morrison, and he was just giving them a little exercise by taking them to Argyle after the chain. I always miss whoever gets sold, but there's babies coming on, and I know the people who get them, like them. James and Charlie will never let that city fellow down. They don't have springs of thing-a-ma-whats that come off in their tummies or anything. OH, this is so much FUN!"

With a nod and a grin, Josie commented, "Yes, I believe you said that. But, America, I'm really so proud of you for being able to read with both eyes. You were always so good with the problems made up by other students when they tried to stump the class. Actually...though I wouldn't have thought about it...I'm not at all surprised that you could figure out what the automobile needed."

Nodding, Josie continued. "I know something else, too. I know that you won't ever be caught in some little town not knowing what's wrong with the car. I know that if you have the necessary part, you'll be able to fix it. Another thing, I'm sure Mr. Brad will let me ride with you, but he may insist on tagging along."

"Oh, goodie! I'd better get on back. I think I have enough gas for that but I just had to show you." Climbing in on the tufted leather seats, she inserted the key and the engine answered with a resounding put-put. Reverse gear growled only slightly, and just a low dust cloud followed her out onto the road.

Miss Josie's face still wore a smile. So flattering that her former students were eager to show her their latest successes. Rosalie and Carmelita she saw every day, but Francine came with her poetry, Pat and Bridie insisted she needed the best lace on her hankies. The McLaughlin sisters brought their bookkeeping ledgers to her to help set up what they were well capable of doing for themselves.

Raymond waved happily when he saw her, and the two young Kiowa boys stopped in often. And here was Miss America, tiny and delicate as a cowslip flower growing down by the river. Soft and dimpled as a kitten, but she treated Raymond's massive horses as if they were trained dogs, caring for their every need. She shoveled muck from the stalls and drove the spreader to fertilize the fields. Her gun had saved a couple of her employer's horses.

Was it any wonder to anyone that America would be the one to repair and drive the town's first car down to the Prairie Academy to show to her! She had heard of one or two automobiles that had been driven past but this one was brought into her yard. Just for her to see.

Josie watched as the dust cloud settled and sniffed softly as she tried to swallow the lump in her throat. Looking up reverently into the blue territorial sky, she knew, for a fact, THAT was where her happiness came from. Only from Him could such a gift be given her. She knew she was not the teacher, but she didn't have to be. There were at least six teachers within a ten-mile circle who definitely were teachers.

And now Carmelita had told her that little Bernice Bramwell had agreed to stay over another year to practice teach so her score would be higher and she could say she was "experienced." She said she had decided to do that because Homer, America's brother, had said he wanted her to. He had told her it was for her own good, because he wanted her to do like the others who got schools nearby to teach. It was certain that her parents would help her to get settled. She would make a good teacher, Rosie and Mellie had said.

"Dear Lord, You are so wonderful! Thank You!" She could not have arranged this happiness if she had thought and planned for a million years

Raymond tried to put it all together.

His sisters had conferred and Francine told him the result. What she had told him earlier still applied…however an important factor had to be considered. It was true, still, that a way to get a girl's attention was to offer her something that she liked better than what she had, but that all depended on the girl. With some girls a better way might be to make sure she knew that you would not take away something that she valued highly, and that you were in position to remove.

If this sounded strange, perhaps the best thing to do was spend some time finding out what the girl had already, that she really liked. She had told him that it would help if they had more information, but he assured his sister that he had no more than he had given her, but he was sure she did not fully believe him.

Anyway, he would see what the girl actually had that she liked. Well, Merry Forrester liked taking care of his horses…which was somewhat strange for a girl, and he was certainly not thinking of taking it away from her. So Francine's advice didn't really fit. She didn't go out of her way to see Phillip or Edward, though she seemed to enjoy their company. So how did that information figure in?

With a weary sigh he went over the part of his sister's advice that he really didn't want to think of. True, he hardly had a moment that he was not working or at home eating or sleeping. No time to look around...or even think. So, what to do about that?

That he needed to move out of his parents' home was Francine's advice. Where would he go? "Build yourself a house with that money you're making." She made it sound so simple. "Face the fact that you'll need it sometime," she had assured him. Likely that was true. Where would it be? "Raymond, you dummy," she had told him. "Look at all that land you have north of the barn up toward the Bramwells. Nice trees...level land." Well...yes... that was true.

With another weary sigh he decided to leave the problem of Merry, which he didn't understand, and attack the problem of the house, which he also didn't understand, but which presented a different set of obstacles.

Who could build a house? The first name to pop in his mind was Phillip. He seemed to have done a good job on the church, and even the cabin for his parents. And he certainly did a good job on the fence. The land had been efficiently plowed and planted in alfalfa, and it should help on the hay purchase.

So...Phillip. He found the fellow over at the Cookie Jar. Speaking of Cookie Jar, that was part of Francine's advice. Phillip had found a problem in Gwinnie's life and had taken it away. Sometimes taking away a problem was better than a gift. If Phillip had given a gift to Gwinnie, maybe jewelry, or candy or...? The thing was, Gwinnie could get any of those things for herself, but she could not straighten up the storm-damaged privy and she was scared to go in it while it was leaning and crooked.

So...fixing the privy was better than a present in this case. That was rather like those backward problems Miss Josie gave them…that he had been so good at. Having part of the problem, and the answer, the students were expected to furnish the missing part of the equation. But it still didn't fit his situation.

Back to the house. Yes, Philip could get at it in about two weeks. And, say, would it be all right if Edward Morrison helped? Things went so much faster with two men…help with lifting and all that? It was certainly no problem to Raymond. It had lately been his habit to turn every problem over to someone who could handle it and go on the next one.

He did, however, have to decide exactly where he wanted it and how big. Also the number of rooms. Well, he could go step it off, or even better, he could enlist his sisters.

Rosalie and Francine had not giggled together so much since they were five- and six-year-olds, snuggled in bed and supposed to go to sleep.

The huge oaks would make a wonderful surrounding. Shade and wind protection. There was a good place for a driveway. Four rooms down and two up would be perfect. Maybe three up. He could certainly start with less, but he had the money for the best. Windows here and over there. Summer kitchen in the back.

At the Cookie Jar they sipped lemonade and enjoyed the slightly guilty feeling that they were doing something fun that should belong to another girl, the one who would live in the house. Somehow that made it even more fun. Merry had joined them for a few minutes, then got bored and went back to her barn. Obviously, Merry and Raymond were not in each other's sights. Yet.

The hammering and sawing did not faze the horses, but the goats were intensely interested. Leaning on the fence and poking their heads through with their ba…a…a…a.

The girls decided on the paint for the upstairs interior and wallpaper for the parlor. Curtains, of course. And there would be furniture…would they get to pick it out, too? Why not?

It took most of the summer, but Rosalie and Francine were on hand most weekends making sure things were going well. Raymond's house caused a lot of talk around the community, but none of it got to Raymond. He was just appreciative of his sister's efforts, and if they enjoyed it, so much the better. Meanwhile, there was dirt to be moved. He KNEW about that!

At one point, Merry had hauled the sisters away to admire the twin kids produced by one of the nanny goats. Proud as a parent, she was. She explained that goats were parents by nature, especially the nannies. They assumed all other four-legged animals were in their charge. Sometimes they were even disturbed by a flock of migrating geese that had stopped to feed on the back pasture.

And scary times came. It started when Winnie's mom had become pregnant for the first time. Merry had been so excited when Winnie had entered the world, a long-legged, gawky filly, struggling to stand. She had been in attendance with Winnie's mama, Henryetta, and she had been singing, "In the sweet bye and bye" when baby Winnie had arrive, a soggy little heap at her mother's heels.

She didn't stay a heap very long as her mother's slashing teeth quickly freed her. Before the count of ten, she had struggled to position her legs beneath her. Merry's papa had said to always count to ten and let a new-born animal try to right itself with its own strength. After that, move it a bit to make sure it was breathing properly. Give it a push, if necessary, but get it on its feet as soon as possible. Especially with horses.

So now, Winnie herself was going to be a mama. Merry had spent a lot of time with her, brushing her and talking with her, and insisting that she be taken from the work rotation when she began to round out. A deep-down fear seemed to surround this pregnancy. Was she just being over-protective? Maybe. But there seemed to be protrusions that should not be seen on a pregnant mare. She stroked the smooth hair on the lovely face and brushed her mane. She talked and sang to keep her relaxed, but there was still that fear.

And then she knew for certain. There absolutely was something wrong, and she informed Raymond. Did he know of a horse doctor anywhere that they could bring? Sadly he shook his head. The territory hardly had a people doctor. The horses just had to do their best on their own. Maybe Winnie would do better as the days passed…but she didn't.

Strange contractions began, and Merry spent the nights in the stall with her. Her breathing seemed to be all right but there were still those knobby bumps where they shouldn't be and the mare had a nervous, flighty way about her. On the eleventh day after she had first noticed the mild contractions, she had spent every night with animal. Now the contractions had started in earnest. Winnie, in confusion and puzzlement, circled and lashed out at her stall walls. She doubled her neck back seeming to try to see what was causing discomfort in her belly.

Raymond had come in from work rather late, and Merry had called him to come and look at Winnie. Nodding sadly, he decided to stay, though he could offer no help or advice. It was just after dark that tiny hooves appeared. Five of them. When the contraction died away, the hooves were withdrawn, leaving the watching pair to look at each other in total puzzlement.

In silence, they held vigil. Steaming coffee to comfort their nervous hands, but nothing to rest their concern. Hooves again appeared. Only four this time. The tiny feet held themselves in sight through the contraction and were joined by a hairy ear. Head sideways. Not a problem.

Merry came to its aid. Rubbing her hands and arms with the slippery preparation, the miniature head was righted, bringing a nose into place instead of the ear. Pushing back a pair of the legs. Homer, rubbing his eyes, came out of his sleep to join the painful vigil. The strange protrusions moved within the huge belly of the mare. Raymond looked imploringly toward Homer, who sadly shook his head. It had been Merry who had helped Papa with the animals. He knew no more than Raymond.

Winnie was obviously tiring rapidly. She spread her legs to brace against the turbulence within her. A mighty groan and a squeal of pain and then a soggy, furry mass followed the small nose. Hooves were withdrawn, legs pulled backward, and the whole mass slipped out onto the pile of hay.

With a small cry of joy, Merry knelt over the tiny filly. One, two, three, and all the way to ten. No movement. Firm hands straightened the neck, lifted the head and pressed gently on the delicate ribs. Two quick breaths, then strong and even intakes of needed air followed. The tiny animal seemed all right, only exhausted.

The little thing certainly had a right to be, but she couldn't be permitted to lie there if she was able to stand. Up...and up! Balance on the spread-out, stick-like legs. Steadily stronger as unused muscles came into play.

It was at this moment that Winnie went down. The labor had taken all strength from her legs, but still the contractions continued. Groans and desperate whinnies, as a wadded wet tail appeared beside one tiny hoof.

Merry watched and released a groan of agony. Bad. Very bad!

She tried to insert her hands around the small rear end, but there was no room. She tried to push the foal back but the strength of the contraction was too great. She leaned her face over the flanks of her favorite horse and wept as her employer and her brother sniffed and wiped eyes, desperately searching for something to be done.

It was quick after that. While she leaned over the horse, she felt the last of Winnie's breath leave her huge body and her head finally relaxed onto the bed of hay. Merry screamed, "NO! NO!" and beat her fists on the motionless flanks of the animal.

Homer could keep quiet no longer. "Merry! Sis! You can..." he did not finish his sentence...as he watched his sister crumble over onto the hay behind the horse. She had wilted as completely as a plucked flower in the sun.

Something broke in Raymond, and unaccustomed tears streaming down, he knelt and scooped her into his arms. Homer opened the gate to the stall and the door to the little cottage, following as Raymond put her on the bed.

He stood back and stared. What to do now? "Homer, stay with her while I go get my mother."

CHAPTER 8

N O! You stay…I'll go. I'll grab a horse, and I don't need a lantern in this moonlight. But I think…maybe, you should build a fire. I think she might be cold when something like this happens. I'll hurry."

Raymond felt her arms. Yes, she was cold. Well, building a fire was a thing he knew how to do.

It was hardly twenty minutes later that his mother came through the door, running in her eagerness. Still in her gown and nightcap, with only a robe wrapped around.

Smoothing her gnarled, experienced hands down Merry's limp arms, she looked up and nodded. "Son, look for a quart jar and fill it with hot water. Wrap it in a towel and hurry. She'd got to be warmed up."

In the tiny cabin, the stove was not far from the bed. Raymond begged for reassurance. "Ma, do you know…what…?

"No, but I think it's something called 'shock.' Old Miz Gray Owl had another name." She did not tell him the old Kiowa doctor's name for it meant something like "leaving body behind." Instead, she told him, "It happens when something terrible happens to a person at a time the person is not equipped to handle it. At least, that's what we'll start with. Homer, will you get all the quilts you have in the house? Bring them."

The frightened young man rushed eagerly…desperate to do something…anything! Tossed the quilts from his sleeping loft into the small kitchen. Raymond handed the wrapped jar of water to his mother who tucked it under Merry's knees.

"Son, I'm going to get in the bed with her and lay close to her. It might help furnish heat and it's the only thing I can think of to do. I want you to cover us with all the quilts you have and keep the fire going."

Julie Canfield stretched out onto the bed beside the girl and wrapped her arms around her. She was not aware that her husband had turned and walked away.

Raymond's father took himself to the barn to view the stricken animal. The well-kept, glossy coat of the mare was quiet and motionless. The enormity of what must be done weighed heavily on him and he knew it was up to him to do what had to be done. Leaving the barn, he walked the quarter of a mile to the north and knocked on the door of the mill.

"Bram, got us a problem. Need your help. The girl passed out and she got a dead animal that's gotta be moved 'fore she has a chance to see it. My son's got a sled and plenty'a horse power, but I'll need help to get the body on the sled."

Minutes later, the two men were hurrying back. Sam Canfield spoke of the next problem. "Losin' a mother…that leaves the foal to be fed. I'm thinkin' he's got a goat that's come fresh. That'll be better'n nothin'."

But when they reached the silent body, they saw the filly had taken care of the immediate problem. The tiny nose had located the source of the first milk… the milk that was so valuable for a newborn. That first milk would immunize the tiny animal against diseases that attacked the very young. Front legs bent at the knees, the filly's head was tucked under the flanks of the mare, accepting the last gift that could be given her by her mother.

By the time the men had attached ropes and pulleys to the inert body, the living baby had her fill and had curled up in the corner on the hay.

In the light of the moon, the two Clydesdales leaned into their harnesses and the sled moved forward. "Let's take it on up to my place to make sure the girl don't see. I got land a-plenty to dig a place…."

Sam Canfield nodded as King Alfred and Louise pulled the sled that gave Winnie her last ride.

"Much obliged, Bram. Felt that needed to be done and my son weren't in no shape to do it. He's pretty much caved in over what happened to that girl."

"Don't give it no thought, Sam. She's special to us, too, same as her brother. You need help puttin' the sled up?"

"Nope. That's somethin' I can do. See you later."

Sam Canfield restored the animals to their stalls and looking around he found the bottle with the rubber nipple kept for this sort of thing. In a pail, he extracted milk from the willing nannie and filled the bottle. He'd feed the filly again before he left, but she seemed to be contentedly asleep. Enough for now.

In the cabin, Merry moved her hand under the heavy quilts.

Julia Canfield spoke. "Son, I think she's comin' around. Help me get up so she won't be startled to see me. Here, take my hand for a little help. This room is so tiny, how does that girl survive? Like the old folks say, "You couldn't cuss the cat in here 'thout getting' cat-hair in your mouth!"

"I don't know, Ma. She's never complained." Actually, he could remember no time that she had ever complained about anything. He had just taken it for granted she had enough room.

One o'clock in the morning.

Raymond had sat for two hours staring at the girl in the bed. Leaning forward toward her with his forehead in his hands. Staring into the darkness outside the window. Fidgeting to be doing something…anything.

His memory tormented him with visions. He saw her perched on the supply shelf like a trinket doll, singing to a mare during her confinement and delivery.

He saw her sitting in the meadow among the wildflowers practically under the belly of one of his beasts. A huge hoof would be in her hand as she peered intently for something…he never knew what. The animal above her would be balanced on three legs cropping nearby grass and turning to chew and watch what was being done for the hoof.

He saw her with the pitchfork in the loft moving straw to fill the many, many hay nets. Important job. Hard working animals often wanted a nighttime snack so the hay nets must be full. He saw her as just a form against the sky when she climbed the windmill tower to adjust...something or other. He had never thought to ask what she did up there, hanging to the metal braces.

He saw the prints of her bare feet on the light snowfall as she had not waited for shoes when her four hoofed charges were in danger. He could imagine the startled thief when the shots rang out on the snowy, moonlight night. The thief would never know how lucky he had been that her hand was steady enough to miss him.

He saw her in the Detroiter, turning the wheel to keep it in the road. Smile of interested satisfaction. No questions to him about his stupid trade. And later, he saw the delighted wave as he had met her in the driveway after she had finally figured out how to get the piece of tin to move on its own.

He saw her in the slim white dress...white kid-leather, pearl-button shoes. The honey-colored hair loose and flowing. He saw her at a table in the Cookie Jar. He hadn't even noticed what she might be eating.

He saw her dangling bare feet in the watering trough, holding her shoes in her lap and singing to the horses after they had spent a day of work. The animals would be brought back wet and dripping, rounded and shiny from being washed down. Itchy dust removed.

He saw her feet protruding from under the Detroiter as she lay on her wolf-fur bedroom rug inspecting the machine's underside.

And then he saw her bent over Winnie's motionless body, beating her small fists on the rounded, well-groomed flank attempting to restore life. Refusing to let go of her friend. He saw her crumble at his feet in heap of dejected agony.

So now, leaning forward over her quilt-covered form, he wept. The strong, hard-hitting businessman within him, cried... tears streaming through his fingers and down his arms.

His concerned mother wrapped her arm around his heaving shoulders. "It's all right, son. She's going to live. She just had a bad thing happen, but she's strong. She'll come around."

Homer had walked circles in the miniature kitchen. Past the stove. Around the chair. By the cupboard. Always with an eye on the quilt-covered figure.

Merry opened her eyes in the dark room. She was weighted down by a heavy heap of bedding and strange figures were moving around her. She screamed and bolted upright.

Julia Canfield called, "Homer, son, bring in the lamp so she can see who we are."

Light flooded the room, but Merry's mind was no clearer. What had happened that Raymond and his parents were here in the dark of the night? Frightened eyes took in the scene.

She pushed words from her mouth. "Oh, I must…. Can I get you something, I just…." She struggled to extract her feet from the pile of bedding.

Raymond steadied her. "No. You stay right there. I don't want you standing up and risking a fall. You'll be fine…." Where were the words he should say? Now was the time…. Surely he…?

Her wide eyes stared at him, questioningly. "But I…."

"No, you didn't do anything. We just had a bit of trouble in the barn, but it's past, now, and you have to rest. Everything's been taken care of. I think Homer has tea he's been keeping hot for you." Words at last, but were they a help? Was there any word that could help?

The thick, hot mug was put in her trembling fingers. Raymond steadied her hands within his. Fingers still cold. "Take a sip if you can. My ma thinks it'll help."

Merry turned to see Julia Canfield's smiling relief. Something terrible was going on, but Raymond didn't seem to be worried. And she was so, so tired. Drawing her knees up under the bedding, she braced her elbows on them. She tipped the mug to her lips and drained it. Comforting warmth spread into her arms. Her legs….

"Is there more tea?" Homer, glad of something he could do, quickly filled and returned the cup. Then her memories returned. The tiny filly. And…Winnie. She wailed dismally, "Oh, Winnie! She's gone! I tried so hard and oh, how can I stand it! She was…." The girl could not form enough words to cover all that the animal had meant to her.

Handing Raymond the mug, she buried her face in her arms and sobbed, shoulders heaving and breath ragged.

Raymond cast a desperate look toward his mother who shook her head in admonition. "Let her cry. She has to do it sometime, and it's best done here and now, with us around. The shock was so sudden, and now she's lost time she's gotta make it up. Just pat her arm or something so's she'll know someone's close."

He reached out but his fingers could not pat. He put his arm on her back as she sobbed into the circle of her arms propped on her knees. He moved onto the bed beside her, tightening the arm across her back, and waited until the sobs turned into whispers and more ragged breaths and then into agonized groans. "My friend. Winnie was so special."

Raymond sought for comforting words. His mind refused to help him. Finally, "But she left you a present. The little filly you delivered is well and happy. She'll be looking for food before too long."

"Oh, yes, she.... There's the nursing bottle, and I'll...? Goat milk? It's what we have...?"

At that moment, Sam Canfield stepped into the miniature kitchen seeming to take up all remaining available space in the tiny house. He held the nursing bottle filled with white liquid.

"She come around?" Seeing for himself she had, he continued, "I saw to feedin' the little girl out there in the barn. Got 'er to sleep. She's doin' good." He sincerely hoped what he was saying was the actual truth.

His glance took in his sober, unemotional son with his arm around the tiny "hired man," her hair a tangled halo around her head. His gaze traveled on to his own helper of a lifetime, and she shook her head and put her finger to her lips. Homer watched with interest as the signaled conversation passed around him.

Julia Canfield stood and took up her usual duty of directing the activity. "Sam, you and me, we ought'a be getting on down the road. This girl needs her sleep, and Homer, too. He's got 'im a workday in front'a 'im. I'm thinkin' it'd be up to Raymond to tend the stove and keep this place warm. That way he'd be there to send for help if we was needed again. Homer, son, you get on up that ladder. Thing like this is hard on youngens, and you need to sleep. Take a quilt with you. Come on, Sam." And they were gone.

Homer climbed up the ladder as directed, and Raymond moved into the kitchen. The stove needed stoking and fresh tea made. He DID know how to do that. Then he went back to the bed.

"Merry, don't you be a'thinkin'a getting' up. I got nothin' to do today that can't be better done by someone else." And, in his state of mind, that was the honest truth. "In a couple'a hours I'll go feed the little girl, and you can help with the feedings after that."

And now he pulled the remaining quilts up to her shoulders, tucked her arms inside and walked away. Merry, though not quite knowing what was going on, could still follow orders. She turned her face to the window and shut her eyes, relieved. She was so, so, exhausted.

Raymond took off his shoes and propped his feet onto the warming rail of the stove. The heat felt good and the tea in his hand was comforting. His thoughts were very much alive. They strayed back to where they had been for the last weeks.

What was it that Merry would like, that was better than what she already had? Nothing came readily to mind. Then…what was it that she had that she didn't want to lose, something she felt might be getting away from her? He had a vision of Gwinnie McLaughlin's pleasure at having the Cookie Jar privy strengthened. He felt himself grinning just a little but he realized the privy at Merry's cabin was just fine. Besides, he wasn't sure his hand fit a hammer handle. At least, very efficiently.

Back to the puzzle. His mind re-played the pictures it had been furnishing to him and settled on the happy smile as she had guided the Detroiter home. And the excitement and pleasure when she got it running. He hadn't even complimented her. He just assumed she would do whatever she felt needed doing. Whatever she wanted to do next.…

He looked around the kitchen at the bare walls of the place he had made for her to live in. Rosie would have colored the walls and hung pictures. Francy would have put up a mirror and would have installed a kerosene stove so she wouldn't have to wait for wood to heat the iron stove if she wanted food or water for tea.

Neither of his sisters would have been caught by human eyes wearing a pair of their brother's overalls. A slight smile as he pictured a pair of his work pants on Francine.

Where in this tiny kitchen was her food supply? All women and girls knew what to do with food, didn't they? Wasn't it born into them? And they insisted on a supply, surely? Why, just look at Gwinnie and Kristie, handing out food at all hours of the day and part of the night. Didn't it just happen with girls?

Girls liked to make clothes…but not Merry…? She let Pat and Bridie dress her just because they had such fun at it. She let them hang her new clothes in the Cookie Jar for a day or two as advertisement. However, she did look really pretty when they went to Argyle for the car. Some kind of a pick flowered scarf on her head. She had attracted a lot of attention, but she didn't seem to notice the fellows gawking at the proceedings with the lizzie. Or when they were looking at her as she had studied the connection of the steering wheel to the tires.

Apparently she dressed in a way that she thought suited the occasion. So it must have been that she considered the occasion to bring back the car to be special.

She didn't mention shopping while they were there. She was intent on the car, only, but he sensed that she would not have suggested anything anyway. She would surely know he was intent on getting done what he had brought her there to get done. And he was her employer.

Daylight was breaking in the east, and he realized with a frown that he had become more acquainted with his hired hand in the last three hours than he had in the last three years.

It was about time for the Cookie Jar girls to be waking up and getting the food ready. He slipped out quietly and walked across the road. Wide eyed surprise greeted him.

"Hey, fellow, your eyes look like burned holes in a blanket. You been up all night?"

"Pretty near. We had a difficult delivery last night and lost a horse. A favorite of Merry's. Its kind'a got her down so I need some food to take back."

"Bad luck. Thing is, though, whatever horse it was, it would'a been her favorite, I'm thinkin'." Raymond hadn't thought of that. Strange....

Pleasant sizzles came from the kitchen along with the aroma of bacon. What should he take her?

"Kristie, do you have any idea what Merry would eat if she didn't feel very good?"

Guinnie called from the kitchen. "She'd want an egg and a bacon burrito. I'm puttin' on the egg now, and what else do you need?"

"Triple that order and add a half a dozen biscuits."

Food wrapped up and hot in a sack, Raymond re-crossed the road. Homer sat in the kitchen rubbing his eyes, and Merry was straightening her wrinkled clothes. The wild whirlwind of hair had been tamed down to a mild breeze.

He stationed her in the chair by the stove and insisted her feet be on the warming rail. Finding a pile of saucers on the cupboard shelf, he transferred an egg and bacon burrito onto a saucer, and adding a fork, handed it to his patient.

Homer stared in amazement, but finally sat himself in the indicated chair, and Raymond took the other. "Don't be scared when I ask you two to do something. We had us a scary night and Somebody's got to be thanked for the outcome. The only One I can think of to thank would appreciate a bowed head. I think."

Three heads bowed for a moment, and Raymond pronounced "Amen." Then he began to eat as though he did this every day. Actually, he was proud of himself for getting this far with the plans for rest of his life, though he knew he had a way to go. Maybe more tears were ahead.

Homer looked at the food on his plate. "I most usually go on to work and eat there. I leave food for sis."

Raymond still gave the orders. "All right. But take the burrito with you and don't worry about your sister. I'll see that she eats."

With a final glance at this person who looked like Raymond Canfield, but must be a stranger, Homer decided to trust him with his only living relative. Donning his hat, the one to keep grain dust from his hair, he walked away with the burrito in hand. Raymond was right…it had been quite a night. Someone must have helped, and Homer had more than a suspicion as to Who….

Sketchy parts of the horror that happened at Canfield Grading had been imparted to various persons who had come into the Cookie Jar, thence to be repeated to a wider group, and before noon, the community of Corners knew that Julia Canfield had sat up with America who had suffered a traumatic experience. Also, there had been a loss of one of the horses during a difficult delivery. That these two incidents were, of course, unrelated was assumed by many. But not by those who knew America.

To those who knew her, the loss of a young healthy horse, itself, was enough of a trauma to put her in shock. It was Raymond's sisters, however, who absorbed, with wide eyes, their mother's account of their brother sitting with her all night, even though his mother was there.

"It's true, I tell you. I was at the foot of the bed, but he pulled chair up beside her and for more'n two hours, he watched her, keepin' the quilts pulled up like I told 'im. And changin' the hot water jar when it cooled down.

"Wasn't too much we could do but wait, and me only knowin' about what might be wrong from listenin' to old Miz Gray Owl. We could sure use us a doctor around here."

Francine's head was shaking in disbelief. "You talkin' about Raymond? Your stone-statue son? Our brother that we share a dinner table with? He held Merry while she cried?"

And her sister, Rosalie, "Mama, you sure you're remembering the way it happened? 'Cause if you're right, could be we have the answer. What's the matter with him could be that he's finally took a look at Merry, and that'd be why he's asking how to get a girl's attention."

Then Francine again. "She's been working for him for over two years. You'd think…well, maybe not, being that we're talking about Raymond. While other boys were learning about girls, our brother was starting his business. So, Mama, what happens now?"

Julia Canfield shook her head slowly and whispered, reverently, "God only knows. For sure, that boy's in love with that girl and he don't even know it. What to do with this is something he'll have to do for hisself."

She paused for a thoughtful moment and came up with a well thought out comparison. She added, "It'll be hard for 'im, though. Those two are exactly alike in a different way. Seein' her clear and actual for the first time...it could be scary to him. Like lookin' in a mirror. Backwards!"

"What are you meaning, Mama? There's nobody like Raymond, and we've about decided there's no one like America, either."

The older woman was nodding. "That's how they're alike. They figured out what they liked and went to it and decided to find a way to keep away from what they didn't like. Both of 'em.

"He worked, he come home, ate, went to bed. Those Kiowa boys he's got workin' for him, they work hard, get off work, clean up and go lookin' for fun. Which'a those things is normal for a fellow not even out of his teens?"

Finally Francine nodded with understanding. "And Merry doesn't care a pin about her house or what she eats. She likes to read, but those horses are what she likes best. I think the only reason she let Pat and Bridie make her some dresses was that they wanted to and she wanted to give them what they liked and thought was fun. I'd already figured that one out, but I didn't see how they were alike."

The morning after the loss, Raymond and Merry had taken the warm nursing bottle to the orphaned filly. The tiny animal quickly recognized the nipple as food, after the midnight feeding by Sam Canfield. She attacked with vigor and much tail switching and lip smacking. Foamy milk drippings fell from her tiny chin.

Merry was silent. No glances toward the fateful stall, no questions. It was as though it had not happened, and the lone, lip-smacking animal before her was an everyday occurrence.

"Raymond, I'm thinkin' I'll go up and move some more hay to the chute. You'll be havin' the cured alfalfa forked up in a couple of weeks if it doesn't rain." It was not a question, just a statement of what she knew was his intention.

He hesitated. "Well, it depends on how you feel. You had a rough night. The thing is, I have a few things to do around here at least till noon. We'll see how you are then." Back to the old Raymond. He felt a pressure in the pit of his stomach like he should have done something…said something…anything…but didn't. Like he missed an opportunity. But he just shook his head sadly. Habits took time to…deal with? …change?

He walked north out of the barn to the new house. Pretty well finished out by now. His sisters had done a good job and seemed to have had fun. He had some sketchy plans for the near future and his mind worked better if the facts were committed to paper. He'd do that now.

He was certain, sure, that he now had a real-life partial problem. In Miss Josie's class, he had been rather good at them, figuring out which part of the problem that was missing, if one expected to get the given outcome. If you had part of the problem and the answer, you had to back up. Three and what made seven. Turn it around and say, seven minus three is…four, of course.

During the horrors of the night, a fact had become crystal clear to him. He did not know how, yet, but he did know that he wanted this girl in his life…now, later and likely forever. That was the answer. All he had to do was turn it around and make the answer part of the problem, then the other part of the problem became the answer. Simple.

Simple, that is, unless part of the problem was a girl. She was hard-headed and a bit stubborn, but every successful person really needed to be what was called stubborn. One would readily admit she was successful.

She liked what she liked and she made moves to get it, and may have sacrificed other things on the way. What was wrong with that? How else did one get what they wanted? Raymond clearly understood that.

The first thing he was going to do was move into the new house where he would be closer to his problem...or situation, perhaps. It need not be a problem, actually, only a circumstance to be adjusted.

It was not in Raymond's nature to plunge into anything without thought. Therefore, the move, itself, was enough for the moment. That evening he went about packing the few possessions that he would take with him immediately. He had a feeling of peace about it. It was a peace, the way that one has who has been lost, and finally finds what looks like the right path, feels peace. He spent the night in his old room...for the last time, possibly.

Julia Canfield held her tongue, difficult though it was. What mother did not want to impart last minute advice to her son... whatever his age or circumstances? There was, however, one piece of information that she intended to pass on. Now was as good a time as any.

"Son, if you have your boxes packed, come sit with me for a cup of tea. I just got it ready."

With her tall, handsome son across the well-used dining table, she began. "Son, knowin' a lot of folks like you do, I thought to pass along a little situation. Could be, you can be a help. We got new neighbors down the road named Santorini. Folks came from Italy. Young fellow not much older'n you with a wife and the wife's two little boys from when their pa was killed in the battle. The fellow got hisself a good wife and she loves takin' care'a the family, except for one thing. His old ma has to stay with them, and she feels like she's in the way. She loves her daughter-in-law, but the girl wants to do everything for her family all by herself, leavin' nothing for his ma to do. Bella, that's her name, she's been goin' up to the Cookie Jar of a afternoon just to get out'a the house thinkin' that she's bein' in the way. Could be, she is.

"Now, we got to talkin', her and me, and she said she'd really like to have a job. Says she loves to cook and clean and take care of a house but there just ain't enough work for her. To take up her time, that is. Says she can cook anything that's she's got the recipe for. Likes to wash and iron nice clothes. Now, I know that's the kind of help a lot of women'd like to have, only they don't have the money to pay for it. She'd not expect much, really. She says she can't spend so much time at the Cookie Jar, even though the young ladies there are nice to her. She'd like to help them, but they don't seem to need her help.

"I was thinkin', the way you see so many people, goin' around the county like you do with your work, you might know of someone that'd need her. She says her son'd take her to work and pick her up, if it weren't too far, and she'd work by the day. Havin' the kitchen cleaned up and supper cooked before she left to come home.

"I can see how she'd feel, livin' in a house she couldn't feel like was hers. It seems to be hard on the girl, too, and on the young man 'cause he cares about the both of 'em.

"So, I was tellin' this to you, so's you'd know if you ran onto someone like that." A short pause. She knew her son and she knew he was filing away the information, just as she had asked of him.

After a moment, she commented, "I 'speck that girl's come around good as ever? Miz Gray Owl thought the weakness of a shock only lasted a while, and for some folks, they got over it quicker'n others. I thought that girl'd be one of them to get over it quick. Sensible girl, she is."

She watched as Raymond nodded, then she added, "Sort of the way you'd be. Steppin' back and lookin' at things that happened, like, and decidin' what to do, and then doin' 'em." Enough said, she thought, and sipped noisily at the tea, reaching for a cookie. Anything more to be said about Merry should be said to him by his sisters. They could get away with more than she could.

The first rooster crow found Raymond leaving the house, his boxes in the buggy seat beside him, and old heavy-footed Mike between the shafts of the doubletree. Half the contents of his mama's cookie box had been emptied into his jacket pocket. He touched the reins to Mike's rounded rear and spoke softly.

Mike leaned into the traces and pulled the buggy and the man with as much ease as if they were not even there. After the six years he had worked on the road with the grader and the dirt scoop, this pulling was nothing.

Raymond's crew showed up, and they were soon on the way to the job site. The day, itself, went pretty much as usual. A cold burrito for lunch and water from the creek nearby. There was a lot of work to be had for a man who had the equipment, and the summer days were long, tired and dusty.

Merry had given a lot of thought to the welfare of the orphan. Now, there was Dollie who had just succeeded in weaning little Rowdy, though Rowdy didn't really agree to it. A few gentle kicks by mama on his sensitive nose were getting his attention, but Mama still let him nurse occasionally, to relieve her own pain.

Merry turned over and sighed. Maybe. In the morning she'd do it. No. Today. Right now. Worth a try, anyway.

After a lone cold biscuit spread with peanut butter, she went to the barn. Noticing Raymond's buggy beside the new house, she commented to herself, *I wondered when he'd move in. Figured it'd be when Rosie and Francy got it ready, fixed up the way they liked.*

On to the filly. The little creature met her with a searching nose, sniffing around her clothes for food. Slipping a lead over the delicately formed neck, she gently led the filly toward the pasture, singing softly, "When the roll…is called up yon…der. When the roll…." The little thing followed eagerly. Surely there would be food connected with this journey if she kept following.

Finding Dollie grazing contentedly, as she was not yet being put into the working rotation, she brought the little filly to Dollie's face, patting and stroking the mare around her nose and eyes, and continuing to sing. The filly nosed along the older mares' lips and chin, startling sharply when Dollie blew a huff at her.

Good news. Dollie would not have blown a huff if she had been disturbed or displeased. Instead, she eyed the young animal with her beautiful eyes and long lashes. Continuing to sing, Merry drew the baby away and moved her toward Dollie's belly. Dollie turned her head to watch, but she did not step or move her feet.

The filly was no dummy. The smell was right, so help was close if she could just find it. Nosing inside the mare's leg, she found what she looked for, and if the meal happened to be a bit scanty, that did not mean it wasn't appreciated.

Merry left the filly busily at work and moved back to Dollie's face. "You're such a good mother, Dollie," she crooned, "I was sure you'd help me with this little girl."

When the baby seemed satisfied, she took her back to the barn. Now Dollie would be more firm with Rowdy because she would have no bag pressure, and, with luck, would be ready by noon to let the filly have a little more.

When the work crew came in, it was past sundown. Raymond cast his eyes around looking for his hired man. He spotted her where she looked most natural, in the horse pasture. Squaring his shoulders, he told himself it was time to make up for past mistakes. He was through with ignoring his hired hand.

Walking on out there, through the many wildflowers that bloomed in the pasture grass, he found the little orphan busily working at the rear of Dollie's belly and his hired man petting and stroking Dollie's face and singing, "Near...er...my God...to Thee. Near...er... to Thee...."

Meeting him with a smile, she explained that this was the third feeding for the day, and that she had needed only a little of the goat milk to fill out. Good news. Being drained would help Dollie continue a degree of production if she would only continue to let the baby nurse. Anyway, every occasion was important now, with the baby so young. Every drop was a plus.

Together, the three of them returned to the barn. Behind them, Dollie grumbled sociably and blew her breath, then lowered her face into the prairie grass.

Having finished her work, Merry locked the filly away, then went on to her cabin. Raymond watched. Discouraged with himself. He'd have to do better than that. He sighed and shook his head. Had to do better....

The new homeowner made the unaccustomed trip to the new house. Empty and echoing. No warm kitchen with a mother stirring around softly. No background sound of conversation between his parents. No coffee aroma.

Well, there was only one thing to do. Washing his face and changing his shirt, he walked across the road. The Cookie Jar was pretty well crowded. In the small community most everyone was well known to everyone else, and three more of the little ice cream tables had been wedged in. The patrons didn't mind being close together.

If a table was occupied by only one, it was acceptable protocol to request to join that person. Raymond was very hungry. Eyeing a vacant chair, he headed toward it. Hand on the chair, ready to ask permission and pull it out, he looked into the face of his hired man. No overalls or blue and white scarf. Honey-colored hair framed her face. Cheeks lightly tanned with rosy tints, not bluish white like last night.

She had been leaning forward, chin in hand, finishing a bowl of chili beans with goat cheese. With a smile, she invited him to sit. Slightly uneasy, he accepted, then went to the counter to get his food. Kristie filled his plate, looked up at him, glanced back at the table where Merry sat, and produced a crooked, impudent smile. The smile said this should be something to watch. A lot of words had been spoken and a lot of conjectures made. Now they would know the truth. Maybe.

Considering the circumstances of the last thirty-six hours, some conversation would be expected between the two. *Come on, Raymond,* he chided himself. *Say something. Sensible or not, something must be said.*

"You're looking nice. Sort of relieved and pleased with Dollie, aren't...we?"

They managed words, soft and low, and they were observed by many eyes. They left together. Who cared what was said? But he let her enter her house alone.

Raymond selected a bedroom in the new house and stretched out. Very tired after the long day. No sleep came, only thoughts. No person in the kitchen. No sounds that he had not made. No meal ready. And there was no breakfast. *All right, Raymond! Where is the rest of the problem?*

It must be nice to have a girl in the house, but he was a long way from that. There was, however, another option. There was that Italian woman, Miz Santorini, was it? She could be brought by her son and picked up and she could cook anything. Liked keeping house, she said. Well, it would be a start....

Hmmmm. All it would take was money, and he had that. Also, he would be helping her son to give his two women a break from each other. It could be just a trial, he told himself, and she could leave to take another job when she could find one. He stretched and yawned, mind made up. He'd take care of it in the morning.

But for now there was nothing in the house. He would never know the agony of his mother, as she made herself leave him alone and not even, at least, permit herself to take him a sandwich.

When morning came, he was still thinking. At least, Merry had peanut butter for breakfast. And she had the leftovers from Mrs. Bramwell. With a sigh, he dressed and headed for the Cookie Jar. Along with his breakfast, he faced Gwinnie wearing a smirk and a wink. GIRLS!

He should have gone on to his mama's house and ate and asked her to talk to Miz Whoever! Well, this evening for sure. Too many new things were descending on him at once. Too much change that he had not expected and was not prepared for. No place to get control. It was like trying to pick up a five hundred pound marshmallow...parts if it kept breaking off in his hands.

And on top of it all, there was that constant talk about the war over in Europe, and about the way England was being dragged into it because of having to honor a previously made, and possibly unwise, partnership treaty.

Anyone who knew geography, and if they were in Miss Josie's class they would certainly know geography, England was just too small to defend herself...alone. In spite of the war they'd had with each other, America would be obligated to help if necessary, and according to the papers, it was becoming necessary. It was like a couple of brothers fighting each other, but if one was attack, the other would rush to his defense.

It would only be right for America to help, and who would do the helping? Young strong men like himself, Willie and Johnny. Philip and Edward, of course, and Tray Cullen, another school mate.

Who, indeed? There was talk in the blacksmith shop, during farming lunch breaks and even here in the Cookie Jar. There was hardly a way to get a newspaper less than a week old, but what they got brought very sobering news.

Parents of sons in their early twenties were concerned and talked privately. Johnny Black and Willie Elk, for all their fun-loving rowdiness, were thinking serious thoughts. It had been clear for years that they and the "hats and hankie girls" were a happy foursome. There was no one who did not assume they would eventually be married, and it would happen as soon as they sorted out who belonged with whom.

But Raymond and others knew differently. The two young Kiowa boys were far-thinking young men and knew they could very well be required to fight for freedom, to be drafted and sent to the battle. If that should happen, it should be done before going into marriage.

Pat and Bridie knew, as well. Now that their fathers had built them the lovely showroom that they had decorated so professionally. Now that they had the machine that made small, tight stitches and created lock-stitches even better than their needles ever had. Now that they knew, and approved, that marriage would have to wait, they made their own plans. As a business, the venture went well, and instead of taking their van on the road, the customers now mostly came to them.

The new sewing machine enabled them to make the latest styles more reasonably priced, opening a whole new market. Hats and hankies, as well as shawls and scarves, were moneymakers. The brave, innovations created by the girls were in demand. If the style of a hat seemed a bit outlandish, the local ladies knew that the girls created "New York Styles" from the books they had, so if the creation managed to stay on their heads, it was bought and worn.

Old Mr. and Mrs. Morrison, aunt and uncle of Edward, had passed on to their reward. They were lovingly placed to rest at the back of the quarter section of land that had given them so much pleasure.

Edward's plans were successfully coming about. Alfalfa, along with flowering trees and beehives. A patch devoted to the growing of popcorn. It was amazing how much popcorn was needed by the Cookie Jar! Also peanuts.

In the sandy soil required by peanuts, blowing dust was a problem, and in a dust storm the whole layer of a plowed field could lift off in a day's time and blow away leaving exposed roots.

Edward devised a plan to lower the dust loss in the peanut fields. It was so ingeniously arranged, it was rapidly copied as far as six or seven communities away.

So simple. Corn was hard on the fertilizer in the soil, and peanuts, being legumes, enriched the soil. Therefore, he planted three rows of corn, then three rows of peanuts, then more corn, carefully marking exactly where the rows were. The next year, the corn was put where the peanuts were last year, and so on.

The dust? Also simple. When the frisky breeze blew a cloud of the red dust off the low peanut vines, the stalks and long leaves of the corn knocked it down, so that it stayed right there in the field.

The stalks of the corn and peanuts, after harvest, were fed to the animals, especially to the milk goats kept for making cheese. His aunt and uncle had been so interested and approving of the changes, they joyfully helped him set it up. Worked well. Most of the popcorn, peanuts, honey and cheese were absorbed by the Cookie Jar.

Edward spent a lot of time at the Cookie Jar, mainly because the scenery was so pleasing. The best-looking pair of sisters in the county were there, but when Philip used his skills to prop up the privy, thereby gaining Gwinnie's undying admiration, Edward centered his attention on Kristie. Probably would have anyway, but this made the choice easier.

CHAPTER 9

And the girls, now in their early twenties, often hired younger girls to run the Cookie Jar, giving them time to spend time with the fellows. All of the young people of the community shared the underlying apprehension brought on by the war, and short-term plans were made accordingly. Best the fellows went, it was universally decided, and did what they had to do, as there was no way to stop war except to win it. Then they could get on with their lives.

There was the poem…Old men made war, and young men died. The girls and women stayed at home…and cried, helplessly. It had not yet hit the Corners, but it was coming and everyone knew it.

The parents of the four girls were grateful for the work that occupied them. Activity appeared to go on much the same as usual at the Corners, but that was deceiving. There was a brittleness to the laughter. The beginnings of adult conversations seemed to start with "What are you reading in the news?" as though the local mentality was now worldwide instead of centered no farther than Argyle. Which it was.

The mothers of eligible sons had difficulty occupying themselves with their usual tasks and friendly chats of gossip. Many of them remembered, as small girls, the conversation of their grandmothers.

The battle. There was always a battle somewhere, and it had a fascination for their little boys. Games with spears fashioned from a smooth stick. Stones tethered in groups and tied to stout sticks to practice throwing accuracy and hopefully to injure an enemy. Tree trunks were often the targets. Joyful shouts when a "kill" was accomplished. Women stayed at home…and cried. Figuratively.

How could it possibly reach them, here safe in the territory? They had paid their price for peace. Their grandfathers had died for their freedom and liberty, but yet here was another battle to fight. And another, and another.

Gathered groups of young men attempted to make sense of something they didn't understand, but they did not hesitate to see what they thought was their duty.

Edward Morrison was the first to receive a notice. "Greetings, and you are selected to…." The notice was examined and re-examined with sober expressions, and plans were made for what would come to them all.

Homer Forrester married Bernice (Neecie) Bramwell. Married men were given deferments, but that meant nothing, actually. They all knew the war, if it lasted, would gather them all into it, like the hand net scooping into the creek for minnows to use for bait.

When asked why the marriage so soon, and was it for the deferment, Homer gave his wide, handsome smile. He shrugged his muscled shoulders and answered that he had married because Neecie had told him it was time. That always produced a knowing laugh among the men, and the question remained unanswered.

Some mothers suspiciously surmised that the Bramwell parents might be hoping for a pregnancy before Homer had to go. That would keep him tethered to the mill where his services were so sorely needed. For a little longer. At present, Neecie had teamed with a classmate from the Prairie Academy and they were organizing a school between Corners and Argyle, appropriately named "Midway Academy."

Raymond Canfield and his father had a talk. "Son, if you have to go…well, have you given thought to…?"

"No thought needed, Pa. If you aren't up to fillin' in, then I'll just lock the doors until I get back. Gonna be a problem tryin' to operate here without young men. There'll be some older fellows…."

"Son, don't you be concerned with how it'll be done. Just remember that I'll do what I can. I ain't dead yet."

It was two days after Raymond had moved into the new house that his mother brought Mrs. Bella Santorini to see him. She proudly conducted the neighbor through the house and basked in her enthusiasm.

"Such lovely house. Is nice...sofa? Curtains...aw, no...is needing iron. See fold creases?"

Julia Canfield treated herself to a small smile at the criticism of Francine's curtain pressing skill. Finding a problem could only make the prospective job more appealing to Miz Bella.

And the little cook house. "Aw, such food to be made here!" She kissed her fingers and tossed the kiss to the wind. "They have chickens to eat? No...? Then maybe...."

Julia could see that there would be major changes in her son's life. Subtle, surely, but changes nevertheless. Changes that she, as a mother, could never make.

Miz Santorini ("call me Bella") continued on the subject of chicken. "Old country pork and beef...they cost...? Chicken always can have. They increase themselves. Have eggs. Food deli...? How to say...?"

Making a guess, Julia furnished, "Delicious?"

"Aw, yes. I learn more American from your son."

That brought another smile to Julia. Good luck to learning English words from Raymond, but that would be her problem. Miz Bella was willing and eager to try. It was decided she would start the next morning.

Raymond, accustomed to hiring boys and men stuttered a bit before he got the hang of instructing and giving orders to a female the age of his mother. "Your job will be cooking, cleaning and keeping clothes washed. Let me know what you need to get started.

"Also, the girl who cares for the horses? She will eat here or she may want to take food home with her. You can ask her what she likes to eat."

Miz Bella nodded rapidly after his every word. She mustn't let this opportunity get away. A chance to be useful. A place to stay out of the way of her son's wife. It was somewhere to be, while they were still on friendly terms. Where she would not be tempted to win away the love of his wife's little boys. Darling little fellows, but she knew they were not to be hers.

"The girl...? She have clothes to clean? I have...skill...? For girl's nice things and lace...I do from old country. I learn when I was little...girl? You think she let me care for her nice things?"

At this, Raymond stroked his chin thoughtfully. "I think you'd have to ask her. I believe there's a good chance that she'd like that, but I don't know."

And he told Merry. "She's hired to take care of everything you don't want to do. She won't bother the horses, but she likes chickens. She loves to cook and if you want anything special, tell her and she'll make it. She's very excited about helping out, and I hope she'll do things the way you...well, I want you to be all right with her being here."

Merry nodded. Thoughts raced through her head. A cook. Someone to do the washing. "Uh, well, I...."

"Merry, I don't want to say this yet, but I think I have to. I'll be getting my notice soon, and I want to get some things done before I have to leave. I don't want you to be here alone. My pa, he'll do what he can, but I don't know how things will go." He paused, as her face was turned toward him, soberly trying to absorb his words. She seemed to be looking for hidden words that would affect her and her immediate future, and beyond. She was right.

He continued, "One thing for certain, I don't want your care of the horses to be disturbed. I want you to do the best you can with them and make every decision that affects them. Absolutely every decision. Ask for any opinion you want to, but the final decision is yours.

"You will decide whether any are to be sold and which ones they are. Also how to treat the foals, what feed is to be purchased and what hay is planted. Now, you don't have to do this if you don't want to, of course. In that case. I will have to make different plans. I know my pa will have his hands full without being concerned with the animals, so...." And he ran out of words.

The knowledge seemed to explode within her chest as she absorbed his words. It was all hers! But how would it be with him not coming and going and being in control of it all? Still, she had a chance to try...no, to succeed, and to make him proud when he came back in a…what? A year, maybe two…? Maybe…no, best not to think too far.

A deep breath. "I can do it. I will make certain everyone is well fed and I…." A painful swallow. "I really will do this and I thank you for…for the chance."

He responded, "Of course you have the chance. There is no one in the territory who could do half as well as you. I think I should have been telling you that all along. But I'll be back, and then we can…." Words failed him, but he reached toward her and she did not shy away. "Merry, I want you to know this. I'll always you need you. I'll need you here and also in my life forever. And I will always…love…you." There. He did it. He was purely amazed that he had gotten it out so quickly…but now he had accomplished it.

She leaned her forehead against his chest; he stroked the blue and white scarf. Looking up, she told him, "I'll be here. You will be back and I'll be here. Forever." Did forever mean she could love him? Of course! He would know that! No one could accuse Raymond of being slow…except with Merry.

These scattered words must have been a proposal of marriage… or at least a solid engagement. Leastwise, they both considered it that way. So what if it was a bit unusual? Weren't they both a bit unusual? And the separation was staring them in the face.

She was to immediately move into the new house and let Miz Bella have the cabin. The woman lost no time settling herself into the tiny house. Happily. Joyfully. Her own place where she would not be in the way of anyone! She looked up into the clouds in an attitude of thankfulness for favors that could only have come from Above.

The "Farewell Parties" were more like wakes. Volunteers had a bit of leeway, it was said, on what part they would have in the army. Raymond would be leaving with Johnny, Willie and several others. Phillip would be along soon, and Edward had already gone. They would be back, of course, for a short leave to square away their affairs, but that would be more painful than joyful or fun… what with the specter of the war hanging over.

At the induction center there were tests. The first dividing line was the ability to read and write English in an understandable way. So many of the volunteers were new immigrants attracted to the army by the meager pay that was offered and the promised certainty of regular meals. The young men from the Corners were not in that category. They scored highly on the tests. Miss Josie would have had it no other way.

Sorely needed were drivers both in England and in France. Young men who had only driven mules were put behind the wheels of the hastily put together mechanical vehicles. Nothing to it, they decided! Making the machine obey them was a sight easier than controlling a hardheaded mule. The horses under the hood didn't make decisions on their own, except for dying. That's why repair mechanics were created.

Edward had been siphoned off as a driving instructor in England while Phillip was sent on to France.

The accurate marksmanship of both Willie and Johnny was grabbed up by the front line. Sharpshooters were needed both on the ground and in the stick-and-canvas flying machines.

There would be the short-lived training camp before they would report. Endless lines of young men shuffled from one station to another. Eyes? Ears? Reflexes by the rubber hammer on the knees. Pass on to the next station.

Footprint on the paper. Pass on. No, wait. "Canfield! Come back and step again." The medic had looked at the new mark made by Raymond's foot, then examined the foot itself. A dismal shake of the head.

"Go back to Section F."

"Why? What's wrong?"

The doctor had no time for explanations. The next man was already making footprints. "Flat feet," he called over his shoulder to Raymond.

"Flat feet?"

The doctor ignored him. "Next...?"

Raymond retraced his footsteps back to Section F where he had received the sheaf of papers. They had no time for his questions, either. Filling out his rejection papers, stamping 4F, handing them to him, and dismissing him. He stood staring.

What did flat feet have to do with anything? He had always known he had flat feet. His pa had flat feet, and Pa had won a quarter section of land in a race. Flat feet hadn't stopped him. He looked at the stamp of blue ink…4F. The mark of a failure… somehow. "F" for failure!

And he was on his way home.

He was met with puzzled amazement. Raymond Canfield, a name well known all over the six or seven town area. The man who could run a business with government contracts, and who hired employees. Raymond Canfield, efficient and to be admired, but he was not fit for the army. Flat feet, indeed!

But many young men secretly examined their own feet. Would they possibly be flat enough to keep them from being drafted? One could only hope!

Puzzled and still trying to wrap his thoughts around it all, Raymond moved back into his childhood home. Such an anticlimactic happening! *Get a hold on yourself, Raymond.*

Merry met him with gladness, though with a wondering thought as to how she would now be affected. Miz Bella could not find it within herself to be happy, though she tried. She would surely be sent home, now, to give the young lady her cabin.

Raymond found Merry at the watering trough. She had adjusted the speed of the blade and examined all the moving parts for wear. Dabbed a bit of oil here and down there. She nodded to herself, deeming the moving parts worthy of another few months before replacements and she climbed down and waited as Raymond came toward her.

A smile. Outstretched arms. Recent events had seemed to give him bravery. Or stubbornness…flat feet, indeed! Maybe even a bit of anger.

Merry bravely walked into the outstretched arms. He held her, while stroking, once more, the blue and white scarf. "Merry, I hardly know how to put this. I thought there would be more time, but I find I don't want any more time. I want you to marry me as soon as we can arrange it."

Merry's breath caught in her chest. She was afraid. She, also, had thought there would be more time. Time to write letters, to think about the answers. Time to consider… to learn things. To learn more things about each other. This was not supposed to happen yet. She needed time to get used to it.

"Raymond, I can't."

"You what?"

"I can't marry you, at least not yet. I can't do things men need for girls to do to make them happy, and I'm not sure I ever can. Marriage changes a girl's life."

Hands on her shoulders, he faced her. Fear gave him courage. If he lost her, what else mattered? "What things do you think would make me happy?"

She sniffed, but plunged on, bravely. Get it over with. "I can't cook, and I don't think I could learn because I just really don't like to. I can't make your curtains hang straight or keep the dust bunnies out from under the bed. I would do a bad job of it because I would keep thinking of other things I wanted to do. I'm so, so sorry to be so selfish. Maybe in time…."

Still holding her shoulders, he tipped his head to look into her downcast face. Suddenly he felt confident. This was a situation he understood, that of passing out duties and making decisions. That of putting order into chaos and oil into human machinery.

"Merry, my dear," he began, his words sounding strange to his own ears. "I'm sorry to say that you will have no time to be taking care of the new house or cooking meals or straightening the curtains. You will be much too busy with the things I hired you to do. And I might tell you, I was never afraid of bunnies, dust or cottontail. You have a big job to do and you will not have time for anything else, except maybe letting me look at you and talk with you. And maybe take a walk in the evening while you tell me your plans with the animals.

"I hired Miz Bella to take care of the stupid little things like cooking and cleaning. I don't ever want to think of you doing them and wasting your time. You might, however, have to learn how to tell her the way you want things done, because I'm going to be terribly busy. It'll be hard to get along without Willie and Johnny, so you'll need to do the bossing of Miz Bella."

He must have said enough to make himself clear. After all, he was a good businessman and expected to get what he wanted. He gave orders well, and he was proud of the orders he was able to give to his "hired man"…as soon as he figured out what orders she wanted to hear.

The wedding was a quiet affair. It would have been even much simpler if Pat and Bridie had not begged permission to outfit her in a manner befitting her marriage to "such an important man" as Raymond.

Also, she must have this new thing called a bridesmaid. This thing with the war was dreary enough without letting a wonderful opportunity like this pass them by. The local girls tossed names into a hat for the bridesmaid privilege, including Francine's name, though she was not present to agree or object.

Francine was chosen, but then the girls decided they would all share the pleasure. Merry was to be dressed in white, and each of the other girls would choose a color and the dresses would be made alike. Merry, herself, greatly appreciated their efforts on her behalf. She had the horses to attend to, so obviously, she hadn't the time.

Miz Bella stood with the Canfield family at the wedding and wept on Julia's shoulders. "So wonderful! Our little ones to have life together. Such a happy…happiness, to see them! That we should see this day!"

Julia Canfield accepted the exclamation of happiness, though she wondered how the bride and groom turned out to belong also to Miz Bella. No problem, though. Miz Bella's presence might see that the two of them ate properly.

Because of his education and experience, Edward Morrison was snagged to sign in as a corporal. Because of his testing scores, he was designated as an instructor. He was to teach the art of driving an automobile when he had barely learned it himself. As time passed, he climbed the ladder of responsibility very quickly.

It seemed almost no time at all until he was put in charge of directing supplies to the needed areas on the battlefield. That meant working with installations in France, supplying the center that accepted wounded off the field, he re-supplied food galleys and maintained the availability of climate-suitable clothing. Huge responsibility. His duties required giving orders, so further testing was needed, and he was now a captain.

Cpl. Phillip Armstrong was put behind the wheel of what passed as an ambulance. He was given a partner who had been trained in rudimentary first aid training and was now called a medic, and together they answered the desperate pleas from wherever they came.

Working with outlying units, he picked up and brought in broken scraps of what was once strapping young men. Also parts left over from the mortar blasts that were identified only by names on their shredded uniforms. His first aid partners were chosen from whoever was currently available.

A call came and his assigned partner slid into the seat beside him hugging the kit of items that might ease pain of the victims on the trip back. If they were still able to feel pain. This time they were heading for a place about fifteen miles away so they attempted to calm themselves by conversation.

The soft voice of his partner caused him to turn for a clearer look. Smooth face, firm jaw, shapely hands.

To answer his questioning look, she offered, "Yes, I'm a girl."

"But the uniform…and all. Why…?"

"I was needed. Not enough… fellows. Too much battle and loosing… Saving fellows for battle, girls fill in. Is…all right?"

"Oh, very much all right. Just surprised. I hadn't realized things were so bad."

"Most Americans…not realize. Not to know how we wait for them. Wait and wait."

"Waiting for Americans? You were waiting for us to join the war?"

"Oui…uh, yes. I see them come and scare…be scared to watch them come."

"Scared of us?"

"Uh, no…I meant not to say scare, just…disappoint. I think we get men. Our men twenty years old and look forty. Faces all in wrinkles of fear. Skin burned, look old. We need soldiers bad. Or we lose the war."

"But there are a lot of volunteers from America. Didn't they help any?"

"I say more is how I know. French girls were sent to bring back supplies from ship and same ship have Americans coming. We get happy and sing because…finally they come. We gather to see them and they walk off ship. Little boys. No beards. Pink cheeks and soft looks. We say 'why they send us children? We send our own little boys to the country…to keep safe. Now we get American children, how that be a help to us?'"

Cpl. Armstrong steered the vehicle among the pits gouged out by the rockets blast. He knew precious little about automobile engines, but he hoped the strange noises from under the hood were normal, and that the fenders of ripped metal continued to hang onto the vehicle. His partner's words were playing themselves in his mind.

She continued, "Then they come on and our hopes, they… drown? Sink down? We hoped so much for help. Then they go to front where is fighting. The American boys."

She sniffed and wiped her eyes. In a cracked voice, she went on. "They go to front and they fight. Boy children from America have no fear and run to battle. Our men get brave to watch and run with them. They not say go back or give up. They go where there is no room to go and make their own room. Enemy run. They fight like…uh…diablo…?"

"Devil? You say they fight like the devil?"

"Oui. Our men take…uh, courage? They think maybe not lost. I think, why they come and fight with us and they never know us? Why they do this?" She looked at Philip with imploring eyes.

Philip could only say, "Just look at the names on their shirts. So many of them have names you know. It's quite possible that where they kneel to aim their weapons is the same land where their father's grandparents were buried. They take up their weapons to protect the family honor and homeland. They can't help it."

A quick swerve to dodge a crater. Then he added, "I couldn't help it."

A few more miles and the shelling became a lot louder. Puffs of smoke, sod, debris and flames shot into the sky. Philip stared at the torn-up road and ignored the devastation ahead. They could feel the shaking of the ground beneath the wheels of the vehicle.

Phillip looked over at the girl beside him. Eighteen years old, maybe? "Uh, I'll pull over here and let you...."

"NO! I go all the way. Drive fast and careful! We have work."

He did. A waving flag signaled him on. The girl beside him crawled nimbly over the back of the seat and unbolted the rear of the van, opening its doors. He had hardly slowed to a stop when she slid out and hit the ground running. Bag open, syringe in her hand. Calming morphine pumped into veins. If the wounded had any threads of strength left within their torn bodies, that strength should not be used up by screaming in pain.

They were set up to bring back four wounded, but six were pulled aboard. Another soldier sitting on the ground, maybe thirteen years old...maybe just twelve. French uniform. Head down, looking at where a hand should be.

Yanking a gauze strip from her kit, the medic wrapped around and around, stanching the blood flow, and then followed with a morphine shot. There was no room in the van. Still in a daze, the young boy was led to the seat the girl had vacated and the door shut behind him.

Leaping onto the shambling, unsteady fender of the vehicle, her hand grabbed a hold onto the door edge and shouted at Philip to GO! Philip obeyed and turned the wheel, striving to avoid the cavernous shell holes. Pressing his foot to the floor, he sent the van shooting away, the girl holding with fierce determination to the outside as though it was a thing she did every day. Likely it was.

One of the passengers was lost on the way, but the other six were patched up and sent... somewhere. Philip realized he didn't even ask her name. Her shirt said "Bertrand." Maybe she was Nancy, or maybe Mimi, but for certain she was brave.

They were fed and the van was swabbed out and refitted. Another call was wired in. Piling aboard the van, Armstrong and Bertrand headed out.

They had to ford a small stream, tires spinning and slinging mud. Foot to the floor and screaming engine, but the horsepower was enough to pull them out of it. Bouncing over the debris of war, they saw the fire ahead. Signal flag desperately waving. Fire burning fast and the thick smoke roiling and black overhead. Eyes stinging from acid smoke, Philip gripped the wheel fiercely, plunging into the rolling waves of blackness.

Screeching to a halt, he leaped from the door, grabbing up a wounded body and stuffing it into the van without thought. The able-bodied flagman was the only person standing, and he now struggled to remove a wounded man from the water which flowed over an injured leg, washing red as it flowed. Philip came to help, struggling to stay upright on the slippery bank.

The victim had blessedly passed out and was limp as he was dragged up the slippery bank by his arms. Philip startled when a fiery blast erupted at his left side. Something within him just knew the fire had caught up with him and his time was gone. Overhead he heard a whine and a crack, and he felt himself scream when his leg suddenly blazed with unbearable heat, followed by a tearing, searing pain.

Releasing his hold on the victim, he turned to see it was not the rocket itself that had caught him but a half-burned log that had fallen from the burning tree. A fiery section of blazing fury.

The flag bearer leaped across his victim landing behind Philip, and he kicked the log aside but the pain did not follow. His voice called, "Medic!" and Philip was barely aware of Bertrand sliding down the bank beside him. With a knife, she sliced through his pants leg and made an assessment.

"Burned and broken. You load, I fix Armstrong."

The flag bearer left to obey her command, while dragging the limp victim by his arms. Philip felt the coolness of the

Mercurochrome over his wound, putting out some of the fire on his skin. He heard the breaking of a stick and felt the tightness of the bandage. Around and around. He tried to help but couldn't. Leg wouldn't lift. Scenery floated around him in broken patches of unreality.

Then the flag bearer was back to help pull Philip up the bank toward the van. Bertrand shouted above the blasts and the whining of bullets overhead. "Wish I could do morphine, Armstrong. Can't. You drive us out."

Philip heard himself groan as his hands were on fire. Was he holding a torch by the wrong end? "Drive!" she had commanded. She couldn't mean it.

Bertrand was quick with the explanation. "Only one is you. Else we stay burn. Fire is here in minutes."

Between the girl and the flagmen, they positioned him into the driver's seat, bending his hastily and roughly splinted left leg carefully into the small space under the wheel. Fiery pain shot up his leg with every movement.

His hands burned and he felt as though he was holding a bundle of flaming switches. Sometimes he looked at his hands but couldn't seem to see them. He could, however, see the fast approaching flames and hear their roar above the sound of the engine.

He gritted his teeth and grasp the burning branches, the ones that made up the steering wheel, into his hands and turned them. Surprised that the steering wheel turned. He backed up, shifted gears with burning knives in his hands and stepped on the accelerator. Like a grape squeezed from its skin, the van shot away from the smoke and flame and bounced onto the shell-pocked road.

He wanted desperately to scream but the thought of the sound of his voice seemed frightening, so he held it in. He couldn't possibly drive any farther, but he kept his foot on the pedal praying to the Power above to hold the vehicle together under the punishment he was giving it.

The flagman was beside him, groaning and holding his side. He didn't know where Bertrand was, but he was sure she was fine. About five miles to go, but he could not make them. He could not go that far. But he could make one mile. Then there might be help. There wasn't. He knew he could make only one more mile after that. Strength was fading. Then another mile.

He saw the aid station ahead. He knew he couldn't make it that far, but he did. Somehow the steering wheel had become so wet and slippery he could hardly hold to it, but he must. How did it get so wet?

The rescuers saw them coming and the van was met by the stretcher bearers. Philip saw Bertrand leap from the rear of the van and shout to the medic, "Get driver first before...he...."

That was all Philip heard before the pain stopped and he started to fall from the driver's seat. Asphalt paving of the landing field coming at his face. Hands that would not let him fall to the ground. He wanted to fall away from the burning pain that seemed to engulf him, but they wouldn't let him. He heard his sleeve rip but did not feel the sting of the needle. Only the beginning of blessed relief.

When he opened his eyes again, his left leg was splinted and hanging by a chain from the ceiling. Compound fracture just below his knee. Bone crushed, but it had been wired together. Maybe it would hold. Both hands and arms were swathed in bandages, and the heat of the fire had been wrapped up within them.

The needle was coming back. It would put out the fire. For a while. What happened with the hands? Burns, he was told. Two broken fingers on one hand and one on the other. Green stick fracture above the wrist. It would heal nicely. The fingers...well, they'd see.

No, they didn't know how it happened. The medic with him didn't know, either, but she said he had driven ten miles on the rocket-pitted road with a fractured leg and two broken hands. Practically ruined the steering wheel with the blood.

Four days later the fire in his hands had been fairly well put out but the new skin was very tender. The aching, broken fingers were splinted and the green stick fracture had graduated to elastic bandages that itched with a vengeance. He was not permitted to grip his hands unless a medic was in attendance. Healing was too delicate to risk further injury to fragile and hastily spliced nerves. Fingers must be bent a certain way to avoid…well it didn't matter. Rules.

Stared at the ceiling. There was nothing else to do. Thought of the Corners and his father. Wondered how much the Reverend Armstrong knew about what happened to him. Thought about Gwinnie McLaughlin. Hoped, with a grin, that the privy was holding up for her. Spiders were bad enough without a leaning and unsafe privy. Wished he could write to them but he couldn't even hold a pencil.

Then he entertained himself with wondering how his hands got burned. He heard that the flagman had shrapnel in his side. Ruptured an intestine. He'd make it, though. He was a limey, a British fellow, and his squad had fallen into an ambush. Lost one, saved four. Three of them and the limey.

Tough fellow, that limey. He would be patched up and sent back into the depth of hell. As soon as he could walk and hold a weapon.

Here came the medic. No, it was someone else. Boss man with bars on his collar. A snake-on-the-spear medic and a cross. Chaplain. Important fellow.

"Thought I'd stop and see the fellow who did what couldn't be done. I see they've got you strung up. They say you're healing fast. I hadn't been able to check on you because we had such an influx of injured when you were brought in. Quite a battle we had out there, but I guess I'm not telling you anything."

"Don't know, preacher. I was sort of out of it for a while."

"I can imagine. Seems you might have had Divine Help, holding onto that wheel with burned and broken hands."

"I had to, Major Carpenter. That girl medic I had, she told me I had to! She gave me no room to argue."

A smile from the Chaplain. This fellow would make it. "I can only hope to imagine what happened. Is there something I can do for you now that you have no hands?"

"Well, yes, as a matter of fact. If you could send someone to write a letter for me, I've got a pa and a girl who might want to know about me."

"Now, soldier, I can take care of that. They taught me to write back in school and I still remember. I'll get paper."

He was back. "We'll address these envelopes first. I learned to do that, right off. Sometimes a fellow is feelin' good, then suddenly he isn't and if I have addressed envelopes I can send off a few words till he's better."

Phillip sighed, and began. "One is to go to Rev. Armstrong and the other to Gwendollyn McLaughlin. Both to Argyle, Oklahoma, in care of the Corners."

The major stopped, pencil in hand, to stare at the man on the cot. "The Corners. That girl's sister is named Kristallyn. She and her sister operate the Cookie Jar."

Philip was speechless. He swallowed hard. All he could do was stare.

The major continued. "I'm Daniel Carpenter. You must be one of the newer town residents. I've been away for quite a while, in seminary and in medical training. I did hear, however, that the Corners was getting a church. Such good news. I'm sure you've been there since I have and I'd like to hear everything. In time, of course. There's so much to do here."

A short note did it this time, and a short conversation, but the pair of neighbors had more to say over the few days that Philip was there. Then he turned his cot over to someone more recently wounded and was moved to convalescence.

Strange world! Travel halfway around it to fight a battle. The preacher knew nearly everyone from the Corners. His ma went to school there, and he remembered Raymond Canfield really well. Also the sons of Miss Josie.

Two more weeks and Phillip was back in a van, braces on his hands. A slightly better van, this time, or maybe the other one fell apart. He didn't draw Bertrand again, but she had stopped by to see him. "I had to make you drive, Armstrong, or we'd be all... dead? I don't know how you did it, but you were only...hope? They sewed up the limey and hooked him onto another squad. Sent me out again."

"Your country sending a heart to you," she told Philip.

"Heart? Nothin' wrong with my heart. Is there...?"

Shaking her head, she struggled with her English, "Uh...blue? No...purple. Like medal...for having injury."

"Oh. A purple heart for sliding down a slippery slope. The purple heart should go to you for pulling me out."

She grinned, showing deep dimples. "No injury! I don't get one! But I say you get the heart for driving with burned and bleeding hands."

"I have a question. How did you know the pink cheeked American boys could fight like the devil?"

"My, uh...to be married? Boyfriend? He tell me and he don't lie. I hope. Says if there's victory, we thank Americans."

The wedding of Raymond Canfield and America Forrester had been a pleasant break from the horrors of the war. It was the first wedding in the brand-new church over on Cedar Bush Road. Seemed appropriate somehow.

The bride stood surrounded by what seemed a flock of butterflies, in pink, blue, yellow, lavender and green. She insisted her brother stand by her, and his wide grin told his pleasure.

Miz Bella took over her job with intense seriousness. She moved her sparse belongings into the little hired man cabin. She proclaimed it spacious and perfect. At her gentle nagging, chickens began to be pecking and scratching about among the weeds and wildflowers and in the hayloft grass seeds.

The chickens appeared in delectable dishes flavored with tomatoes, herbs and cheese made from the extra goat milk. Eggs appeared in every conceivable concoction.

Clothing appeared clean and folded, all of their own accord as far as Merry was concerned. She still went to the Cookie Jar, but for friendship rather than necessary food.

Raymond went about his work with his usual methodical progress. He hired girls to manage his equipment and even found two who could stand the pressure of the work. Some older men tried it, and Sam Canfield could be counted on if there was no one else.

Raymond, however, bent to his work with even more pressure than usual. He felt, if it must be said, a measure of guilt that he was not in the army. Seemed unfair, somehow. Flat feet, indeed!

The war, halfway around the world, seemed to have everyone's thoughts tied up in knots of concern. Young men spent sleepless nights. Is it time to volunteer…? But all their hopes and dreams were centered on their little part of the Corners area in the new state of Oklahoma. Wait for the summons and keep plans on hold? Volunteer and get it over with? Which?

The entire community was surprised when Tray Cullen enlisted. Tray had come with his family from Tennessee when he was barely five years old. That was the year he set eyes on Lily Gray Owl, granddaughter of the old doctor, Miz Gray Owl.

When their eyes met, Tray's and Lily's, they neither saw another person. No one was surprised, three years ago, when they were married.

After three years Tray and Lily were still childless, and it seemed best for Tray to volunteer now. Because of his test score and his education, he went in as a lieutenant and was sent to the hot spot of France. Due to his obvious leadership ability and the desperate need for leaders, he became a captain in three months time.

He was given assignments in an area called "intelligence" which meant he and his fifteen men set out on their own with orders to locate trouble spots, access the depth of a problem and determine the likelihood of success. They were not to engage the enemy unless cornered, and not to take prisoners.

In was on their fourth sortie that they came upon the remnants of an American company totally pinned down. The enemy surrounded the shallow canyon. It would be just a matter of waiting it out, the enemy knew, so there was no reason to lose troops to attack. In time, the pinned-down company would run out of food and ammo. Mere days, certainly. Maybe hours.

This situation did not fit the specifications of his mission, but the seriousness of the loss, and the good likelihood of rescuing them made him decide to undertake the liberation. Joining them on a hidden path, he accessed the difficulties. Added to his own fifteen men, the company now consisted of twenty-seven persons, including their captain who had injured his foot and another with a broken leg. The captain could walk, but not far. The other must be carried.

It seemed to Captain Tray Cullen that someone had to go, alone, for reinforcement to allow them to free themselves. It was also clear to him who that one person it would be.

Leaving his contingent as guards and moving on elbows and belly, he pulled himself through the undergrowth until he could partially stand, then he ran bent over. So, bent at hips and knees, he forged on, the battle raging fiercely around him. When he had gone perhaps three miles, he almost stumbled over a body sprawled under a low bush.

American uniform. Ill-fitting, but American nevertheless. He turned the body over and felt breath. Alive, but limp and obviously unconscious.

Decision time. He was already on a mission and time was a factor. But here was a countryman. Very young. Looked maybe fourteen or fifteen. Only one thing to do.

Kneeling backward in front of the young man, he held to both his wrists and pulled them up to his shoulders, essentially drawing the body over his own back. It was the most efficient way to carry an inert body over a long distance.

Still running on bent knees, he threaded through the brush as long as possible, but finally had to run for a ways in the clearing. Exposed to fire.

Hardly had he left the brush when he heard the whine of a bullet overhead. It was said that one never hears the bullet that wings himself, so he ran on. He had no other avenue. Another whine overhead, then the jarring thud vibrating through his whole body. That would have to be his end, but he did not yet feel pain.

CHAPTER 10

Kneeling to the ground, he leaned forward from shock, his head touching his pounding chest. He waited. Still no pain. He released his hands to get a better hold on the wrist of the body he carried, causing it to shift and roll to the ground. Still felt no pain.

Again turning the body looking for signs of life, he saw the spreading red as the blood seeped away from the wound in the boy's back. A groan and then a relaxed stillness, and what was barely alive was obviously now gone.

Tray looked at the lifeless body with a mix of emotion. The thudding bullet that had sent him to the ground had entered the back of the boy he carried. The boy had born the bullet meant for him, but in the kneeling he had done, it must have seemed to the sniper that he was killed, as there were no more shots.

Hmmm, too late now for thoughts or regrets. The best he could do was to tell a medic where the boy was. He could, however, take his identification for the records. Searching pockets produced several documents…every one of them in a language he could not read. The papers did not match the name on the uniform. A story here, but he had no time to read it. He could only surmise what had happened.

An important part of his instruction came funneling back into his mind. A young (German?) boy in American uniform meant either he was looking for asylum, had nothing else to wear, or was outfitted as a human bomb. And there it was. In the cargo pockets of the trousers were two grenades. Had the kid been sent to the pinned down company with the hope of infiltrating? Certainly his uniform and obvious youth would have given him a temporary welcome.

Dragging the body into the brush, he pulled the grenades from the cargo pockets and moved on.

Thoughts chased themselves in his mind. It was obvious that the boy had been commissioned to destroy. He might have lived if Tray had passed him by, as he had seemed to be only knocked out.

Tray had, however, tried to save him, and in that act had saved his own life. Now the boy was dead, and so young that his life had hardly started. A deep truth was in there somewhere, but Tray was sure that he would never find it. At least not any time soon.

Another three miles and he found help. A small company, well equipped and rested, and they marched surefooted and confident. Well-fed and heavily burdened with ammo, Sgt. Black was bringing them along with a cadence barely loud enough to be heard.

Long ago I loved to dance
Now I'm traveling into France.
Here and everywhere I go
They speak works I do not know.

Sound off. SOUND OFF!
One
Two
Three
Four

One two... THREE FOUR!

A relieved gasp of breath as Tray looked through the bushes and read the name of their leader. Almost afraid to make himself known for fear of being shot by this obvious top-notch squad, he raised his arms and shouted, "AMERICAN HERE! Sgt Johnny Black Bear!"

"COMPANY, HALT! Tray Cullen! What're you doing here?"

With a wide relieved grin. "Sgt. Black, I came for you. Got a mission for you about four miles as the crow flies. We're gonna be crows because the woods are crawlin' alive with trouble."

"Captain Cullen, SIR! Give your orders...."

"Got a couple dozen men pinned down. Two injuries. Can't get out without help. Only one way to get at 'em. We circle, you fan your men to make it look like they are the company trying to climb out of the depression they're holed up in. My men'll help. It'll be dangerous, because you'll be in the line of fire hiding behind bushes. It'll be elbows and belly all the way after the first four miles."

The men filtered through the underbrush at breakneck speed, running with legs bent at the knee. Tray, already tired, had a bit of trouble keeping up but he had to be there to point out the only hiding place. The only path safe enough to go through.

At the edge of the boxed-in area, Sgt. Black, from his place in the lead, stopped dead still and the entire group of men stopped amid step. The sergeant pointed, and Tray followed his gaze.

Three men were crawling on their knees, obviously intent on an end run around the captives. Tray held his finger to his lips and not a man moved a muscle. Extracting the two grenades from inside his shirt, he drew back and threw. One, then the other. On signal from the sergeant, the men had stooped low and hid their faces, but no shrapnel reached that far.

Cover now blown, Captain Cullen again. "Carry on, Sgt. Black. Go on elbows to about three hundred feet ahead."

They reached the lip of the shallow canyon and spread out, sheltering behind any available bush or rock. It did not look good at all. Tremendously outnumbered, and if the enemy just came on, there would be no way to escape. Sgt Black was working out the best positions for ambush, and Capt. Cullen was scanning for a better plan.

A tiny speck with a clattering engine cleared the horizon and plunged through the rising clouds of black smoke. The noise of the small aircraft barely made itself heard above the ground noise, as the stick and canvas machine dipped precariously into, and then shot back up out of the smoke. The small craft whirled out into the distance and came in again, plunging so low that a well-aimed ground gun could have caused serious damage.

On its second circling, dark cartridges tumbled out of the airplane and fell with deadly accuracy along the north edge of the canyon where the enemy had dug in.

Sudden changes inside the canyon. Incoming fire halted. Flames shot out of the north edge, and blasts of debris, dirt, metal objects and scraps of torn vegetation lifted into the smoky air.

"Sergeant, go down and get 'em. Bring 'em up. Tell 'em I sent you. I'll check up here, but I think it's clean."

The captives came out on a run. Boots trampling down the underbrush, rifles at the ready. Two of the sergeant's men were attached to either side of the wounded captain, practically carrying him.

The sergeant's voice rang out. "Company halt! Form three abreast and let's get out of here. Hup, two, three, four...."

The injured captain commented to Tray, "Lucky break, that airplane coming by."

Tray nodded, agreeably. "He was just doin' his job. Same way as you and me and the others."

Captain Tray Cullen had a cot to sleep on that night. It was a rare luxury. He thought, *one more day closer. Lily, my darling, we made it one more day. Be brave. Just be brave and wait for me.*

Mrs. Lily Gray Owl Cullen was exhausted. She crawled into her bed with aching legs and arms. Raymond had said it was a man's work to operate earth moving machinery, but she had retorted that sometimes a woman had to do it. It was not so much that she could have stayed safely in the house and waited, but that the work must be done. And the men were gone.

Canfield Grading and Dirt Works had just about shut down. Seven of the workmen had gone, one of them her husband. Raymond was obliged to hire just about any who applied, and some did not last more than a week. Some of the old men thought they were still young but found out they weren't.

He hired a Swedish girl who hardly had any English, but she was desperate for a job. She had been on the job a week and had begged Raymond to also hire her younger brother. Thirteen years old. Raymond told her to send him in.

Big boy, the brother was, and Raymond put him with his sister for two days training, then he was on his own. Turned out to be a natural with the animals pulling the equipment.

Then Lily Cullen had come to him. He looked at her and asked himself, if he hired her, what would Tray think of him? Lily, however, was persuasive.

"You hired Bertha Swensen and gave her a chance. Let me try."

Raymond considered the matter. At least, Lily was acquainted with the handling of horses, and she was accustomed to being in the elements, the heat, the wind and the cold. He put her with Bertha for two days, and decided to leave her there. He decided he liked it that way. If help was needed, one of them could go for it.

Parting instructions to her were, "If the horses get excited, sing hymns to them. 'In the Sweet Bye and Bye' is a good one."

She nodded. One doesn't argue with the boss. She had enough else on her mind. The child she and Tray had wanted had now decided to come along. She guessed she had been a couple weeks along when he had enlisted, but she did not tell him. She hadn't known yet but would not have told him if she had.

He had to do what he had to do. Her love for him wanted to spare him the worry and concern for her. He must not be concerned about her or the baby, so she did not tell him she was operating heavy machinery. She wrote cheery letters about the neighbors and the weather.

Of course she did not write about the baby. Love makes people do hard things. Very hard things. She wanted more than anything to share the news with him, but once having decided not to, she would not change. She was beginning her eighth month before Raymond realized her condition and made her quit. An Irish girl whose parents had rented Edward Morrison's house, begged for a trial. Working with Bertha, they did well.

Captain Tray Cullen stretched out onto the unaccustomed comfort of the canvas army cot and thought of Lily. *One more day has passed, my darling, so we are one more day closer to being together.*

While he enjoyed the much-needed sleep on the cot that night, Lily gave birth to a noisy little girl. Pugged nose and a wild halo of coal black hair. Ellen, she was named, and was lovingly rocked by her proud aunt Janine, Tray's older sister.

Still Tray was not told, though Janine could hardly restrain herself. The pleasure of telling and the concern for Tray were the responsibility of Lily. Tray would see the little girl when he got home.

Those who stayed and those who left, each had their own story. The two young Kiowa boys from Raymond Canfield's school class were no different.

Johnny Black and Willie Elk each had a different story. The tall, swarthy young men had arches as high as a bowstring, no flat feet with them. They had lungs that would out-run a racehorse, there was no doubt. But the top crust on the pie, as far as the army was concerned, was that these two young men were educated and could score well on the test. The army had no way of knowing that their education was only two months and two terms under a stone ledge by an uncertified teacher. Test results were what mattered.

They were sent to a "training camp" with the knowledge that if they passed tests there, they would be loaned to the "underdog" country of England who needed them so badly. So much to be done to stop the overseas aggressor before he could decide to attack their homeland, America.

Pass a test? What test? Sure they could read and write, but the army needed more. The two young men sneered at the physical tests. They had better contests than those most any Sunday afternoon in a cow pasture. Jumping, running, crawling, and swinging from obstacles was just good fun, and the food? Man, were these people good cooks! And the food trays were loaded!

The cousins had joined at the same time and trained together and were irritated that they would now be separated. They would ship out as soon as possible.

Johnny hardly had time to tell the folks goodbye and get a last kiss from each of the Irish girls, before he was on a ship with nearly a hundred other fellows. Headed for Britain, then…? But where else…? It all seemed to be a big secret.

On the basis of his ability and his test scores, Johnny was assigned the rank of Corporal, which might or might not be changed later. Meant nothing to him, really. Just doing what anyone else would do when orders were thrust into his face.

The fight was heating up in northern France. The country had no military strength to fight against the enemy from the north and were crumbling before the advancing army. The number crunchers in Britain stirred through the mix of new recruits looking for leaders and naturally centered on Johnny Black Bear, now being called Johnny Black. He was still on the ship at the time.

Before he passed the Channel Islands and entered the mouth of the Thames River, he became a sergeant. Promoted without his knowledge. Just needed a short orientation class. Didn't need target practice. He had scored sharpshooter with his gun and every other category that involved a weapon. They didn't test him on bow and arrow but could have.

He and his assigned crew boarded the small boat and crossed the bouncy channel water to France. A week of orientation and map reading and they were assigned. Simple assignment. Somehow figure out how to stop the invaders. Seemed easy to understand. Officers were scarce and thinly placed. Just get on out there and fight. Do what you have to do. So he did.

He and his men had hardly gotten their breath when they were marching, running and crawling northward. Johnny had always been a confident fellow dating back to when he stood in the center of the seesaw and bounced the board with Pat and Bridie on either end. Making them squeal and threaten him. Wonderful days!

Looking at his map, he took his bearings and headed out. Back in the training camp they had done a thing they said was calling "cadence" and it made the marches less boring. Leading the way, he called out loud enough for the rear of the platoon to hear:

NOW they tell you where to GO!

NOW they call you G. I. JOE.
NOW they tell you what to THINK,
NEXT they'll tell you when to BLINK.

Sound Off! SOUND OFF!
One-
-Two-
-Three-
-Four-

One Two... THREE FOUR!

Each shouted line was repeated by the men. It helped to keep their attention and they must listen closely as they never knew for sure what that tall fellow ahead of them was going to say.

MARCHing on with blistered FEET!
DAYS ago you got to EAT.
EIGHTY pounds upon your BACK
ONE foot, two foot... Muddy TRACK!

Sound off! Etc.

Sometimes the chow wagon caught up with them, and sometimes they had to just think about food. The few pieces of hard candy provided for an emergency did not last long. Their sergeant had no mercy. They were all here because they had agreed to come here, and they would do what they were told to do.

When one of the men stepped on something that blew up, the sergeant helped carry the stretcher until they got help. Shortage of ammo was a problem. There was a limit to what could be carried, and there were times they moved on with no weapon except their strong hands and stubborn minds. Sarge would permit nothing else. But on this occasion, they were armed.

It was on such a sortie that they had been commandeered by Captain Tray Cullen for a rescue mission. Successful.

Johnny's cousin, Willie Running Elk, was spotted by those in charge during training camp when his paper target was examined after target practice. Six shots in the center of the bullseye except for the one that was a half an inch off. His folder was tagged, and he was watched closely and retested. His target record was not a fluke or a one-time thing.

Not only that...he had an education. That part was a rarity with the men brought in from the plains. No schools available out there, and education did not yet have the same value as survival. So many strong fighters among them, but most had to be taught emergency reading ability. Might find themselves alone sometime and need it. But this fellow, Private Elk, he had that well covered.

When he was brought in for interview, he was asked. "Do you have a fear of heights?"

"You mean like the top of a tree?...Sir?" He had trouble remembering that this fellow had to keep being reminded of who he was. You'd think by now he would know he was "Sir."

"No, not a tree. More like on riding a kite. Would that scare you?"

"It'd depend on who it was that had a'holt'a the string...sir."

The interviewer repressed a smile. "What if the person with the string was a big strong fellow like you?"

With a toss of his head, he dismissed the problem. "Nah, I wouldn't be scared then...sir."

A few more questions and the folder took on another identification mark. This and that happened to him until he found himself in Britain with a two-grade promotion. Earning all kinds of money! Grandad Gray Eagle would have been impressed.

Willie's orders said he was a tail gunner? Bomb dropper? Huh! Well, if he was going to shoot, or drop, then someone else had to fly the "kite." He looked the plane over from end to end. Dinky little kite it was. Looked like something a schoolboy would put together on a rainy Sunday afternoon. But here came the fellow who would be handling the machine. The one holding the string, so to speak.

Willie took a look, smiled a friendly smile, and offered his hand, speaking one word. "Kiowa."

His smile was met by a face that could have been a mirror image of his own. The offered hand clasped his in a hearty shake, and the voice responded with one word. "Wichita."

Willie countered with, "Oklahoma Territory?"

"Yep. Name's Larry Raincrow, or that was as close as the interpreter could get to whatever it was my grandmother named me."

Nod of recognition. "Had a bit of the same trouble, only my grandmother rescued me. Call me Willie Elk. I leave out the 'running.' You pretty good at drivin' these kites?"

Wide smile. "Have been so far. Been up a couple'a dozen times already. Been countin' on you to get here and shoot down the interferences."

Returning nod. "Shouldn't take a couple'a Territory boys very long to wind this thing up, huh?"

A few practice runs and the new team aimed the tiny machine out over the white cliffs of Dover, nosing the propeller toward France and their crumbling allied forces.

Nights were best and safest from gunfire, but blackouts hid targets unless the aircraft skinned down to the rooftops, but then the ground forces and their guns could get at them. No good answer. They were pretty much on their own up there. A few good daylight runs. Medium success.

The pilot could not see in every direction and depended on the additional eyesight of the tail gunner. Willie was quick with the help.

"Line it up again, Larry. I'm thinkin' I see somethin' goin on down there. Try to come in straight southeast'a the tower."

The aircraft dipped and circled. The pilot commented, "Got it! Less'n one of the Kaiser's birds heads me off."

So tiny in the sky, like a bumble bee in a garden, the aircraft circled and lined up.

Instructions from the rear of the plane. "Hold it there!" A row of six explosions shot up from the ground.

"You okay back there?"

"Yep. Next target."

"Can't. We're spillin' fuel."

A pause, then a shout. "MOVE OUT! Eight o'clock behind you!"

The airplane rocked with the force of the attack, a pinging rattle sounded against the propeller and the plane began to wobble.

"Wing's on fire! Circle around and duck down so's I can get 'im!"

Eyes darted and muscles strained as Larry sought to control the plane, but there was sense in Willie's command. If they were going down, at least take someone else along. Minutes later they were headed back to base. Lopsided plane looping along like a meadowlark catching grasshoppers.

Summing up the success of the aerial attack, "Best thing was, they're fuel leak was faster'n ours!"

The last of the fuel was gone a quarter a mile from the base, but they managed to glide in over the fence. A few feet from the ground, both airmen bailed, rolling over and over with shoulders tucked in and drawn together as they had been trained. They heard the crunch of the landing apparatus, but that didn't matter as the burning wing had caught the fumes of the ruptured fuel tank and exploded into sparks, while flames and strips of twisted braces, screws and sticks filled the skies and fell around them like rain.

"You okay?"

"Made it! Let's go find some chow and check on gettin' another plane."

Assessments among the desks of the officers at the base. "Took a look at the record of team Raincrow and Elk. Racking up an impressive total of successes. Took out a railroad shipping center, tracks blown to bits. Left the terminal smoking. Took down another aircraft on the way home and came in with a wing on fire and leaking fuel. Young men think they'll live forever! Wish we could clone those two."

Nodding response. "And another thing. I am intrigued at the names of the volunteers from the colonies. McGee, McConnell and McLaughlin from Scotland…Owen and Lewyllyn from Wales. Those Welshmen always made good soldiers. Even the Irish O'Day, O'Grady and O'Neill. It's a good chance their granddaddies fought against us in their Revolutionary War, and now they're here, helping us. Interesting thought, anyway."

Agreeing nods. "Yes, but they sure are hard on airplanes."

Retort. "Wouldn't be, if the planes were any good. They're putting them little contraptions together practically overnight. Can you imagine going up in one of those things?"

Grateful sigh. "Glad I don't have to, but doubly glad someone else will. The colonies are having good luck with volunteering. Though, of course, they'd have to come into the war soon anyway."

And they did, a little over a year later.

Cleaned up and fed, Cousin Sergeant Johnny Black and his men headed out on wheels. A trio of drivers were weaving their way along rutted and blown-up roads heading out to be reinforcement for a spearhead that had marched past their supplies and were falling back. He had lost only two men so far, and he was determined that would be all.

This time he was going to bring back everyone they had given him. There had been a reason that the training camp drill sergeants had made them walk on their elbows and toes, head down and pulling themselves along like so many snakes. A head raised could be a head blown off.

HERE'S a thing that you should KNOW
KEEP your head ducked way down LOW
BULLets whizzing over HEAD
TRY to make you very … UNHAPPY!

Sound Off! …..SOUND OFF!
One-
-Two-
And so on….

Amazing that he had come across Tray Cullen, a hometown boy. Captain Cullen promptly took over his squad on the special rescue.

As it happened, cousin Willie was overhead but the sound of the little plane and the rockets were all alike. The noise of the engine sounded no louder to Johnny's men than the tin lizzies on State Highway headed for Shady Ridge. The two flyers, Raincrow and Elk, had spent their free time comparing notes about their homes. And female friends.

"Which'a them Irish girls you got your eyes set on?"

"Don't know. We're thinkin' the girls'll have that figured out by the time we get back."

Incredible reply. "You ain't carin' which you get?"

"Nope. And if you saw those girls, you wouldn't care, neither. I'd feel lucky with either one, and I'd rather have the one that wants me the most."

"They got any sisters…or anyone?"

"Tell you what. We get this war won, you come on up north to Kiowa country, and I'll show you around." It was said as a joke, but he would have no way of knowing that Larry would find Linda Black Bird from Westridge, all on his own.

Reply from Larry. "What'd ya think your cousin is doin' right now?"

"Wouldn't know. Likely crawling around in the mud on his elbows, hopin' us buzzin' around up here don't attract the Kaiser's birds."

As facts would have it, Johnny and his men were directly below them, sprawled out in the mud and pulling themselves along on their elbows. They were too close to their targets for Sarge to yell out their cadence songs, but he felt they needed to brace up for the battle just ahead. In a stage whisper, he said:

ROCKETS burst and sparks fly HIGH!
LOOK just like a starry SKY.
JUST as sure as you are BORN,
BULLETS sound like poppin' CORN.

Sound off. SOUND OFF!
One-
-Two-
-Three-
-Four-

One, two... THREE, FOUR!

He was relieved to hear the hoarse whispers behind him, repeating his words. *Great fellows. THIS TIME THEY'LL ALL MAKE IT HOME!* He was determined.

Squirming ahead and gaining ground inch by inch, they could see the marks of the retreat of the men before them. Bad news. The enemy would be encouraged and ready. Plane overhead, wonder whose it is?

From within the plane Willie had looked down. "Hey, Fly Boy! Dip down right here. Someone's in trouble and I need to see who it is."

The tiny aircraft lowered itself within range of the ground rockets. Larry Raincrow warned, "Look fast! I'm goin' back up."

"Hey, circle around! Enemy comin' up from the north, out numberin' us ten to one! Got tanks and guns pointed up."

The aircraft eased into position for the rescue, and the bombs fell on the enemy camp, who saw them coming but could do nothing about it.

"Circle again! We gotta take out their guns"

One more circle and more explosions. "Take off, Larry. Our fellows too close to risk another run."

The bee sized plane lifted into the sky and became a speck, but Sarge Johnny raised off his elbows and yelled, "Don't know who you are, but thanks!" A pause, then, "MEN! Stand up and charge! We're goin' in."

Sergeant Black got the credit even though he insisted it was the friendly plane that tipped the scales. Didn't matter. Sarge was due a battlefield promotion to captain and he got it. Then he was ordered to fall back for a rest. Good. His men could use it.

And who could ever know that in about fifty years a couple of old men in gray hair might compare battle experiences and come up with the same memory of this encounter? And how many times has a similar occurrence happened in a war?

It was on a stormy day with heavy cloud banks and rain that the fragile craft again rose up from the landing field. Sometimes bad weather was good and seemed worth the risk. A patch of new earthworks had been spotted, and heavy troop movement tried to fill them in under the cover of rain. Enemy on the move!

Pilot Raincrow nosed the aircraft low for a look-see and there were no gun emplacements yet. He raised the nose, circled around and came in on a swoop, laying a carpet of ammo across the length of the breastwork. It was the direct hit they had planned. Gunner Elk could practically hit the rivets on their helmets at this height, but there were risks.

One quick acting soldier raised his gun and fired, the bullet amazingly striking against a metal brace in the plane's undercarriage. A wobble and a dip, quickly recovered by Raincrow skill, but the damage was done.

The object, now, would be to totally expend their ammo and fuel, as the crash landing at the base would be no better by having explosives aboard. Describing a wide circle, they found plenty of places to unload, but because of the rain they must fly dangerously low. Breathtaking dips and the tops of trees so close, Willie could even tell what kind of trees they were, and as the contents of the fuel tank lowered, they wheeled around and headed home.

In the air they were safe, but the trick would be landing and living to tell it.

Circling twice, Flyer Raincrow positioned himself where he would not endanger anyone on the ground, and he glided as low as he could manage and still clear the river to their north. He had no way of seeing all the damage to his aircraft, but he knew one wheel was gone. Doubled under by that single lucky shot.

At touchdown, the aircraft tipped, dragged a wing…totally destroying it as it was scraped across the asphalt field. As the last of the wing crumbled, he yelled, "Jump now!" Willie jumped while the machine was scooting along at a good twenty miles an hour. Curl up, shoulders in, drop and roll. He only sprained an ankle and skinned a shoulder.

Larry had no place to jump. Pulling himself through the window just as the plane rolled onto its side, he found himself being flung to the ground and part of the twisted undercarriage passed over his legs. Medics were prepared for them and on hand, as they always were, and had the pilot pulled away by his arms and on stretcher between their running feet.

By the time the day was over, Pilot Larry Raincrow had pins and screws in his right foot, and a stump on the left. His natural foot having been left spread over the landing field.

A few days later, Gunner Willie Elk fought tears as he saw his pilot shoved aboard the vehicle that would take him to the ship and back home. His parting advice had been, "When you get up and around, Ace, I want you to get yourself up to Argyle and go five miles south. Ask for Raymond Canfield and he'll take care of introducing you around. One thing though, if you value our friendship, and maybe even your life, you LEAVE THOSE IRISH GIRLS ALONE! You go find your own!"

Larry found breath to ask, "How will I know which they are?"

"Easy. They're the prettiest."

"Thanks, buddy."

It was almost three months later that Larry learned to manage the crutches the medics furnished him and had been promised more work would be done and maybe an artificial foot. That would be later.

He could still ride a horse, however, and in due course he found himself in front of Canfield Grading and Dirtwork. He saw the Irish girls, and he saw the McLaughlin sisters. The Cookie Jar appeared to be a haven in the desert.

It was a week later that he crutched himself across the graded road and opened the Cookie Jar door. What a crowd!

Linda Black Bird was there. She often came, just for a change of scenery from her family and others in Westridge. Today had been exceptionally bad. A month ago one of the young men she had dated was replaced by a folded flag and his medals…both sent to his family. Nothing but tears and sympathy for her. Too much sympathy, and she was weary of it. She was weary to death of crying.

Then, two days ago, it happened again. Another white cross in France and a folded flag received in Westridge. More tears and sympathy, and deep depression. Was nothing to be the same anymore? And who was next? Would there be any men left?

By riding over to Corners, she saw others her age. They were sympathetic but they had their own lives. A very good thing. She was tired of useless attention. She had to find a way to create a life of her own.

The Cookie Jar was crowded today. When one of the miniature ice cream tables became available, she grabbed it. It was set up for two, but there was, painfully, only one of Linda Black Bird and she deserved it as much as anyone else. It was not her fault that she was alone and she didn't want anyone to sit with her. She was sick of losing.

She wanted to sit alone with her whirling thoughts and concentrate on staying dry-eyed for a change. She wanted to erase the sight of those folded flags. What were they worth, anyway, when they replaced the laughing eyes, smiling face and strong shoulders and arms?

She pulled the empty chair from across the table as close as possible to the table and planted her feet on the wire braces. She was determined to humor her anger and depression one more day, then she would make plans. Far away. Maybe Oklahoma City. Somewhere far, far away.

Larry Raincrow edged himself into the full room, preparing to stand aside, out of the way, until there was space to sit. He would like to be unnoticed, but crutches were hard to hide. Bad timing, he guessed. He cast his eyes around the room. Small table. One person. Girl. Head bent and chin in hand. Untouched cup of something on the table before her.

Shiny black hair…cut in fashionable shortness and fanning against her cheek like the wing of a black bird. Arms bare up to the elbow, skin the color of ripe wheat, silver bracelet slipping down from her wrist onto her forearm. Bright stones in the bracelet. Turquoise. No hat…no bonnet. Just the glossy blackness smoothly shaping her head.

A shiver passed over his neck and down his arms, all the way to his strong hands as they held to the crutches. He watched as the girl lifted the mug of "whatever" and raised it to her lips for a sip. The light from the window reflected on the shiny path of a tear as it had made its way down her cheek. Then another tear.

Larry knew tears. Maneuvering his crutches, he moved across the room, standing behind the empty chair. Seeing someone close, the girl looked up and let her eyes travel down the length of the crutches. The tears shone brighter and filled her dark, dark eyes. Pushing back her drink, she buried her head in her arms and sobbed. Deep down, shoulder-heaving sobs.

Larry knew sobs. Pulling back the empty chair, he settled himself into it, leaning the crutches against his lap. Both hands extended and lightly grasped onto the folded arms before him. It took a couple of minutes for her to regain the control that allowed her to raise her face. She stared ahead.

There he sat, weathered skin, wide smile and sympathetic eyes.

Kristie McLaughlin had been watching…as she had been about to find the soldier (he obviously was) a seat and saw that he had found one. A better one than she could have furnished.

Gwinnie McLaughlin brought two fresh cups of coffee, picked up the cold one, and slipped away.

Linda Black Bird focused her red eyes. No folded flag. No white cross in France. Who cared about an absent foot? Who cared about a pinned-together ankle? He was here. Handsome and smiling. His hands held warmly against her elbows. It was as though two disabled ships tethered themselves tightly and held together to try to make it to port.

Before the day was over, they knew they would be together. Only a matter of time, and there should be as little time as possible until that happened.

Willie Elk was sent home for a leave, simply because he had gone through more than enough to cause a mental break up. And those in charge had seen their share of break ups. Strong men, suddenly dissolved into jelly. This one was too valuable to lose, so send him home a while. Yes, send him home for a rest, and get to use him again, later.

If he had made it only a few days earlier, he would have been able to attend the wedding of retired Pilot Raincrow and Miss Linda Black Bird. They would live in Westridge and she would complete the education she desired, having had only sporadic attendance and what she could pry out of her younger brother who was permitted to go to Miss Francine's school full time. Miss Francine (or someone, maybe Miss Eve Adams) would let her help, and learn, as it had happened for the Dutch girl, Margie Van Pelt. Education. Better late than not at all.

Westridge needed a school and Linda could take care of that. Miss Francine had done it, and so could she. This beautiful man who actually made it home and showed up at her table would find something to do. Many things could be done with one foot gone. Just be grateful that it was only his foot that was left in France.

What Larry Raincrow did was acquire a ream of paper and a handful of sharpened pencils. That airplane undercarriage had serious flaws, and they were unnecessary. It was dangerous and also maiming. Drawings and his knowledge of flying teamed up, and most of the ream of paper was trashed with drawing after drawing. Larry was determined, however. Nothing but success was acceptable.

Years later, if one was to examine the undercarriage of the current small fighter aircraft (though, why should they?) but if they did, they might see the RC imprinted into the metal of the wheel struts. The nation of Britain was glad to have help from the colonies and were extremely happy to pay a retired airman for the knowledge that would save not only many of their aircraft, but their pilots, as well.

With the rest of the paper, he set about again. Those tin lizzies could use a few improvements in design. Who knows?

Before that was done, however, Larry spent his time (weather permitting) on the horse-drawn grader. Raymond Canfield had a contract from the state to survey, cut through the native vegetation and build up a network of roads in his county, roads that would get needed cotton and wool to the freight lines.

Just now the roads were to be dirt, but could gravel roads be far away? Maneuvering the horses and the equipment gave Larry time to think.

Very soon the enlistees would be back and take over their jobs. It seemed that the thing in Germany had come to a head and something had been done.

Fighting would stop, but what was that thing called an "armistice"? In a contest and in a war, one side won and the other side lost, but what was that thing in the middle called an armistice?

The graybeards scratched their heads and stroked their whiskers. It was a thing to struggle their minds around, and they were having no luck. Their grandfathers had fought wars in the old country, and someone always lost. It was like sending boxers to their corners and saying, "Thanks a lot, fellows. You can shower and go home now."

They'd yell, "Hey, wait! One of us gotta come out on top!"

Then the boxers would go out the door, face each other in the street and go at it again…with no referee. Their young country had come through two bad skirmishes, and something had to come out settled. Didn't it…?

England got its hand slapped, and America decided to team up in a civil war and make room for all of its citizens.

But no armistice, whatever that was?

EPILOGUE

(Researched and written by historian
Merytaten Franchesca Angelique Evangeline Cullen Carpenter)

Sure enough, there was the cease-fire called an armistice. The only good thing was that their men would be coming home. The older ones had been released first.

Sergeant Johnny Black had been sent home for a rest leave but had returned in 30 days. He was now retained in England on the safe side of the White Cliffs of Dover and set to training newly promoted sergeants.

Good choice. Johnny Black knew, as few others knew, that the sergeants were the fulcrums of the war…much like the seesaw when he had stood in the center and tipped Pattie or Birdie whichever way he wanted them to go.

"Sergeants," he always began with a new group. "You've been around a while and are acquainted with the wheels that run the army. You have experience at being the tread of the wheel, that part that comes in hard contact with the ground.

"You were promoted to being a spoke and you learned how to transfer power from above to those below. But now it's different. Every one of you has become the hub of a wheel, and you will not only be making sure that orders are carried out, but you will be giving them.

"You will know, as no other will know, that it is the sergeants who keep the military machinery moving. You will find yourself where there is no one but you to make decisions. Officers may come and go but you are with your men forever. Difficult decisions will be yours. Some of your decisions will give you nightmares."

And he ended with these words. "Always remember, any time you must give a decision, it will be a fact that, of those present, you were the most able person who was available and would make the wisest choice among the options."

Knowing that even the simplest foot soldier needed focus, he taught the men leaders the rhymes that he had found helpful. Just a minor changing of the words.

He studied the bright, young faces before him, and he felt decades older. He'd learned the best trick for pulling the men together was the cadence.

NO time left for fear or DREAD
SOLdiers go where they are LED.
To EVERY fresh-faced country LAD,
YOU have just become their DAD.

Sound off! SOUND OFF!

SOUND OFF!

One
Two
Three
Four

One Two, THREE FOUR!

And he thought up another one.

LEARN to shout your words in RHYMN
WHEN you're marching double TIME.
ONE foot, two foot, three foot, HOP
KEEP 'em marching till they DROP!

Sound off! SOUND OFF!

SOUND OFF!

One
Two
Three
Four

One Two THREE FOUR!

Edward Morrison was one of the last to return. It seemed that the same skills needed to build up a functional army, were needed to break it down. He was now a major, but how little that meant when his dreams always centered themselves in the quarter section of prairie soil and beautiful lady who spent her time down on the corner of Canfield Road and State Highway.

Before they left the Corners, Phillip Armstrong and Edward had become close enough to know their dreams would more quickly realized if they teamed up, and Phillip had used his accumulated savings to buy half of the tract. Together they decided to press on with Edward's plan, using the tiny house of his uncle's as a place of business and a storage area for jointly own equipment

Phillip came home first. Moving into the current house, he used his muster-out pay to begin his own house. He also made sure that the Cookie Jar privy did not again become overbalanced and frighten Gwinnie. He built an arbor in the spacious yard of the Cookie Jar. It was very popular with older ladies…to sit in the shade and chat over tea.

Hands still bothered him…scar tissue and all, but what did that matter when things had to be done with hands. His leg still ached where the compound fracture had happened. Especially in damp weather the splintered fragments of bone the doctors had wired together instead of amputating what looked as though it would be useless, that caused pain. Phillip found a use for the leg and was grateful for the surgeon's skill and their courage. Ignore the pain.

Both of these concerns were usually a minor annoyance compared to the dreams/nightmares. Fire. Screams. Bullets whining and rockets exploding. Leap from the van and gather up whatever scrap of flesh that seemed alive and wore the correct uniform.

Voice of Medic Bertrand screaming orders. Trying to dig in his boot heels to keep from being sucked into the river as he worked with the flagman to rescue a…. And then the dream always stopped.

Suddenly awake, he relived the horror of the return trip, fractured leg and burned hands. Bertrand would not let him stop. Dying again at every turn, and the firm voice came through the window, because she was riding the rickety and torn running board. "ARMSTRONG! Snap to! No one can do this but you. Remember, six people. DRIVE! YOU CAN MAKE IT!"

Sure, he remembered it all. But what happened at the edge of the water? The injured man was pulled free, and he had learned the limey flagman had worked beside him with a shrapnel fragment in his own side.

It was like a mental sandwich with no filling. He strained to remember. Rockets. Huge tree above them on fire. Crackling of flames and a rain of falling twigs glowing like shooting stars.

Digging heels in the mud. Smell of sulfur and smoke…and death. What came next? It had recently become so important that it affected his daytime activities. He just had to know.

He should have asked Bertrand. Too late to find her. Hoped she was now carrying her boyfriend's name, the one who had fought with the American "devils."

As soon as Philip had a roof, he moved from the equipment house to his own. Bed on the sawhorses. Pillow and quilt that had belonged to "Aunt Sybil." Smell of new wood and resin. And dreams.

Digging heels in the mud. Crackling fire overhead. Screech of tearing splinters and a rain of fiery sticks. Aw, this was new! In previous nightmares he hadn't remembered those sticks.

DIG HEELS DEEPER! A pillar of fire was descending, end over end, and seemed the size of the stove pipes to the pot bellies back at the Corners. FEET STEADY!

Hands leave the injured body in the uniform and lift overhead. He watched them…mentally detached. Fiery pillar in front of his eyes falling onto the injured man. And the hands reach into the flames to the solid wood, lifting and heaving the massive ember up and over his own head.

HEELS SLIPPING IN THE MUD! Pain! Leg on fire for certain. Sensing it was his time to go, he gave over to the pain and felt himself slipping away. Into the water. What did it matter, anyway? Water would put out the fire. Along with the life.

Now back in the safety of the corners, he sat bolt upright on the sawhorse bed. So that's what had happened! In the spot of moonlight through his glass-less windows he studied his hands. Stretching his fingers carefully to keep the scar tissue from shrinking his palms. Slowly…as the therapist had instructed.

That's what happened. He could now see the whole picture except the part where he slipped away into the water. The enemy rocket had dislodged a burning limb, and his own reflex had reached forward and upward, tossing the blazing log over his head and away from the man they were saving. It had landed on the calf of his bent leg. Heavy. Two splintered breaks below his knee.

Limey flagman with a fragment in his side had leaped over the victim and pulled him up from the water. He remembered part of that. It must have been the medic who had finally rescued the original victim. Leastwise, he had been told that the soldier had "made it."

He suddenly knew why Bertrand had not chosen to fill him in. It had lost its importance among the many rescues she had attended. He had "pulled through" and that was the goal. All that was needed was to, somehow, live through every horrible incident.

Later, he had had a better van. He had a new partner, and he drove with bandaged hands, but he had a record of getting the ambulance there and back so he was pressed, again, into service. Fractured leg in a brace from heel to knee.

And there was the time he was speeding down a muddy track trying to follow a dirt smeared hand-drawn map. They were NEEDED BAD!

Immediately in front of him was a civilian huddled by the road, and apparently not looking or hearing him. Young woman with a baby and a toddler by the hand. Bowed protectively over the child.

Phillip screeched his good brakes, flinging his medic against the windshield. Succeeded in missing the woman.

Then behind him a whine, a flash of fire exploding into multiple smaller fires. A roar and a scream of metal with billows of fire-tinged rolling smoke. Dirt, sticks, garments and glowing pieces of metal. A ping and a crack as the windshield of his good van suffered a split from east to west, with a web of cracks north and south. Glass splinters showered around the two men.

Smoke cleared, and through the glass-less windshield, they saw a shawl drift down into the road ahead of them. Following it was a child's shoe, turning over and over in what seemed to be slow motion.

The two men looked at each other, tossed the larger splinters of glass through the window and the medic calmly pinched a needle-shaped splinter with thumb and finger and drew it from his wrist. Blood erupted, but he staunched it with a firm thumb.

Philip drew in a breath, restarted his van, edged around the hole in the muddy road and proceeded. Medic with the map advised, "Watch for a big tree, it looks like…and then take a sharp turn left."

Philip answered, "Roger." He tried to remove from his mind the sight of the falling shoe, but so far he had not been successful. Somehow the ambulance with no windshield made it back.

Lying back on the sawhorse bed, he sighed his eyes shut. Tomorrow was another day. At least, now he knew. He'd sure like to thank that limey flagman.

Master Sergeant Johnny Black had begun to get letters from Bridie, with just a note from Pattie and sometimes one from the Cookie Jar girls.

He'd like to see if his cousin Willie was getting letters from Pattie, but he wasn't sure where he was. Sure to be somewhere overhead, though, taking advantage of the marksman skill he had earned from shooting squirrels for stew.

He grinned as he remembered their agreement. Let the girls decide. No use for the fellows to pretend that they had any influence over a determined Irish girl. He had stood on the fulcrum and bounced them both equally. If he and Will could just pull this off.... In the meantime he had work to do.

With determination he called his new cadence and trained new sergeants. Told them what they were facing and how to save their lives. As often as possible.

Willie's new pilot was a limey. A lot different from Larry Raincrow, but he had a good reason to be different. He hated. He hated with a passion. Most of all, he hated the Kaiser's bird that had invaded the White Cliffs of his homeland and had dropped a fiery missal into his parents' house. They'd had to move in with his brother who "flew" a desk in London and was just as angry as he was. Not only that, his girlfriend was driving the top brass around.

She had wanted to try to come to France, and he had demanded that if she had any love for him, she would stay where she was. Just a little bit safer, he thought. He wasn't sure she'd do it but the "brass" usually had the safer places to be. So would she. She was a hot-tempered Irish girl and was just about as mad as he was. This war had not been in her plans.

It hadn't actually been in Willie's plans, either. It had just been something that he had to do in order to live with himself during the rest of his life.

Maybe the limey wasn't as much fun as Raincrow, but he knew what he was doing, and when Willie wanted to come in close, they got CLOSE. More than once, by the time the pilot had decided to roll away, the aircraft actually turned upside for an instant and just missed the ground fire. Skillful hand on the stick. He seemed to have a second sense about danger.

The tail gunner smiled and mentally patted the bulge in his jacket pocket. Letters from Pattie O'Day. Short notes from Bridie. Sometimes one from America Forrester, when she could tear herself away from her horses. Pardon, it wasn't "Forrester" now. It was

Canfield. Good for her. Old Raymond must have been a challenge, but if she could manage those Clydesdales, she could manage him.

Now that it seemed the girls had decided, it was mainly Pattie who occupied his dreams.

The battle raged on.

Captain Trayler Cullen looked soberly at the map. He knew exactly where that spot was. Terribly and dangerously close to enemy headquarters, but, of course, that was where the best intelligence was to be found.

He was permitted to select his own crew. Six men. If he couldn't do it with six, then twelve couldn't be successful either. Peters, Scroggins, Butler, Peabody, Longstreet and Mobley. Four Americans and two limeys. Peabody and Longstreet were both sharp and able. Being limeys should not be held against them.

The vehicle took them as far as it could…within two miles. Heavily loaded with ammo and rations, they proceeded on foot, unheard and unseen, to within spitting distance of the target, if the wind was right.

A furrow of old earthworks led past the target building. That would be a plus. Huge, huge liveoak tree with low spreading branches that would bring darkness on early. Also a plus.

Send Butler up the tree to attach the restraining strap for the lookout man. Sleep could attack the most well-meaning lookout and he couldn't afford having one doze off and fall out of the tree. Hook around a large limb and attached to a belt. Always think of safety, first.

Orders from the captain. "Men, find a place in the earthworks and sleep. I take the first watch. This looks like a thoroughfare beneath the tree and there's a good sight of the building. Sentries and all.

"We go in just before dawn unless you hear the code word, 'boxer.' If you hear the code word, we attack immediately. Three on the north, three on the south. Close in fast and stay below the windows. Have your fire power in hand while you sleep. Scroggins will be the next watch. Dismissed."

Quietly as a dropped feather, the men disappeared as though they had sunk within the ground. The captain tossed a leg over the lowest limb and swung up, just as quietly. On the fourth limb up, he seated himself by the strap and hooked his belt to the limb.

Northern France was just an incredibly beautiful land. Through the branches he saw the sun casting its last rays. Quiet. So unlike the noise and fire of the battle. He sighed and spoke to Lily as he did so often. *Lily, my love, one more night closer. Remember that. One more night closer.* He could almost smell her fragrance in the breeze that ruffled the leaves. Lily. His Lily. He was so fortunate.

Dusk fell onto the French landscape, and darkness settled into the dense leaves of the liveoak. He sat on a limb and leaned comfortably against the trunk.

Then the soft flapping of wings as a night bird (owl?) fluttered in among the limbs and startled at the strange presence in his tree. A squawk and a screech split the decibels of the whispering leaves.

On the thoroughfare below the tree a group of men in uniform passed by, chatting amiably within themselves. One of them looked up at the bird squawk and aimed his weapon. Four shots in rapid succession, and the bird left the tree with a flutter of loose feathers and a lifeless body.

The group of men made out to proceed on their way, just as the Captain Cullen felt a streak of fire from his right wrist to his elbow. In reflex, his left hand reached for his right elbow and felt the gaping hole of his jacket and the dampness of the blood.

Decision time. Fact one…he didn't know how seriously he was hit. Fact two…he was seriously right-handed and it was his right that was injured. Fact three…considering the number of men passing below him, there wouldn't be many left in the building. Maybe just the sentries. Fact four…this could be the time.

Some of the men were looking up and would certainly see any movement. He quickly ducked behind the tree trunk and yelled, "boxer."

As though they were on springs from a jack-in-the-box, six men appeared and shots whizzed past the liveoak. Tray was working his way down, staying behind the trunk and pressing his mind for the next action. On the ground, he stripped off his belt, winding it as best he could around and around his forearm.

Ignore the fire, he demanded of himself, "It's no worse than a skinned arm sliding down a hay pile." The firing had stopped and he stepped around the tree. His six men were standing.

"All here, Captain."

"Move out as planned. Peabody, grenade the top. Butler take the back."

With no other orders or response, his men became shadows among the other shadows. Captain Cullen moved into position at the front. Sentry on a limb, just a dark lump among dark limbs. Another sentry on the ground by the door.

Tray, your arm does not hurt. Take aim. Two shots should do it. Lifting his right arm with the help of his left, he aimed into the tree. As the shot went off, he thought he had shot his own arm, so great was the pain. And with the second shot, he was absolutely certain he had. Flaming pain had exploded in a hundred directions.

No matter. Don't think on it! There were NO lightening streaks of fire within his sleeve. NONE at all! It had to be controlled by strength of mind. No pain.

Another shot at the door lock. Quicker than using a knob. Door swung open. Two rapid shots from where Mobley should be. How could he see in this darkness...then Tray could see. Just before he stumbled over the body on the floor. The last sentry.

Instructions whizzed through the pain and into his brain. Always work as though you have only thirty seconds to do the job. Butler had scanned his area and set the fires. Longstreet and Peters were searching through desks and shelves. Anything loose was stuffed into their jackets.

Tray aimed his weapon at the safe and gathered its contents before the smoke cleared. Drawing acrid sulfur into his lungs.

"MOVE OUT!"

Silent as a sigh, the building became empty and the flames shot toward the ceiling. Immediately, the answering rocket fire came and bullets rained in on all sides. Behind them. *Thank you, Lord, for the liveoaks and their thick trunks and dense limbs.*

They were more than a mile away when he called a halt, again in a grove of the beautiful liveoaks of northern France. "Count off."

A reassuring "One."

"Two."

"Three."

"Four."

"Five."

"Six."

"Injuries?"

From Butler. "Bullet graze. Lost my hat." A chuckle followed.

"Good. Think I might need a little help with my arm. Just to hold till daylight."

Scroggins' eyes widened as he saw the belt-wrapped arm. With eyes accustomed to the dark, and with the faint light of the moon, he gently unwrapped the belt. Sleeve soggy and heavy. Gaping hole in the elbow.

Tray felt the knot forming in his throat. He held it there. Perhaps the knot would halt the scream that would not take away the fire in his arms but might draw the enemy rockets.

"Captain, you got a sleeve full'a blood. Can you keep standin'? I'll put the belt on straighter."

Tray did not answer. That would have removed the lump in his throat and for certain released a scream. Scroggins efficiently re-wrapped the sodden sleeve against whatever condition was under it. Apparently there was no break, though he was certainly no medic.

When he could speak, the captain ordered, "Divide up the papers and hope we get enough." No one needed to ask why the loot should be divided. There was a good chance not all of the seven would make it to the meeting place.

Another mile. Conceal position until more light. Silently seated in dense shrubbery of what was once someone's home, they waited.

Flames crawled up his arm and the captain forced his mind to remain sharp. He would live. He looked up into the starry sky. *One day closer, Lily. Wait and watch.*

Daylight gave direction and they moved on. Climbed gratefully aboard the waiting van. The fire had now reached his shoulder and he dreaded to see the damage that was sure to be inside his sleeve.

A bed. Sleeve stripped away. A magic needle that began to erase the pain, then blessed oblivion.

It was a week before he was told the truth. It seemed a bullet had entered his sleeve at the cuff, followed the length of his forearm muscles to the elbow and exited. It was still retained within the thickness of his jacket fabric.

On its journey, the bullet had plowed through the flesh and muscle, exposing a bouquet of torn blood vessels and tendons. Surgeons were hours sorting and re-stitching torn flesh and reattaching, they hoped, blood vessels and nerves. As they worked, the surgeons had agreed that what had saved enough of the arm to work with, and possibly saved his life, was the first act of binding the sleeve to his arm, packing the blood clots tight enough to stop the bleeding.

A commendation of valor, a purple heart and a promotion to major. And a trip home to the Corners. He looked at it and sighed. *We're one day closer, my Lily. One day closer.*

While he recuperated, he was given desk duty. Writing down what had actually happened that had brought needed information that would save an uncountable number of lives. Then he was on the ship.

It was during that time that the "armistice" had been arranged. What in the world was the value of that, and had he and others paid for something that actually meant nothing? If the word and the intentions of the enemy were good, then this war would not have happened to start with. Why was it not clear to everyone that the enemy was not to be trusted? The ship rocked on the waves and his mind rocked with the strange puzzle of the armistice.

He did not tell Lily. He wanted to see her in their house. Likely with her fingers working with the knitting needles or perhaps the darning egg. Relief was so great that he could have cried, but he had not cried when the bullet tore up his arm, so why cry now? Useless waste of energy.

In Oklahoma City he bought a shiny new Ford, Model T. Savoring the thought of what was closely ahead, he leisurely followed the road to Argyle and made the turn south. Among the times he thought of Lily, there were occasions when he thought of the Corners, and the picture that formed in his mind was that of the side-by-side buildings of the Cookie Jar and Hats and Hankies.

He was doing fine, smiling and happy. Ah, look, there was another school. Called Midway Academy. *Hmmmm.*

Bramwell's mill and the well diggers. Just ahead was Canfield Grading and Earthworks. Smiles and a pounding heart. For no reason that he could imagine, he pulled the little car over to the ditch and got out. A flat stone marked one side of Canfield's drive, and he sat down on it, facing Hats and Hankies and the Cookie Jar.

He sat with his knees pulled up and held by circled arms, being careful of his injury. He thought to feast his eyes on the sight of the symbols of the Corners but his eyes had something different in mind. To his dismay, the brave Captain…no, Major…Cullen began to cry. Leaning his forehead on his knees, his tears flowed as they had not since before he could remember. The Cookie Jar! It was not a dream or a mentally constructed vision. It was real. Siding. Roofing. Smoking chimney\. Fragrant aroma of home.

Mrs. Raymond Forrester was adjusting the blades on the windmill after replacing a blade with a dent, and she used the moment to look about. She was always on alert for something that should not be. And there was someone by the driveway. On the rock where she had sat when she had been so down…now, someone…else….

Maybe a traveler…maybe a bum. Either way, he needed a cookie and a cup of tea. Maybe there was no money for the Cookie Jar. Armed with the cookie and the mug of hot drink, she made her way toward him.

Seating herself beside this stranger, she asked softly, "Sir, could you use a cup of tea?"

The brave and tearstained Major lifted his head and looked toward the remembered voice. America! God bless America! Tea and cookies, the other symbol of the Corners.

Merry startled slightly as she recognized her neighbor, Tray, Lily's husband. Recognized him through the sodden face and red eyes. He reached for the tea. "Tray, it's so good to see you home." She held out the cookie and he took it. She had done what she could so she just sat quietly.

Slightly refreshed, he attempted to explain. "I don't know what came over me. I just...."

Merry stopped him. "Say no more. It's what they have all done. Willie and Johnny, they had red eyes. Phillip is battling his injuries but Gwinnie has been a help. Philip added his own tears right here, staring at the COOKIE JAR. I could name a lot of others, but you want to go to Lily. I'm thinking she has a surprise for you." Reaching for the empty mug with a smile, she stood up as a dismissal.

With a final swipe across his face, Major Trayler Cullen climbed into his little car and went on down Canfield Road. To Lily.

He parked the vehicle and walked slowly up to the house. Sound of humming inside. He looked through the door, and Lily was not knitting. She was rocking gently and singing softly. She held something in her arms. Someone must be here visiting with a baby. Lily so wanted a baby.

Lily knew he was on his way, but she didn't know what day. He stepped through the door and with the light behind him, he was not readily recognized, except by the way he walked. A well-remembered stride.

"Tray..." she moaned softly. She could not move. "Come see your baby...our baby." No more words...and no one saw much of them for at least week

Things happened fast for a while. Edward Morrison finally made it home. Major Morrison, that is. It had taken a while to get his countrymen back where they belonged, paperwork and all. It was amazing, really, at the commendations that came with them.

He bought a car with an American motor and a French name. A Chevrolet. Speeding through Argyle, he kicked up a pillar of dust behind him. He was going to be brave, but, like all the rest, he was no match for the tears.

Just the sight of the building brightly proclaiming Cookie Jar, and the long sign in the yard proclaiming WELCOME HOME, brought tears and a pounding heart.

He stepped through the door and heard Gwinnie's voice scream, "KRISTIE!" He had been gone almost three years and he had not forgotten how Kristie looked, but how had she become so much more beautiful?

In his arms there were more tears on both shoulders. It was over and he was home. Standing right here in the Cookie Jar where he belonged. Where he would stay forever.

Gwinnie had married Phillip a month ago and moved into the partly finished house. Who needed a big fancy wedding? It meant nothing now that the fellows were home.

Kristie and Edward were married before the month was out. They lived in Aunt Sybil's house among the stored supplies and equipment. A house would appear for her in due time, but what did it matter where she lived, now that the fellows were back.

The tail gunner was mustered out and given an array of medals. They were well made and shiny, but they were outshone by the mental picture of Hats and Hankies setting across the road from Canfield Grading and beside the Cookie Jar.

There was the Big Ben clock in London and the Eiffel Tower in France. Also the little mermaid in Denmark and the windmills of Holland. These landmarks, however, counted as nothing when compared to the Cookie Jar and Hats and Hankies in Carlile Corners, Oklahoma, USA.

There had been no talk of marriage except when it would be. When Pattie wrote only notes to Johnny, and Bridie only said "Hi" to Willie, the fellows knew who they would marry. And they knew the girls would tell them when.

Lily, of course, was first with the babies, then Francine, from Shady Ridge acquired her stepdaughter, Violette. America was next, much to the delight of Miz Della Santorini and Julia Canfield. A strapping handsome fellow she named Emil after her father. Then, after that, small, new residents appeared here and there and they came on at frequent intervals. By choice.

Miss Josie, the originator of the Prairie Academy, noted with interest that most of the girls from her classes had not married in their teens. Here they were almost in their mid-twenties! Practically unheard of. It was what they chose to do.

America Forrester had been almost twenty when she married. Eve Adams had recently married and continued teaching in the private school in her parent's yard. A baby for her would be a future decision.

Like a ripple in a pond it had been for Miss Josie. A tragedy had ripped her life apart, and a prairie community had helped her put it back together, with many added pleasures. Just look around!

She often came, of an afternoon, and had tea and cookies at a little place called Cookie Jar. It was right next door to Hats and Hankies, located in Carlile Corners. And that was where her heart was.

Just one more sentence from the Historian. A very private one and one that was close to her heart. Josie's only daughter had shared the buckets of tears as the warriors came home and relived their horrors for the journal required by Miss Josie. But one and all had insisted that the tears shed in the telling had helped to wash away horrors and allowed their happiness to shine through.

For that, Josie's daughter was grateful. There was still a soldier unaccounted for, but he would be home sometime. It was known that Old Miz Gray Owl had placed the white feather of peace on his infant forehead. It would protect him.

UNDER THE HAYSTACK will tell his story. This is your invitation to come along and share it.

-BONUS EXCERPT-

A FOOTSTEPS IN THE CANYON
ANTHOLOGY

VOLUME
1

FOOTSTEPS
IN THE CANYON

VOLUME 1
- A GIFT FROM THE PAST
- THE BIG WIND
- TWO BONUS SHORTS

JOANN KLUSMEYER

A GIFT FROM THE PAST

High on the mesa sat the large ranch house, square and solid against the blue of the sky. Beside it were the three guest cottages and the long bunkhouse. Farther away were the buildings for the many kinds of animals. Fenced corrals surrounded the large barn, and many horses grazed in the pastures or stood dozing in the sun.

Thirteen-year-old Caitlyn Bradford yawned and rubbed her eyes. The bright sunshine outside her window called to her every time she looked away from the unfriendly face of the computer monitor. She had no way of knowing that this was a day that she would remember forever.

The lesson she had just downloaded, Beginning Algebra, was somewhat confusing, so she had put on the CD of the teacher's instructions, and now the lesson was no clearer than before. She decided the teacher didn't know how to do it either, so she must have studied long enough.

Home schooling from the Internet had its plusses, and it also had minuses. It meant you could study when you wanted to, and you could take a break when you got tired. It even meant that you could make the teacher "repeat" the instructions twenty times if you had trouble understanding something.

That's what home schooling had, but what it didn't have was other students. Caitlyn was always alone. Her bedroom was her classroom. The closest she got to other students was through email, except on picnic or party days, and they only came several times a year.

Clearly, it was time to treat herself with a break so she stepped outside. The sun seemed unusually bright after the dimness of the computer screen, but it instantly cheered her.

The "BB" name of the ranch was for her great grandfather Bradford and his brother, the original Bradford Brothers, but the neighbors had other names.

Other times it was the "BumbleBee", the "Bouncing Betty", and "Bouncing Bee" and even worse names sometimes. The official name was The Bradford Guest Ranch, but nobody cared.

Caitlyn hurried past the bunkhouse and went on to the stable where her horse might be. Then again, the horse might be in the corral, or in the near pasture. Josh Hunt would know. He always knew where every horse was at every minute. He knew because it was his job to know.

Josh was the head wrangler of the BB Ranch and he was in charge of the string of trail horses that were ridden by the ranch guests, and he also cared for all of the work horses. Probably forty animals in all, maybe more... and it was his job to keep up with them.

A loud whinny beside her ear told her where her palomino pony might be. The animal poked her golden head out of the half-door of the stable and whinnied again. She was ready for their afternoon ride.

"Hello, Golden," Caitlyn greeted the pony. "Are you ready?"

What a question! Of course she was ready. She had been ready and waiting for hours, so she tossed her head and snorted her answer!

Caitlyn tossed the light saddle over the back of the palomino. She had saddled her horse so many times that she could have done it in her sleep. It had been one of her father's rules. If she was big enough to ride, she was big enough to saddle and care for her horse without help from the wrangler. Even her little sister, Nelda, only ten years old, could saddle her own horse.

The girls had been told that Josh, the wrangler, had a job to do and he was not their servant, so the girls must care for their own horses. They brushed the animals and cleaned the stalls. That was the small price to pay for having their own horse to ride whenever they wanted to.

It seemed to be a good afternoon for a long ride, so Caitlyn put an apple and the cell phone in the saddle bag and tossed it over the golden back of the horse, just behind the saddle.

On impulse, she put in her camera. She was a rather good photographer and hoped to get better. She loved to take pictures and one never knew what they might see when riding out over the grassy mesa.

The sun shown warmly on her yellow hair and the breeze fanned against her face, waking her up from the boring bout with Beginning Algebra.

The tall grass reached as high as the belly of the pony. It was a mixture of yellow-green buffalo grass, and the gray-green stems of the prairie bluestem grass. Flat as a tabletop, the meadow spread all the way to the lip of the huge box canyon.

A small river flowed down from somewhere in the far off foothills and poured over the lip of the canyon in a silver spray of a waterfall that would be the envy of the wedding veil in any bridal shop.

The river water was made up mostly from snowmelt from the distant mountains and it flowed across the high meadow, cascading over the lip of the canyon, and falling with a roar into the rock-bottomed pool. From there it spilled over into a small lake.

When it flowed from the lake, it gathered itself back into being a river, and wound its way across the floor of the canyon. After that, it flowed away, maybe all the way to the Mississippi and into the Gulf of Mexico.

Caitlyn loved the box canyon. It was called a 'box' canyon because it was surrounded with walls like a huge bowl. It was located on land leased by the ranch for their horses and longhorns, but a lot of other animals claimed it as well. Wolves and foxes and smaller animals were often seen there, as well as bison, often called buffalo along with a herd of American elk, an animal that was originally called wapiti.

The only reason she was allowed to ride out alone was that she carried the cell phone and could always be located, and also could call for help if she should need it.

Across the familiar tall grass the golden pony trotted, joyful to escape the stable. Caitlyn bounced happily on her back, just as joyful to escape her lessons.

At the narrow trail that led down into the canyon, Golden slowed, picking her way on careful hooves. The steepness of the trail tried to pitch Caitlyn forward over the pony's head, but she had ridden this trail many times. She knew just how to hold on.

Finally on the canyon floor, the palomino lowered her head to grab a bite of the juicy grass, but Caitlyn reined her up. "You can eat later while I climb on the rock ledges."

The pony trotted around the wall of the canyon, stopping by the rock outcroppings where Caitlyn often brought her. She lowered her head and again began to graze, as she had been promised.

The girl leaped to the ground and ran to the rocks. It was such fun the way the flat stones jutted out from the wall of the bluff like the steps of a very wide ladder. She could climb from one to the other, though some of the steps were quite a long stretch for her legs.

Today, the stretching felt incredibly good.

High on her favorite ledge, she sat and swung her feet over the edge while she watched her grazing pony. Then she looked, with dismay, down at her feet. In her haste to be gone, she had not changed into her riding boots and here she was, climbing the rough rocks in light casual loafers.

Bad idea. The slickness of the soles made them a bit dangerous and she could get hurt. In addition, the climbing and scuffing was not doing the shoes any good either. Oh, well...

And it was at that moment that one of the loafers dropped off her foot. Oops! Toe over heel the shoe tumbled, kicking dust puffs here and there, and it came to rest on a small ledge much closer to the canyon floor than the ledge where she sat. Well, she'd get it when she came down, and now she would just have to be sock-footed on one foot. She'd also have to watch out for the cactus stickers in her sock.

Caitlyn climbed about on the rocks until the sun lowered to the canyon lip and that was her signal to head for home. Working her way down, she reached the place where her shoe waited.

The shoe was full of dust and gravel, so she whacked the heel against the rock ledge to knock out the dirt. It was then that a chunk of the clay between the rock ledges slid away, revealing something behind it.

She had been warned never to poke her hands into a strange place. Who knew what might be in there? So she used a stick to work the object out from under the rock ledge.

It seemed to be something wrapped in cloth and the old cotton fabric of the wrapping was very rotten. It broke into crumbles when it was touched.

An idea!

Jumping to the ground, she rooted around in the saddlebag for her camera. Aiming the camera high, she took a snapshot of the ledge containing the strange package, while standing on the ground, then climbed back up and took another picture. The hiding place was hardly more than eight feet above the canyon floor.

Now, to get it down without tearing it up!

Another good idea! She slipped off her shirt and then her undershirt. Putting her shirt back on, she carefully slid the crumbling package onto her undershirt. Gently folding the soft knit around it, she slid down the bank and put it on the ground. Then she climbed back up and got her shoe.

Crouching on the ground, she carefully peeled back the rotted fabric of the item and what she saw made thrill bumps raise up on her arms. A little shiver of suspense played along her shoulders and down her back.

Right there before her on the old cloth was a small book and a tiny rag doll, hardly longer than her hand. The old, stained cloth fabric of the doll's body was not much better than the wrapping, so she lifted the doll carefully with both hands and slipped it into the loafer beside her. So what if she rode home with one sock foot in the stirrup!

Carefully she put the shoe into the saddlebag so it would not tip over and spill the fragile toy. The small book was in somewhat better condition, though it was yellowed and crumbling. Beside the book was a stub of a pencil that appeared to have been sharpened with a knife.

Slipping the wooden pencil into her shirt pocket, she carefully opened the book. On the flyleaf was printed, This Book Belongs to, and then there was a line. Still readable was the name on the line, Annie Jo Cantrell.

The shiver of thrill bumps again raced down her back. A diary! It seemed this book must be the diary of a girl named Annie who, for some reason, had hidden her book in the rock ledges of a box canyon on the tall grass mesa of Oklahoma.

This was clearly the beginning of a mystery, and no one loved mysteries more than Caitlyn.

Carefully she lifted the flyleaf of the small book and a chunk of the yellowed paper broke off in her fingers.

Oops! She would have to be more careful, but first she needed a picture of the flyleaf. Raising her camera, she snapped two shots, just to be sure one was good.

With a stiff blade of grass she lifted the flyleaf and turned it over. The words said, "They gave me a book to write in so I would have something to do while I ride. I would rather not have to ride, but Pa says it is a thing to be done."

Ride? Was there another girl who sometimes rode her pony here to play on the rocks? Probably not because no one could write while they rode horseback.

Golden snorted, startling Caitlyn, and she noticed the sun had passed the canyon rim. It was time to be on her way. Closing the undershirt carefully around the book, she slipped it into her other saddle bag and climbed aboard the pony's back.

- END OF EXCERPT -

ADDITIONAL BOOK SERIES BY JOANN KLUSMEYER

The Great I Am Bible Story Series for Kids
6 books

The Young Pioneers Adventure Series for Kids
5 books

The Wentworth Triplets Mystery Series for Young Teens
3 books

Footsteps in the Canyon Adventure Series for Young Teens
4 books

Burnt Tree Junction Historical Fiction Series for Adults
6 books

Ozark Mountains Historical Fiction Series for Adults
7 books

Taming the Wilderness Historical Fiction Series for Adults
4 books

The Sheltering Stones Historical Fiction Series for Adults
5 books

The Trilogy of Wishbone Hollow Historicial Fiction Series for Adults
3 books